John Silverton was born 1945, a Man of Kent. He is a former freelance journalist, newspaper columnist and magazine features writer, although most of his commercial life has been in sales and marketing. He has two children from a previous marriage and lives in East Sussex with his partner.

John's mother was an artist and that inspired him to take up the brush. Many of his artworks include text and his affinity for words led to writing this novel.

A second novel, *A Murder of Crows,* is in progress plus a collection of flash fiction stories inspired by works of art, six available to read on his website.

www.johnsilvertonwrite.co.uk
www.johnsilvertonart.co.uk

A Pearl Amongst Oysters

JOHN SILVERTON

First published in 2022 by Independent Publishing Network

ISBN 978-1-80068-638-0

Type set in Garamond 11 pt
Cover image by Julian Bailey
Cover design and typography by
Julian Sutherland-Beatson

Printed and distributed by KDP Amazon (UK)

www.johnsilvertonwrite.co.uk

A Pearl Amongst Oysters

In the Cimetiere du Père Lachaise in Paris is the grave of a beautiful young Russian woman, Tatyana Rachevskaya. When separated from her Romanian lover she committed suicide.

Moved by this event the renowned Romanian sculptor Constantin Brâncusi created a headstone in memoriam, the inscription:

To all unknown couples of the world who loved each other before suffering the agonies of separation.

This book is dedicated to lovers separated against their will.

Chapter 1

No one goes to Grimsby unless they have to, the name so appropriate to the grim, unromantic nowheresville on Britain's east coast. The town was my new workplace and, I discovered, harboured more than fishing boats. There I met her, the one to quell desire for greener grass on the other side of the cliché.

February 1976, the country was in the grip of the coldest winter for thirteen years. Sleet stung my face as I hastened along Cleethorpes Road, past run-down Victorian terraces and interventions of small shops, ventures once pregnant with potential now miscarried with time: a grocer with a whiff of Indian spices; a newsagent plying risqué magazines; an open-all-hours greasy-spoon café.

A frigid wind from distant tundra swirled litter in an empty shop doorway and carried the odour of gutted fish from the harbour's filleting sheds. A discordant chorus of incontinent seagulls circled like vultures. Stooped raincoats with upturned collars and downturned heads scurried past, candidates to model for the last Lowry painting.

I was relieved to arrive. A battery of glass panes adulterated the Victorian grey brick facade and neon signage emblazoned "Lotus House", the lettering inferring its oriental character. Condensation rendered the menu illegible but I was here by recommendation: "Feast your eyes on more than the food" a work colleague commented with a wry smile.

Accompanied by an unwelcome draught I ventured inside, shaking the icy snow from my coat and hat. A young firmly built Chinese man approached; his smarmed jet hair and black attire redolent of my father's undertakers. His inscrutable expression betrayed no sign of welcome. I followed to an outer row of tables, removed my coat and sat on the red faux-leather couch seating. I chose from the "Special Businessmen's Lunch" selection before considering my new surroundings.

A blend of food aromas and smouldering joss sticks garnished the warm atmosphere. Businessmen in dark suits munched keenly, the drone of their conversation and clinking cutlery vying with the resonant oriental muzak. Paintings of mystical rural scenes and glowing red lanterns endeavoured to create a Chinese ambience. A dozen white-clothed tables, religiously arranged in rows before the altar of an illuminated bar, completed the visual mosaic.

A cheerless waif-like waitress served. The chicken and cashew nuts, egg fried rice and vegetables in oyster sauce impressed more than both she and the decor suggested, but my contented digest was interrupted when the door from the kitchen swung open to reveal a second waitress: the "Feast your eyes ..." intrigue.

Her uniform of white blouse and black skirt hugged graceful curves and a waterfall of lustrous black hair splashed her shoulders framing ebony eyes and a joyous smile. She wandered around the tables and captured every gaze. I watched, not with the dubious motive of a voyeur, but with the appreciation of an enthralling work of art.

With an escorting waft of perfume, she paused at my table. I looked up in admiration; her softly sculptured face fissured by a thrilling mouth with lips enticingly proud asking to be kissed. She asked only after my dessert. The dulcet tone of her voice charmed with its hint of mirth and characteristic lallation with which the

Chinese modulate spoken English.

'Lychees and a black coffee please.'

Her eyes glowed like burning embers and ignited a fire that would only be extinguished by making love to them; a fire incinerating my marriage vows.

She moved away and an over enthusiastic pinstripe-suit attempted to detain her with conversation, his eyes wandering distractedly from face to figure. He reached and touched her arm but she turned away with a reproachful frown and entered the kitchen. The door swung to-and-fro to a stop; I looked on hopeful of her return. The waif served my white dessert and black coffee.

I stood at the bar waiting to pay. *She* whooshed through the kitchen's swing door like a genie from a bottle able to grant any man's desire.

'You wish to pay?' Her smile was worthy of a cover charge.

'Yes.' I nodded.

'Did you enjoy the food?'

'Better than expected.'

She handed my change. I tipped her smile.

'Thank you. Your first time here.'

'Yes, recently arrived to work in Grimsby.'

'Will you come again?'

'I'll come again if *you* serve me.'

She sighed and a quizzical look inferred I was yet another chat-up suit on the make. My gaze toured down to the landscape of her blouse; although aware of the impropriety of this excursion my eyes had their own agenda. She must notice men's eyes detouring regularly; I regretted falling victim to type and hoped she hadn't noticed. She had noticed, reflexively folding a protective left arm.

'Maybe if you sit this side.' She gestured, extending her free arm.

I stood entranced, the embarrassing pause between us an invisible barrier. She wasn't doing anything except making me nervous. I was anxious of reacting too eagerly too soon; I wanted to go but I longed to stay.

'Okay, see you tomorrow,' I said cheerfully.

She returned my smile with palpable warmth and a natural sentiment to drive any man to distraction. So it proved; I was unable to concentrate on work. The mischievous Eros had loosed his arrow.

A five minute walk from the Lotus House the premises of International Weighing Scales loomed large on a windswept corner. Built on a site bequeathed by the Luftwaffe, this concrete and glass blight of post war brutalism was incompatible with neighbouring Victorian buildings. The showroom resembled a graveyard: rows of dormant scales the tombstones, green vinyl floor tiles the turf.

Behind a desk a half glazed door accessed the repair workshop. In his cramped office Danny Parker, the ponderous branch foreman, sat drinking tea. I had a preconceived perception of Yorkshire men of which Danny was archetypal, calling a spade a spade and clouting you with it if riled. He viewed the world via a cynical scowl and his brusque brogue implied his short fuse.

'Aye, she's a good looking lass,' agreed Danny. 'You've no chance lad, I know several guys who've had a go. She's sure to have a boyfriend, or maybe she's a lesbian.'

With the looming obstacle of a boyfriend, even worse a girlfriend, my initial elation ebbed.

'Anyways, you're married.'

'Six long years of monogamy,' I said with a sigh. 'This Chinese girl though ... she's special, I felt an immediate connection.'

'I know the connection you want to plug in,' he quipped.

I ignored his innuendo; Danny was too macho to comprehend the profound, sensitive, emotional reaction I had experienced. I picked up my briefcase and left to drum up some business, but my heart wasn't in it, my heart was back in the Lotus House.

My move from Godiva's Coventry to grimy Grimsby was a promotion, as International's representative for South Humberside and half of Lincolnshire. I sold expensive new weighing scales to shops and factories that had, most often, perfectly serviceable old weighing scales.

Although it sounds uninspiring, cold-calling was challenging and not without perversely exhilarating incidents. On one occasion I was chased down the street by a cleaver wielding butcher threatening to add my tadger to his sausage display – my persistence for an order had outstayed the butcher's welcome. There was also the incident involving ... but never mind, some other time.

I admit to not being a natural salesman and averse to the coercive companions of monthly targets and commission earnings, but a decade ago I was seduced by the regalia of swish suits and current model company cars and the prospect of a better life.

I also admit to not being a natural when it comes to selling myself to women. I experience a nervous uneasiness when aroused by the presence of an attractive woman, lacking the confident chat-up lines and gregarious charm gifted to more successful rivals. Even so, the notches carved on my proverbial bedpost had, by dedicated perseverance, climbed to the respectability of double figures – although a modest tally for a twenty-eight year old.

In matters of the heart I struggled with the diffidence kindled by too many rejections in my teens, when tears were the only dock leaf to alleviate the sting of unrequited love. So why risk further heartache and jeopardise my marriage? This girl was different; the sexual allure an expression of a more profound impact on my emotions.

As the afternoon wore on I realised I couldn't wait until tomorrow to see her. I returned to the showroom and left an answerphone message for my landlady.

'Hello Cynthia, I'm detained on business in Grimsby and will not require dinner tonight.'

Cleethorpes Road improved its appearance after dark, the daytime drab of the buildings masked with shadows or the glow from street lamps. The camouflage of snow on the roofs radiated an eerie moonlit blue tinge. Icy pavements reflected the colours of neon signs and the curb side slush puddles were stained with oily rainbows. Light poured across the pavement from the all-night café from where the streetwalkers plied their obvious wares. I and most other pavement users averted our eyes, hurrying to indoor havens away from the john proposals and harsh weather.

'I've come back to see you,' I said chirpily.

She smiled politely, pen and pad at the ready. 'What would you like?'

'I like you.' I held her gaze.

'I'm not on the menu,' she chided, with a sigh and frown of disapproval.

She waved an admonishing pen held like a blunt hypodermic filled with potassium bromide to cool my ardour. I echoed her martyred sigh. She must realize that approaches from customers were a price her beauty exacted. I regretted my gauche approach and tried again.

'I know a recommended restaurant at Laceby if you are available for dinner one evening?'

'I have a boyfriend,' she said emphatically.

'Just a date for dinner.'

'It's never just dinner,' she said sagely.

'You're right ... with you it could never be just dinner.'

I looked at her hands, encouraged by the absence of a ring. She bustled off to give my order to the kitchen. When the food arrived, I picked up the chopsticks.

'Will you show me how to use these?'

'You have knife and fork.'

'Yes, but I would like to learn, I'm sure it will enhance the food experience.'

She reluctantly demonstrated the grip and finger movement; her fingers had the slender delicacy of a pianist, her manicured nails without added colour.

'Now you try.' A hint of derision gilded her tone. She moved off to tend other customers. Passing by later my proficiency surprised her. 'You learn quickly.'

'You're a good teacher.'

'Hmm ... I think you already knew how to use chopsticks,' she said accusingly.

'I think you're right.' I gave her a droll smile. 'What's your name?'

'You don't need to know.'

I ignored her rebuff. 'My name is Chris Patterson.' I proffered a hand to shake. She looked at it warily, like an unclean utensil and declined the gesture. 'Okay, if you won't tell me your name I will call you ... Aphrodite, goddess of love and beauty.' The intended compliment was immediately reproached.

'I think not. She slept with anyone. I'm not like that, and you're no Adonis.'

'Ouch!' I winced in mock hurt.

Concerned she had caused offence she sheepishly recanted.

'Sorry; I meant you have brown hair and eyes.'

'I would dye my hair blond and wear blue contact lenses to become your boyfriend.'

'Adonis is not my type,' she countered with a smug smile, turning to the beckon of another customer.

I lingered over the food, savouring the pleasure of discreetly admiring her. Later, the undertaker man drifted by and I collared him for information. His face had the solemnity of the straight man of a comedy duo, no inner smile daring to emerge to crease his impassive expression. His name was Jimmy, apparently common practice for Hong Kong Chinese to adopt an English first name. His wife, Lucy, was the joyless waif who apathetically served lunch. I now sympathised with his sombre demeanour. Perhaps he also fancied Aphrodite; maybe Lucy thought he did too.

'What's her name?' I indicated Aphrodite with a directional nod.

'Have you asked her?'

'She won't say. Come on Jimmy, it's only a name.'

He hesitated, fixing me with an appraising gaze.

'Her name is Fong, Leung Yuk Fong. Leung her family name; Chinese family names come first.'

'She said she has a boyfriend. Does he work here?'

'Not here.'

I sensed his tone to be evasive. 'Okay, thank you Jimmy.'

My dessert arrived, juicy lychees huddling in a small bowl like eggs in a nest, the one fruit I preferred tinned to fresh.

'Ah, thank you Fong.'

'Only friends call me Fong,' she rebuked.

'Let me be your friend.'

'I've told you, I have a boyfriend,' she huffed, before turning determinedly away.

I imagined Jimmy received a reprimand. The evening ambled on and I observed her whilst pretending disinterest, but she felt the touch of my gaze upon her.

'Why are you always looking at me?'

'I'm sorry. I don't mean to embarrass but I feel strongly attracted to you. I want to take you out, to get to know you.'

She shook her head. 'Not possible ... little time off work and boyfriend *very* jealous.'

'Your boyfriend doesn't need to know.'

'I'm not like *that*,' she admonished.

'Of course not. I apologise. What time do you finish here? I could drive you home.'

'I live many miles away.'

'That doesn't matter, I have a company car,' I boasted. 'This is a rough area and it's freezing and dark. Allow me to drive you home.'

The answer remained 'No.' My sales training advocated persistence in closing the sale in one way or another, that is, until the chef comes out of the kitchen wielding a meat cleaver. But I judged a campaign of persuasive attrition was more likely to succeed with this personal sale. Unfortunately time was not on my side.

Chapter 2

The historic Georgian market town of Louth nestles at the foot of the Wolds sixteen miles south of Grimsby. In 1976 its heritage and architectural charm remained unsullied by modernity and multiples – save for a mini Boots and diminutive Woolworths. Eastgate, the main street, was an oasis of quality independent retailers plying local produce. Every Wednesday, Friday and Saturday the town centre congested with gaily coloured market stalls, vibrant with the wit and bawl of hustling traders. Thursday's livestock market paraded breeding stock in a bovine beauty pageant, whilst the less fortunate fattened sheep huddled in pens nervously awaiting the auctioneer's death knell.

Louth's pastoral character proved an agreeable refuge from the likes of Grimsby and my family associations with the town – mother's birthplace, father's resting place – decided my intended residency. Meanwhile, as the sale of the family home in Coventry and purchase in Louth inched through the legal system, I was ensconced in Highholme House, a B & B run by harridan Cynthia Howard and her disabled husband, affectionately known as Mr H.

Located on the northern outskirts of Louth, the detached Edwardian house displayed a faux Tudor facade of brick and stucco with blackened timbers and leaded windows. Over the threshold the hall was wide, with oak panelled walls and parquet floor. The measured heartbeats of a longcase clock were drowned by hourly chimes, refusing to let time pass quietly. A side table displayed a notice, thrown down like the gauntlet of a challenge: "GUESTS ARE NOT ALLOWED VISITORS TO THEIR ROOMS."

From the hall the staircase turned back on itself to a balustraded landing. My room was plainly decorated in a blue borrowed from Picasso and simply furnished of Edwardian vintage: mahogany veneered wardrobe (with wire coat hangers jangling like a wind chime); matching chest of drawers (lined with yesteryear newspaper the colour of toast); and an upholstered chair (of Victorian straight back discomfort). A card table deputised as a desk. The double bed was comfortable although when put upon the mahogany frame creaked like a becalmed galleon and the springs protested with atonal dissonance.

The ground floor rooms were veritable galleries of pictures, objets d'art and comfortable furniture. I enjoyed the ambience of the house with its past feel, a preference inherited from my parents for antique furniture and properties of period character.

Scrumptious breakfast fry-ups and ambrosial roast dinners were dished-up by a cheerful motherly cook with flushed cheeks and heaving bosom who bore the weight of her own moreish creations.

The next day's business kept me away from Grimsby and I returned to my lodgings frustrated by not having seen Fong. The clang of the dinner gong and enticing aroma heralded the evening menu: thick vegetable soup followed by leg of lamb garnished with rosemary, complimented by mint jelly, crisp roast potatoes, Brussels sprouts, and carrots in a honey and garlic glaze. Delicious!

The other guests were a motley group of business suited sales reps, from balding weary old hands to hairy spirited neophytes straight from university. Everyone heartily tucked in. Topical discourse included the artistic legacy of L S Lowry, the escalation of the Icelandic fishing dispute – with its implications for Grimsby – and the impending obscenity trial of Warhol's provocative *Deep Throat.* The relentless physicality of the weather – officially the most severe winter since 1963 – was de rigueur: the perilous ice and snow creating havoc on the roads and railways, the hurricane force winds wreaking damage to trees and buildings.

I left the table ahead of the others to forgo the stodgy treacle pudding, not one of cook's best. From the hall I knocked on the second door on the right before entering to give a message to Cynthia. She was not there. Mr H half turned towards me, rolling backward the right wheel of his wheelchair. The loss of his right leg ended his career as a civil engineer, but the industrial injury compensation enabled him and his wife to purchase the B & B a few years ago – a life alternative and income stream to retirement.

He sat with Buddha like calmness and corpulence, resignation of a spent life implied by his invalidity, monkish pate and mournful expression. He looked up over his horn rimmed glasses.

'Oh, it's you Chris,' he muttered with the phlegmatic croak of a hardened smoker.

I glanced about the room. The air was a stale fug of aromatic pipe smoke and the open grate fire burned low in its tiled surround as if starved of oxygen. An antique mantle clock ticked his life away. An opened novel rested on his lap. A side table supplied the trappings of his virtual imprisonment: Ogden's tobacco, silver lighter, box of Kleenex. A briar pipe rested in a glass ashtray and a half mug of cocoa had died waiting to be drunk, the thick skin its body bag. A framed photo stood on the windowsill next to a dead fly. A Bush television on spindly legs slept in the far corner.

'I was looking for Cynthia.'

'Wednesday is whist night at the Community Centre.'

'Tell her I'll be eating out tomorrow night; fancy a Chinese in Grimsby.'

'Lucky you. I love Chinese food. Brings back happy memories of my time in Hong Kong.'

'I can bring you a take-away.'

'No, Cynthia wouldn't approve.'

'Your son?' I said, picking up the framed photo.

'No, me. Hong Kong 1949; last tour of duty, a sapper, repairing infrastructure after the Japanese occupation.'

'See any wartime action?'

'Never a shot in anger; support detail, always behind the front line.'

'Did you like army life?'

'Only for the overseas deployments. Hong Kong was the best – the food, the girls.' His eyes softened and his expression engendered wistful musing. 'Halcyon days.' He breathed an exaggerated sigh.

'My father had a spell in Hong Kong,' I commented. 'He was an officer aboard the battleship HMS Anson which helped liberate Hong Kong and accepted surrender of the Japanese occupying forces. Before that his ship was shepherding Arctic convoys carrying supplies to Russia. Winston Churchill called it "The worst journey in the world." Sub-zero polar conditions were as much an enemy as the German U-boats.'

'Sounds awful. What about after the war?'

'He started a catering business but died fighting the enemy within ... cancer,' I said mournfully.

'I'm sorry. I know how boys need their fathers; mine died in a bombing raid on Grimsby.'

He failed to suppress a hippo yawn and on that tired note I took my leave. I loped upstairs and completed company paperwork before climbing into bed. Aroused by the discussion with Mr H my thoughts returned to my father's demise.

At seven years old my faith in God was buried along with my father's coffin. A kind, generous and humorous character, he brought joy to the lives of many; everyone spoke well of him. Not only was his life cut short – a meagre forty years – the pain convinced him to attempt suicide by jumping from the hospital ward window. In those few weeks of illness he aged thirty years becoming a gaunt, grey wraith I hardly recognised.

The funeral service played out as a ceremonial drama, irrational to the comfort of private grief that mother and I needed.

'Ask God why his life was cut short. Ask God why he was made to suffer,' I hollered from the pews.

'God works in mysterious ways, it is not in our wisdom to question His motives,' the vicar reprimanded.

As clods of wet earth pounded the coffin lid, I had looked to the heavens for an explanation of God's motive; but God was found wanting. There was no reason to inflict such suffering and rob us of the fulfilment of a long life well lived. I had an ulterior motive for looking up at the dissonant concert of thunderous storm clouds, the raindrops on my cheeks might pass muster for the obligatory tears I was unable to summon in my anger. The torrential rain appeared integral to the occasion, washing away a precious life on a flood of memories.

My father's early demise, the vicar's enigmatic act of God, railed against all the religious pronouncements that God was merciful, God was love. Mother became a reclusive broken spirit, all the gaiety of life rinsed away by the rain that cried for us in that dank, windswept churchyard. Henceforth she lived the odyssey of his absent future: she grew old, grey and arthritic whilst he remained young and handsome in her memories, blocking out his last anguished days. She became a convert to atheism and at my wedding stood defiant in the church's graveyard, a portent for the future of the marriage.

* * *

Like the hallucinations of a drug addict, images of Fong impeded sleep until the early hours. I contemplated strategy, deciding on both lunch and dinner the next day in an assertive sortie against her defences.

The lunch session went well. She served and exchanged a few pleasantries and half acknowledged my attentive glances with her own stolen looks. I was captivated by her easy smile that radiated the warmth and kindness of a gentle happy nature. When paying, I stood before her, long enough to be significant. She tilted her head with an enquiring look.

'You want something else?'

'I want you not to have a boyfriend. Isn't he due for replacement?'

'I've not thought about that. Obviously you fancy yourself to replace.'

'Yes I do. How about it? Will you come out with me?'

'Sorry ... boyfriend would not allow.'

I sighed wistfully. 'If you were my girl, I would be equally protective. Your smile touches me, brightens up my day.'

'Nice thought.' She smiled on cue.

I proffered my right hand; she left it hanging with uncomfortable hesitation before gently shaking goodbye. Her hand was soft, warm and dry, somehow sensuous. Her touch engendered disquieting sensations of excitement tempered by apprehension, feelings that harked back to teenage first dates and loss of virginity.

My annus mirabilis concurred with Philip Larkin's assertion: "Sexual intercourse began in 1963." Aged fifteen, the alarm bell of my biological clock awakened me to the attractions of the opposite sex. However I soon realised seduction required an expertise untaught by the education system. I was inarticulate in the parlance of chat-up and thus denied girls' interest by an invisible force field of shyness and inexperience; they were either equally shy compounding my irresolution, or streetwise self assured leaving me timidly gauche. I remained marooned on an island of nervous diffidence until rescued by "Mrs Robinson".

Following the screening of *The Graduate*, the name "Mrs Robinson" became synonymous with mature women initiating young men in their rite of passage to manhood. Her name was Janet; we met at a neighbour's barbecue party. Her shock of wavy auburn hair framed a mellow porcelain complexion with arresting emerald eyes, the classic muse of the Pre-Raphaelite painters. The confidence of maturity, fall of her breasts and fine lines about her eyes were the only betrayals of the length of her journey as the mother of school mate, Terry. Her gemstone eyes engaged my appreciative gaze and, I suppose because of her maturity, conversation flowed. After a few glasses of wine she revealed the disillusionment of her marriage.

'I am a perennial bloom in need of regular watering, a chore my gardener is neglecting. Do you have an interest in gardening?'

Janet was not the cynical, scheming, smoking bitch of *The Graduate*. My "Mrs Robinson" was humorous, cuddly and giving, generously relieving my self-conscious virginity for which I remained eternally grateful. There was no need for a hotel, her house vacant on a Saturday afternoon, Janet's husband and Terry spectators at an away football match.

When she exposed my erection, she cheerfully said, 'Bloody hell! That thing should have a notice on it, not for internal use,' before gleefully climbing astride and devouring it whole with the ease of a fireman descending his greasy pole.

It was an unforgettable baptism of pleasures previously unknown. I had been emancipated, manhood had arrived, my school cap and blazer discarded to the dustbin of juvenile history. Cycling home I passed a Methodist church; outside a prophetic poster proclaimed: "This is the first day of your new life." And it was. Armed with enabling confidence I ventured into the sexual jungle.

There was something deliciously thrilling in hanging out with Terry knowing I was secretly sharing his mother's bed. The amour lasted a year or so until her husband became suspicious. Our liaisons lessened from regular to occasional, with a last night of passion engineered seven years later on the eve of my marriage to Mary.

That evening at the Lotus House I resolved to stay until closure to get a look at Fong's boyfriend – a good salesman knows his competitors. In the absence of the boyfriend, I would again offer a taxi service.

'Is your boyfriend coming tonight?'

'Maybe, if not busy.'

'Well if he's not here to take you home, I will. You cannot be out on the streets in this area so late without an escort.'

'I've managed so far,' she responded indignantly.

The unease of her backward glance inferred she was mindful of restaurant owner Mr Zhang, her uncle, who sat quietly smoking in the far corner, watching. His keen eyes were at odds with his sallow, weathered face; a face too old to have been known young by present company. His tombstone smile could be adopted for tooth decay adverts.

I sat supping coffee waiting for the restaurant to wind down. With Fong in the kitchen, I paid Jimmy and slipped out to retrieve the car. I parked on the double yellows with a clear view of the rear kitchen door and impatiently waited.

The wind had calmed, the snow crunched under foot as I padded up and down to keep warm. A freezing mist veiled the dimly lit street lined with the backs of buildings to which the Victorians had applied no aesthetic obligation. Piles of rubbish awaiting collection strayed and bled into the gutter. A burping drunk relieved himself against an alley wall adding to the unsavoury cocktail.

There was no sign of the collecting boyfriend. At last Fong emerged accompanied by a woman from the kitchen. I opened the passenger door like a chauffeur awaiting instructions. Fong hesitated, spoke to her companion, and with waves of an arm encouraged her to walk on up the street. She stepped warily forward, maintaining eye contact.

'Your carriage awaits.' I gestured she enter.

'Hmm ... are you sure you'll take me all the way home?'

'Yes, wherever it is.'

'It's a long way,' she cautioned.

'No matter how far,' thinking the farther the better.

She paused, weighing up the situation, glanced around at the restaurant and looked up the street to her colleague. Her eyes questioned mine but found no reason for further excuse.

'Hmm ... alright,' she said slowly, shyly smiling and slipping into the passenger seat.

I closed the door, acutely aware of my whole being on heightened alert. 'Which way?'

With a wry smile she gestured straight ahead and we moved off slowly down the street. After barely a hundred yards she placed a gloved hand on my arm.

'Stop here!'

'Why what's wrong? Have you forgotten something?'

She alighted from the car with a mischievous chuckle. Her eyes twinkled with triumphant merriment.

'It's most kind of you to take me *all* the way home,' she said, laughing.

She playfully ascended the steps to her door to be joined by her chuckling companion. I should have seen it coming, but she was too distracting. I stepped from the car, but happy with her ruse she bade farewell with a fluttering wave. Unlike the snow, I sensed a thaw had begun, hopeful that tonight was the prelude to a first date.

Chapter 3

On Friday, with business to conduct in Louth, I had no time for lunch in Grimsby. There had been overnight snow but the main roads were passable, so mid afternoon I commenced the slow-moving, convoy style journey to Coventry for a weekend of familiar joys and labours of family life.

I arrived early evening, the kids overjoyed to see me. To witness their jubilant faces erased the tiredness of the journey as they clamoured to receive and give affection, impart their latest achievements and disclose each other's misdemeanours. Mary was relieved to be rescued from her overworked single parent role. The cat rubbed against my legs and purred his welcome.

Both kids proudly produced artworks of Mary, me, the cat and the house. The naive style suggested acolytes of Alfred Wallis, with perspective overlooked and the most important objects looming largest. I was grateful to note my dominance in both pictures.

Judging the best artwork required tactful diplomacy, highlighting aspects of each. Critically though, I did draw their attention that at six feet tall I was not as tall as the house, my eyes were brown and not blue, my hair brown and not black. In self defence Samantha blamed Simon for the loss of the brown felt-tip pen, starting the first argument of the weekend arbitrated with the promise of a new set of pens.

In the first couple of years of marriage I didn't particularly want kids anytime soon, now I couldn't envisage life without them. I adored doing things with them, seeing them learn and develop and experience life's bounty. Each had a strong character as different as the colour of their eyes – Simon's brown but Samantha's blue – whereas Mary's and my eyes were brown; something to do with random selection I supposed.

Saturday was taken up by the weekly shop at Sainsbury's and visits for the kids to be spoiled by two indulgent grandmothers. Fong invaded my thoughts and Mary commented on my perceived preoccupation. I blamed the icy road conditions for hampering efforts to reach February's sales target. Thoughts of Fong made me frisky but Mary claimed another headache.

The Sunday morning late lie-in did give rise to sex, although annoyingly interrupted by the children. I had climbed aboard an apathetic Mary in the missionary position and was humping away when the bedroom door swung open. Apparently Samantha and Simon had been listening to the squeaking bed springs and peering through the keyhole.

With hands defiantly on hips, Samantha loudly entreated, 'Daddy! Stop bouncing up and down on Mummy, we want our breakfast.'

Falling snow slowed my return journey to Grimsby but I arrived in time for a late lunch, hungry to see Fong.

'Thank you for driving me *all* the way home,' she jested, milking her ruse. 'Shall I pay for the petrol?'

'A kiss would be acceptable in lieu of payment,' I said, hopefully.

She smiled and waved an admonishing finger. 'Oh no, boyfriend would not like.'

'I won't tell him if you don't.'

'That would be dishonest.'

'Would I get a kiss if it was my birthday?'

'Is your birthday today?'

'Not today, but I will accept a kiss in advance.'

'When is your birthday?'

'November.'

'November! You cheeky boy.'

'A kiss for your birthday?'

'My birthday's even further away.'

'A kiss for Chinese New Year?'

'Too late; New Year end of January.'

I enjoyed the banter, encouraged by her friendly repartee.

Business kept me away from the restaurant until Wednesday lunchtime. To my dismay Fong was not serving.

'Jimmy,' I beckoned, 'where's my favourite waitress?'

Jimmy had become friendly now that I was a regular diner and I hoped to adopt him as an ally to my cause.

'This Wednesday's her half day; she will be here tonight. You like her, yes?'

'Yes. I want to take her out, but she says she has a boyfriend. Do you know anything about him? Is the relationship serious?'

'Many customers like her, but she not go out with them, not much time off work.'

'So she has no steady boyfriend?'

'I should not tell,' he said cagily, gingerly looking around to see no one was in ear-shot; he put a hand on my arm. 'No boyfriend; she's from Hong Kong, in Grimsby only two months,' he gestured with a victory sign.

'Thanks Jimmy.'

Coerced by my enthusiasm he reciprocated with a smidgeon of a smile.

In the evening I sat at my preferred table, the other tables yet to be engaged by diners. She approached to take my order, but without her usual smile. It would appear that Jimmy was a double agent.

'I don't want you to ask Jimmy about me,' she said firmly.

'I'm sorry, but I have to get to know you. You're upsetting my life: I can't work; I can't sleep; I can't stop thinking about you. I feel we are meant for each other. I want to take you out, to make you happy.'

She was visibly startled by my fervent revelations. Confusion lined her brow, hesitation arrested her lips. I sensed her eyes questioning: are his feelings genuine? I broke the uneasy spell.

'Maybe I could drive you *all* the way home again tonight?'

Her seriousness dissolved, the smile returned. 'Perhaps, but only if I'm alone,' she cautioned, looking around.

She sat uneasily in the passenger seat, coupled hands seeking comfort with each other and fiddling with the strap of her bag. I captured a restless hand, tenderly caressed and lightly kissed it, a lingering kiss, gazing longingly into her eyes.

'Allow me to take you out on your next day off.'

'Oh, I don't know; busy on day off. So little free time. People already talk.'

'So let's give them something real to talk about.'

'I'm not sure. I'll think about it.'

The dreaded sales pitch put-off, "I'll think about it." The hundreds of times I had heard potential customers trot out that dismaying phrase. I decided to let it ride; I was making progress and her reluctance for a date appeared to be disquiet over what colleagues would think of a relationship with an Englishman.

Perhaps she had seen *Love Is a Many-Splendored Thing.* The film relates the moral dilemma of a 1950s inter-racial affair. In a case of art mirroring life, the reputation of Han Suyin, a doctor and later author, was destroyed after her passionate affair with *The Times* correspondent Ian Morrison. She met with disapproval from her Chinese family and was ostracized by medical colleagues; the British expat community cold shouldered him. Attractive unmarried Chinese women on the arm of a colonialist were tarred with the stigma of moral laxity – Tsip Sze (concubine) inference. Fong's cautious reluctance had understandable justification.

Friday lunchtime she took my order before mischievously asking, 'Are you dreaming about me?'

'Yes. I dream about you every night. Why do you ask?'

'You keep me awake,' she whispered. 'Chinese proverb says: "If you can't sleep it's because you are awake in someone's dream."'

Unsure whether this superstitious belief was serious or an oblique research into my feelings, I played along.

'I'm afraid you are destined for many sleep deprived nights. You will be in my dreams for the rest of my life. But ... if you were to come on a date, I may need to dream less.'

'Hmm,' she frowned, sceptical of my logic. 'I'll get your order.'

She served with a few brief exchanges between courses. The restaurant filled and she was too busy to linger, but I was aware of discreet smiles of complicity when our looks collided. When paying, I told her I was away for the weekend in Coventry.

'No dreaming,' she said, wagging her index finger.

'I will daydream instead and send you a special card so you know I am thinking of you.'

Monday lunchtime, seated in the Lotus House ready to order, I looked up into her big, guileless eyes. We smiled. How I longed to kiss those inviting lips so tantalizingly close. I looked back at the menu.

'Did you get my card?' I said nonchalantly.

'I did, Saturday morning; a beautiful card, but who is Valentine?'

'She's the patron saint of sweethearts. A card is sent to someone special, someone a man loves.'

'Why me? You don't know me.'

'How could it not be you?' I smiled with a tilt of the head. 'Give us the chance to get to know one another. When is your next day off work?'

'Half day Wednesday.'

'Keep that time for me and I will take you out.'

'Oh, I don't know,' she said half-heartedly, 'my boyfriend ... '

'Ah yes,' I interrupted, 'the mysteriously elusive boyfriend no one has seen, a piece of Chinese mythology I think.'

'Jimmy doesn't know everything,' she responded indignantly, as if not to have a boyfriend was an insult.

I raised my eyebrows with a frown of disbelief. She stared sheepishly back, her lips parted with hesitation, consternation ploughed her brow and a blush of embarrassment suffused her cheeks – a criminal's alibi exposed. Loss of face is a serious concern with the Chinese and I hastened to console.

'I understand why you defend yourself with the boyfriend pretence to deflect unwanted attention; it's an effective ploy.'

'Many men ask to take me out, but I not want to,' she protested.

'Compliments your beauty,' I absolved sympathetically. 'If you let *me* take you out, I would be a real boyfriend, no need for pretence. Keep Wednesday free.'

She frowned and compressed her lips, the look of a chess player resigned to the loss of the game.

'Okay,' she sighed. 'Wednesday afternoon,' quickly adding the proviso 'but only for a short time.' She looked warily around. 'We cannot meet here, they are not to know.'

'I understand.' I nodded reassuringly.

As I opened the door to the street she semaphored a discrete farewell.

'Yes!' I shouted, punching the air like a winning sportsman. My breath was smoke on the wintery air but I no longer felt chilled, warmed by the kindle of expectation.

Later, I sat in the office drinking tea and pondering a confusion of elation and guilt at what I had initiated and why. There was a definite ambiguity to my marriage, love for my children but not for their mother. The marriage survived like a patient on life support, drip fed by love of the kids. Mary-the-mother had lost her womanly luminosity and sexual appeal, her appetite for sex replaced by tiredness or euphemistic headaches. I doubted she loved me other than as a home provider and father to her children. If I had no love in marriage, then ... This *then* helped assuage my conscience with the confidence of justification.

Marriage to Mary had compromised my life by bowing to societal pressures when my friends had jumped ship to board HMS Matrimony. I married prematurely, not having the confidence to wait for the one to make me forget all others. Fong was a definite candidate. Unlike previous purely sexual temptations, Fong had the profound attraction of love at first sight; I was drawn to her as if I had no choice. I'm getting ahead of myself in assuming she may come to feel love for me, but the strength of my feelings compelled me to find out.

With Mary in Coventry – well over a hundred miles distant – for the next few months of the conveyances, there was time to forge a meaningful relationship with Fong without the chance of discovery; or so I thought.

Chapter 4

After lunch the following Wednesday Fong hurried across the pavement to the car, the raging arctic wind peppering her with snow. So, where to go in Grimsby on a first date during an afternoon tempest? Cinema? Not ideal for getting to know each other with conversation. Restaurant? We had lunched. Pub? Wrong lifestyle impression. Art gallery? Did Grimsby have an art gallery? Was she interested in western art? No, I decided the only viable option was the recently built sports and leisure centre, one of Grimsby's few redeeming features.

The centre boasted an indoor ice rink and I was a competent skater. Fortunately, Fong was suitably dressed for the ice – white polo neck jumper and woven three-quarters length auburn skirt – the weather my co-conspirator.

If you think about it, ice skating is an ideal first date if the girl is a dependent beginner. The necessary physical support affords a hands-on informality avoiding any tentative, embarrassing manoeuvres to engineer a first embrace.

We set off along Cleethorpes Road and when the car approached the front of the Lotus House she shuffled down in her seat and raised a hand to shield her face.

'They must not see me with you,' she excused.

'It's okay, I understand.'

'Where are we going?'

'Have you ever been ice skating?' She slowly shook her head; a look of disquiet replaced her smile. 'Don't worry, I can skate. It's easy; I'll show you ... a new experience,' I cheerfully assured.

Sceptical of my presumption, she looked fazed and stared ahead with an "Oh God, I wished I'd never agreed to this date" look of resignation.

Half-an-hour later, heavy, white leather skating boots imprisoned her dainty stocking covered feet and with my reassuring support we hobbled towards the rink. Fong's eyes had the nervous look of a trapped animal uncertain of its fate. After much encouragement and firmly enfolded in my arms her white knuckles let go of the safety rail and we launched into the flow of boisterous bodies.

I felt her tension as she clung to me like ivy to a tree. Her closeness and trust within my arms were reward for the weeks of longing; I was as grateful as she. Our first tentative laps completed with both bums dry, she relaxed and enjoyment and confidence replaced her qualms.

After several more laps we rested at the barrier rail, my arm about her waist in continuing support. She turned full face towards me, looking up, lips slightly apart. She wore minimal make-up, a little rouge to the cheeks and a hint of auburn eye shadow; with her beauty, less was more. I lightly caressed her cheek. We were engrossed in a sense of intimacy, quietly gazing at each other.

'May I kiss you?'

A coy smile creased her face, she slowly nodded. Her lips were cool, soft, yielding and naked. That exquisite, gentle, lingering kiss would be forever remembered for its hope and promise, not meant to lead beyond itself then but arousing a future commitment.

'I've wanted to kiss your lips since the first time I saw you,' I said breathily.

'I know,' she said, smiling playfully, 'I know.'

Our lips met again, our mouths a natural fit. The merest tips of our tongues gently parried; my heart pounded and I felt the thrill of an electric current course my veins. I suggested a couple more laps to finish before going for tea. The inevitable happened, she lost her balance and we acquired wet bums. We laughed it off, left the rink and dabbed ourselves with handkerchiefs and paper towels.

After reclaiming our shoes we climbed stairs to the first floor café, a glazed structure affording panoramic views over the centre's many facilities. We drank tea and munched crisps. The kisses relieved the first date tensions and we enjoyed a relaxed familiarity to chat and impart personal details suggestive of a continuing relationship.

'What made you decide to come to England? Why Grimsby of all places?'

'I was encouraged to come to Britain by my Buddhist priest and my younger sister, Mai Ling. She and her husband work in Watford this year and I stayed with them when I first arrived three months ago. Uncle Zhang offered me a waitressing job at the Lotus House; I needed money so I came.'

'How come you speak such good English?'

'I studied English at college and later worked in the University library with access to many English language books. I also learned by watching films. I enjoy the cinema.'

'Me to. Tell me some of the films you've seen.'

'Many British and Hollywood films,' she said proudly: '*Casablanca, Brief Encounter, How to Steal a Million, Love Is a Many-Splendored Thing, The World of Susie Wong,* and all the Bond films.'

She has seen *Love Is a Many-Splendored Thing.* I thought best not to mention it. '*How to Steal a Million* is one of my favourites. Audrey Hepburn and Peter O'Toole had such chemistry. There's a wonderful scene in the museum's broom cupboard when she apologises for endangering him with involvement in the heist; she naively wonders why he agreed to help her. He kisses her full on the lips. "Oh, that's why" she coos, realising love. I felt the same emotion when I kissed your lips.'

Fong dipped her head.

'I'm sorry if I've embarrassed you.'

'No, its okay. I see your feelings in looks ... and in trousers.'

'Now I'm embarrassed,' I chuckled, hoping not to blush.

'Don't be embarrassed, it's a natural response to kissing.'

We buried our looks behind sips of tea. I was captivated by her playful candour.

'*Casablanca* is my favourite film. He loved her so much he let her fly away to better life,' said Fong wistfully.

'My favourite too ... the song '*As Time Goes By* ... such a mournful lament for lost love. When Dooley Wilson starts to sing, it brings tears to my eyes.'

'You big softy.' She smiled warmly.

'Yes, afraid so; a sucker for old Hollywood romantic films with happy endings. I often compare life to scenes from movies,' I said pensively.

Fong nodded agreement. The serving girl came to reclaim the mugs and took the empty crisp packets.

'Would you like more tea?'

She shook her head. 'Tea not good here,' she said, wrinkling her nose.

'Tell me what else you like to do. What do you read?'

'Chinese literature and I enjoy the fantasies of Greek myths.'

'Ah yes ... my faux pas regarding Aphrodite. I will never forget your deflating rebuff, I am no Adonis.'

She laughed and put a hand on my knee. 'I apologise, but I didn't want to encourage you then.'

'Apology accepted.'

'I've recently read *Lady Chatterley's Lover* to see why banned,' said Fong.

'The reason I read it too. At school in 1962 the Penguin paperback edition was handed around with all the juicy pages earmarked. A career as a gamekeeper beckoned,' I jested.

She glanced at her watch. 'I have to go soon, working tonight. Tell me about yourself and your family.'

'The Patterson's are not close knit, gatherings restricted to throwing confetti or scattering ashes. I'm an only child, born in Gillingham, Kent, a nowheresville rival to Grimsby for Britain's most dismal place to live. Father was a naval officer and took part in the liberation of Hong Kong from the Japanese. Mother was a café waitress. It was love at first sight for my father. Like father like son it's said; I fell in love the moment I saw you. It doesn't only happen in movies.' We gazed intently at each other and slowly smiled.

'After the war the family moved to Louth and started a catering business, but my father died when I was seven ... cancer.'

'I'm sorry ... do you miss him?'

'Not so much now, but during my formative years, yes. I remember a particular occasion at the school's sports day. I was running a race against another rival for first place. We came off the final bend into the straight and his father was there waving and egging him on. My father wasn't; I came second.'

'Oh, how sad.' She frowned sympathetically.

'Anyway, when father died in 1955, mother sold the catering business and moved to Coventry to be near two of her sisters. I've lived and worked in Coventry until my promotion here last month. What about you, I presume you were born in Hong Kong?'

'Yes, although parents are from Shanghai. In 1949 the family fled by boat to Hong Kong to escape Mao Tse-tung's communists, the so-called People's Liberation Army. Liberation! What irony. Tens of millions died ... our family lost several members, murdered by student red guards. Mao emulated crimes of the first emperor, Qin

Shi Huangdi, intellectuals condemned as counter-revolutionaries, books burned and scholars buried. Mao trained as a school teacher and yet he abolished children's education.'

'Unbelievable,' I said, shaking my head.

'When Mao dies we will have a big celebration.'

'The world should celebrate his demise,' I said with a nod of sympathy.

'When my mother arrived in Hong Kong she only had what she could carry. Paper money was worthless, but my father had gold and managed to rent a flat. Mother was a good cook and ran a popular dai pai dong (street food stall). One day, a British soldier stopped for lunch. He wanted to take her out. He came every day. Like you, he wouldn't take "no" for an answer. He helped her through hard times, gave her money, bought her clothes, and took her to restaurants and dances. She loved him. At the same time she met my father. He drove them in his taxi one evening.

The soldier's tour of duty ended and he returned to England; she did not see him again. She was pregnant but unsure who was the father, soldier or taxi driver. She married the taxi driver. When the boy was born he was not Chinese. Husband was angry and left, but our priest mediated and I was born 1952, my younger sister, Mai Ling, two years later.'

'Are your parents alive?'

'Yes, mother runs a grocery shop, Kowloon side; father drives a taxi.'

'What about boyfriends,' I said sheepishly.

'No one special.' She smiled. 'My priest wants me to marry his brother. He's older, with a baby daughter. His wife died giving birth. So sad. He's a good man, but I want romance ... to marry for love, like in films.' She paused in reflection. 'You have a girlfriend?'

'I want you to be my girlfriend.' I reached for her hand and gently squeezed.

'Hmm, maybe.' She smiled, tilting her head and cheekily looking me up-and-down.

I bit my tongue as the pang of guilt wrestled with my conscience. I am not wearing a ring so she didn't ask if I was married. I decided not to lie if directly asked, but offer mitigation of unhappiness and future divorce. I wanted to confess, but was too afraid of losing her. If we carried on seeing each other I knew the deception would come back to haunt me. For now it was prudent to change the subject and I explained the reason for returning to Coventry at weekends due to the sale of my house.

'What's Coventry like?'

'A major cathedral city, culturally more exciting and cosmopolitan than Grimsby. The town centre is modern, rebuilt after the German blitz. It's famous for Lady Godiva, who rode through the streets naked on horseback a millennium ago.'

'Why ride naked?'

'A wager with her husband, Leofric, Earl of Mercia, to reduce taxes on the poor; unfortunately the tradition died with her.' I smiled ruefully.

I described Mr H's guest house and told her about my work in selling, based in an office up the road from the Lotus House.

'What do you like to do after work?'

'I love the escapism of films and most forms of music, especially classical nineteenth century romantics. When I have time I read novels – thrillers mainly – and play chess. Selling is much like chess, composed of strategy and manoeuvring for advantage, gradually whittling down defences. I had to sell myself to you and combat your defensive boyfriend strategy.'

She smiled sympathetically. 'Many men pester but you keep trying; I think you different: honest feelings, good humour, reassuring deep voice and kind eyes. When you kissed my hand in the car ... such a look of yearning,' she gasped, placing a hand on her heart. 'I wanted to see that look again.'

'And have you?'

'Yes, when we kissed today. No other man has looked at me like *that.*' She paused; we looked longingly at each other. 'I enjoyed this afternoon but now you must take me back.' Her tone inferred reluctance.

We didn't say much on the drive back, exchanged looks and smiles, held hands at times. We intuitively knew what we had in common was more imperative than merely similar interests; something special occurred on the touching of lips.

The Lotus House was closed on Sunday but I needed to return to Coventry at the weekend for mother's fiftieth birthday. Fong had the following Wednesday evening free – one of only two per month – and agreed a date for dinner. As she waved good-bye it was like the end of an engrossing romantic film, but with a trailer promising the screening of a sensual sequel.

Thereafter entering the Lotus House Fong's body language was discreetly welcoming. I kept a watchful eye on male customers attempting to chat-her-up; I am already protective. Fong's shared room with a co-worker prevented an invitation for coffee, so for a few precious minutes each evening we chatted in the car outside her flat, cuddling and kissing under the cloak of darkness.

We transferred to the rear seat but could not be more intimate with our clothes on. The strength of our feelings required the proper ceremony of a romantic candlelit dinner followed by the all night comfortable luxury of a cosy double bed. The cold and cramped back seat of the car would reduce our act of love to shallow gratification. Our first experience needed to be profound and sensuous, time later for playful romps in cars when the weather was warmer and we knew what we meant to each other.

Chapter 5

More snow was forecast; dark cumuli stained the slate blue sky and menaced the Moon's attempt to reveal the countryside. A few miles west of Grimsby near the village of Laceby, we approached a grey-stone Georgian manor seated at the foot of the Wolds. A cordial wash of soft amber light escaped the windows and filtered through the driveway's colonnade of leafless trees. Gravel crunched noisily under the tyres as we parked.

The house had undergone conversion to a hotel and restaurant, but its Grade II listing ensured retention of the building's architectural heritage. The mansion's engaging history included an overnight stay by George lll in all his regalia and regaling madness.

'What a lovely building. Do you bring all your girlfriends here?'

'Only you. My sales manager stayed here early January and I joined him for an evening drink.'

Hands clasped we hurried through the biting wind, up the footfall worn stone steps, through the imposing arched entrance to the foyer with its welcoming warmth. Shorn of my sheepskin, I slipped Fong's fur from her shoulders and she emerged with the beauty of a butterfly from its chrysalis.

She modelled a delicately embroidered pink silk cheongsam with allure cut into the design. The short sleeved bodice contoured the swell of her breasts and possessively hugged her profile before dropping to the ankle; two slits extended above the knee allowing ease of movement. No couture catwalk model could be more irresistible, no opium induced vision more beguiling. I slipped a protective arm about her shoulders as she sheepishly smoothed the fabric to her sides.

'You look stunning, so sensual,' I whispered.

'Thank you Chris.' She shyly dipped her head. 'Cheongsam is for special occasions.'

'I am honoured.' My conventional dark blue suit and sober tie served to heighten her impact. 'Let's get some drinks and go through to the restaurant. I have a table booked.'

We walked past the grand sweeping mahogany staircase to the bar where all eyes focussed upon her, men enviously distracted, women jealous of their attention. Pride straightened my back, expanded my chest and broadened my smile. I gratuitously basked in the glory of envy as we sat and sipped our sherry aperitifs.

'Tell me about this gorgeous dress.'

'Mother made it in Shanghai before the war, fashionable then; but she's too good a cook, the dress no longer fits. She hoped I would have occasion to wear in England.'

'I remember Nancy Kwan similarly dressed as Suzie Wong.'

'In the 1960s Kwan's outfits created a fashion trend in the West for cheongsams. Mao decreed the style decadent and banned it in China. In British Hong Kong we continue to wear.'

'Colonialism has its benefits.'

The grandeur of the restaurant impressed and we paused to take in the scene. The central ceiling panel portrayed a colourful fresco of halcyon Bacchanalian revelry. In a tranquil wooded landscape, naked men and women cavorted with intent, their modesty preserved by artfully placed strands of foliage. Disapproving putti floated across the pastel blue sky on fluffy cream clouds reminiscent of magical Persian carpets.

Oils of idyllic Lincolnshire landscapes, encased in ornate gilded frames, adorned the pale green walls. The furniture was modern but ambient, the napery thick and starched, the silverware heavy and traditional, the waiters stiffed back and liveried.

The hotel was owned by a businessman who also operated a fish merchant close to the quayside in Grimsby. Accordingly the fish was particularly good: North Sea, last caught top of the boat, firm of flesh, lustrous of eye, luminous of scales, landed and filleted the same day. We decided two courses would quell our hunger. Fong chose the poached halibut dressed with hollandaise sauce accompanied by brown long grain rice and a green salad. I decided on the baked salmon with parsley sauce, sautéed potatoes and winter root vegetables.

We raised our glasses of Sauvignon, 'To us.'

The food met expectation and we were spoilt for choice when the desert trolley arrived. We decided on poached pears in cherry brandy, a single portion intimately shared with two spoons.

From a corner dais a balding, bespectacled pianist caressed the ivories into a medley of popular dance tunes. Although athletic at several sports I was never a natural mover on the dance floor. In my teens the steps rehearsed at a Victor Sylvester franchise were long forgotten, although I recognised the tempo of a waltz and the opportunity for a legitimate cuddle. Taking Fong's hand we slalomed through the formation of tables to join other couples on the island dance floor.

She slipped into my arms; I drew her close, nuzzling her hair and inhaling Chanel or whatever. My left hand affectionately traced the contours of her back and waist, sliding easily across the silk's sheen. I rocked from foot to foot as if waiting for a bus on a cold day; she followed my lead.

The truism of the old adage "Dancing is the vertical expression of a horizontal desire" was never more apt. When the music ended we parted reluctantly and sat quietly at table sipping coffees. She reached for my hand and our fingers entwined suggestive of what our bodies wished to do. Our eyes spoke to each other with longing.

Coffees drunk, I suggested an exploration of the hotel's facilities. We entered a comfortable lounge with subdued lighting and deep piled carpet. Button-back green leather armchairs sat by mahogany side tables with glass ashtrays, redolent – except for the presence of ladies – of a gentlemen's club.

A life-size portrait of mad King George hung above the white marble Adam fireplace, the glowing log embers a magnet to clusters of couples. Waiters ferried the amber of brandy and the ruby of port on silver salvers. Gentlemen puffed cigars; a few ladies drew on cigarettes. Murmured conversation occasionally erupted with peals of laughter.

A panelled door opened to a library furnished with glass fronted mahogany bookcases the shelves laden with leather bound, gold embossed tomes. Their titles and bindings indicated a relevance to a bygone era and a faint mustiness savoured the air. Above the cases, painted grandees peered out of white lacy ruffs as if to question our intrusion.

French doors opened into a large Victorian conservatory populated with potted plants and comfortable reclining chairs. Beyond the throw of lights the gardens receded to a woodland gloom. Flurries of snow had begun their fresh camouflage and we stood cuddling to take in the beauty of the changing scene. With a strange sense of unreality we became characters in our own snow globe. I moved behind her, enveloped her in my arms and kissed the nape of her neck and upper arms.

'I love you ... I need you ... stay with me tonight,' I implored.

She turned, placed her arms about my neck and answered with a lingering kiss. With trepidation and crossed fingers I approached the reception desk.

'My wife and I would like to stay over until morning because of the snow. Do you have a double room available?'

'I'm afraid we are fully booked sir,' he replied leafing through a folder.

'Another time,' consoled Fong.

'I couldn't dishonour you with the presumption of booking a room in advance,' I said glumly.

'Next time you may book a room,' she said quietly, coaxing me down to touch foreheads.

Her eyes showed the disappointment and frustration reflected in mine. Another hotel was out of the question; traipsing around from one to the next to find a bed would be unseemly and destroy the romance. We returned to the lounge and sought the comfort of a leather sofa by the fire. I gazed into the flames with thoughts of what might have been, although heartened by Fong's assurance of a mere postponement.

When collecting our coats the receptionist approached.

'Does sir still require a room for the night? A cancellation due to the weather.'

I looked encouragingly at Fong and nodded, yes? She nodded back.

'Yes, we do, my wife and I not wishing to continue our journey for the same reason.'

'Does sir have any luggage?' he said haughtily.

'No luggage. We were not expecting to stop over.'

He glanced in judgement towards Fong. Annoyed by his inference, with a smug smile and theatrical flourish I signed the register "Mr and Mrs Smyth." The name played to the man's unspoken presumption, the '*y*' a gesture to the hotel's four star rating.

Coats in hand we steadily ascended the carved mahogany

staircase to the first floor. Creaking floorboards beneath the carpet alerted life size portraits of past notables to our approach; each pair of eyes seemed to question the intention to break my marriage vows. I paid no heed. We walked on hand-in-hand, silence its own language; I put a comforting arm around her shoulder and her huddling response spoke more than words. The red carpet felt appropriate to the occasion. I opened the door to room eight.

Fong ran her fingers over the embossed brass number as if reading Braille. 'In Chinese numerology, eight is favourable,' she said, smiling confidently.

Chapter 6

The room was spacious and furnished ambient to the Georgian architectural style, although no four-poster. When pushing down on the mattress to appraise its comfort we looked at each other like bashful virgins. A Chagall painting – depicting a kissing couple floating in ecstasy – suggestively hung over the bed and a hint of cigarette smoke alluded to the post-coital puffs of previous lovers. I turned down the bed cover and crossed to draw the curtains, shutting out the blustering snowflakes.

Fong withdrew to the en suite. I switched off the ceiling light and undressed in the modest glow of a table lamp. The silence of the room was deafening. My heart pounded with expectation. From a jug on a side table I gulped a glass of water to irrigate my desert dryness. Fong reappeared looking pure and demure wrapped in the hotel's white towelling bath robe; she folded into my waiting embrace. We kissed and kissed, our tongues enacting a mute duet.

I gently peeled away her cloak of modesty. Her naked flesh – delicate, vulnerable, warm and willing – pressed against my firmness, our breathing excitedly shallow in concert. We eased into the bedding; the cool starched linen threw our bodies together cuddling for warmth. My hands and lips caressed her curves with tender reverence before I gently entered, becoming part of her.

Our rhythm was tempered to the languid momentum of a sultry summer afternoon, prolonging the pleasure until the intensity was beyond control. The rapture of release surpassed previous knowing.

Later, entwined as if one body, we savoured our intimate harmony and temporary languor, impatiently awaiting the next swell of desire. Our eyes coupled in a visual embrace, the endearing gaze of pure love.

'I think we belong,' she said softly.

'I'm sure we do.'

'My first orgasm with a man,' she said coyly. 'I felt beautiful, floating in the heavens like the Chagall heroine.' We gazed at the painting. 'This image will always hang in the gallery of my mind.'

Her sentiments moistened my eyes.

'Chinese proverb says, "Orgasms join souls." Now we're soulmates Chris.'

'We are. I feel I've been waiting for you all my life, only to find you in Grimsby of all places.'

'Not so strange; Chinese believe soulmates have the same hiding place.'

Awaiting my ember to rekindle its fire, Fong – like a detective searching for forensic evidence – observed, 'You've no top skin.'

'Foreskin,' I corrected.

'He handsome with no foreskin. Are you Jewish?'

'No, not Jewish. I have the cock and the nose, but not the faith.'

'You're Christian though.'

'I was christened, an event of social convention, but neither I nor my parents were committed believers. Mother and I lost faith when father died young.'

'You must believe in something.'

'Now I have met you, love is the only belief I need.' I smiled and kissed her. '"All you need is love" is not only a Beatle's lyric; it's the ethos of life.' We kissed again. 'I'm ambivalent about religion and doubtful of the existence of God as represented by the Christian faiths. What I do miss is not having anybody to blame when things go wrong or to thank for a deliverance of good fortune, such as meeting you.'

'Maybe a god had a hand in sending you to the Lotus House.'

'Could be. My landlady packed sandwiches each day for lunch. The day I forgot to take them I lunched at the Lotus House. I put it down to the oft attributed *fate*. What about your beliefs?'

'Chinese people are superstitious with a god for every occasion in life. God Kwan Yu is the patron of restaurateurs; Mr Zhang prays to him every day. My family attend a Buddhist temple to meditate and to appease the gods with offerings and ask for their blessing. Our priest is a good man, fat and happy, like a smiling Buddha; I confide in him, he's a good listener. He studied in England and encouraged me to come.'

'So I do have someone to be grateful to. I would like to meet him one day.'

'You could if you come to Hong Kong,' she said wishfully.

I nodded approvingly. 'One day I will.'

After making love a second time I brewed tea. Fong candidly admitted desire had been an intrusive visitor to her bed after our first date. She had been many months celibate and had to pleasure herself in order to sleep. I confessed to the same offence.

'We will no longer need to reoffend,' I jested.

Over sips of tea we recounted our first sexual encounters. I narrated the fable of my "Mrs Robinson" of *The Graduate* fame, and her dissimilarities with Anne Bancroft's bitchy portrayal. Fong remembered the film but didn't know of the cachet applied to "Mrs Robinson."

Fong lost her virginity to a boy from the same school. She was sixteen, her breasts arrived and she literally stood out from the other girls. Her breasts were magnets to the iron resolve of male students to make their conquest. Her mother warned, "Your legs are like two best friends and should stay together where boys were concerned." But the unknown experience of pleasures of which the older girls boasted induced those two friends to part. Afterwards, she was still in the realm of the unknown, the procedure comparable to a surgical incision without anaesthetic: quick, painful and bloody. Her consolation was graduation to join her peers shorn of the burdensome virginity.

Fong confided about her emotional struggle before her lips had intemperately said "yes" to me. For her, making love was the natural end to the perfect romantic evening, but she had worried I would not understand the naturalness of making love so soon. In my famished state I might take her hungrily and in the cool aftermath of satiated ardour think unfavourably of her fervid surrender. How could she be sure of my love, sure of my understanding? She was not sure then, but she was sure now.

'My mum says "Love remakes a virgin." No other man has taken the virginity of my heart.'

'I feel the same; I never experienced genuine profound love until tonight.'

A little after 2 am we snuggled down intending to sleep, but my impudent erection suffered from insomnia and our conspiratorial smiles suggested sleep would be deferred.

The daylight and general hotel activity woke us. I sauntered over to the window and drew back the drapes. The evening clouds had dumped their snow and given way to blue sky and bright sunlight. The starkly undressed trees shivered in the wind. Fong called my name. I looked across to her. Motes from the bedding surfed on the sunrays streaming across the room.

'Come back to bed.' Her voice had the beguiling timbre of a siren's call.

I slid back between the sheets to luxuriate in the warm comfort of her nakedness and she felt my arousal. Later, we cuddled in blissful exhaustion, the kind I imagined you only get with someone you could love for a lifetime.

After a few minutes Fong donned the hotel robe and padded to the bathroom; the shower gel's humid fragrance escaped through the half open door encouraging me to join her. The warm water temporarily washed away the tiredness from the exertions of the night. We stood and hugged, drenched in happiness. My hands fondled the luscious, warm, slippery wet feel of her and we soaped and rinsed each other with intimate familiarity.

Wrapped in the hotel robes I helped brush her hair to shapely obedience. Fong produced a camera and we photographed each other's jubilation before dressing.

The aroma of fried bacon and toast crept under the door seducing our appetites. In the dining room, Fong again turned heads, the cheongsam not usual morning attire. We enjoyed a first breakfast: bacon, eggs, tomato, mushrooms, toast and Earl Grey for me; porridge and black coffee for her.

'What would you eat for breakfast in Hong Kong?'

'Congee and crullers most days. Congee is similar to porridge, but made from rice and served with various toppings; crullers are twisted strips of deep fried dough we call Yu Za Kuei (fried devils).'

Fong related the legend of two government officials in the time of Confucius who falsely accused a renowned scholar, Yueh Fei, of treason. The crullers symbolized the two corrupt officials being burnt in oil for eternity.

We were content to eat with little conversation, comfortable in our quietude, absorbed in our worldly seventh heavens. From the speculative glances of waiters and other guests I imagined we had the post-coital glow of a self-conscious honeymoon couple: she the blushing bride, he the lucky bastard.

By midmorning, the Sun had begun its slow thaw, the main roads black and wet in stark contrast to the pristine white carpeted countryside. In Grimsby, the drab Victorian streets looked bleak, the snow trodden, stained and slushy.

Outside Fong's flat we hugged and kissed in the car reaffirming our feelings; there was no morning-after disillusionment and we parted reluctantly. She was tired but with no time to sleep before the lunchtime shift; she hoped for a siesta before the evening session. I stopped off briefly at the office to see if any matters were urgent before continuing on to Louth in a mood of euphoria but yawning tiredness, keen to catch up on sleep.

I awoke late afternoon and relived every precious, passionate episode of the night. Thirsty, I dressed and ambled downstairs to make a mug of tea. Cynthia was seated at the kitchen table with a younger neighbour, both adoringly attentive to a gurgling baby rocked in a pram.

The pram caused me to recollect a scene from *Brief Encounter*. The errant couple are seated in a cinema watching the trailer for an adult film, *Flames of Passion*. The closing scene of a man and woman in a passionate embrace is immediately followed by an advert for baby prams. Laughter from the audience, but babies is no laughing matter; despite the forewarning of the restaurant's putti, I reflected that such consequences had been ignored last night.

Like a Catholic I loathed condoms and a layer of latex between us may have disparaged the romance of the moment and suggested my expressions of love were not genuine. My intention had been to withdraw on ejaculation, but I had not the will; the will was to pander to the lure of her body and our intense feelings, recklessness not previously experienced in my hitherto cautious nature. Pregnancy would be an unwelcome complication; I must tactfully suggest Fong attend the NHS Family Planning Clinic.

* * *

Thereafter when I entered the Lotus House our eyes exchanged the emotional empathy of covert lovers. I felt uncomfortable being served by her, but the Lotus House was unavoidably the venue for much of our time.

It was not without a measure of guilt and self-reproach – deceiving Mary and missing time with the kids – I decided not to go back to Coventry the following weekend. My life was in turmoil with two loves pulling in different directions as I lived a lie with both women and my children. The arctic weather conditions conspired to be an acceptable excuse for Mary.

I insisted on room eight when rebooking the Laceby hotel. The room and bed had a comforting familiarity and we made love with a recurring passion. During a resurrection interval she said, 'You know I like Greek mythology stories, but I don't know any English legends.'

'Okay, let me think ... the most famous legend is King Arthur and The Knights of the Round Table.'

With my body between her thighs, kissing her cupped breasts, I modulated my voice to a near whisper as I tell bedtime stories to my children. I began as all such stories do.

'Once upon a time, many centuries ago, King Arthur ruled the heart of England with his Queen, the beautiful Lady Guinevere. They lived at Camelot, a commanding castle guarded by twenty courageous knights resplendent in shining armour and the royal colours. Sir Lancelot was the king's champion and most loyal protector.

Arthur was required to lead his army to quell a rebellion in the north of his kingdom; his trusted knights would guard Camelot and the Lady Guinevere, although Arthur harboured suspicions his knights might succumb to the temptations of his gorgeous queen. So he instructed the blacksmith and saddler to construct a secure chastity belt containing a hidden miniature guillotine, "to protect m'lady against infiltrations to her privacy."

The craftsmen toiled through the night and next day the belt was ready. Arthur was pleased with a demonstration using a large carrot, which when inserted was decapitated. Lady Guinevere was locked into the belt and the key affixed to a chain around Arthur's neck. The king rode off to battle assured his Lady's honour was safe.

A week later, the victorious Arthur returned to Camelot to be welcomed by Guinevere and his knights. Guinevere was released from the chastity belt but Arthur was curious as to whether his doubts had been founded. So he instructed his knights to parade in a line with Lancelot at the end and ordered them to drop their trousers. To Arthur's dismay, every knight had a bandaged injured cock, except Lancelot, whose proud member hung unscathed.

"Oh Lancelot," hailed Arthur, "of all my knights I knew you, you I could trust. You shall have one-hundred guineas in recognition of your abiding loyalty to your liege."

Lancelot bowed reverently before replying in a tongueless mumble, "Oh fank oo fir, fank oo."'

'You cheat,' Fong giggled, as I slithered down her body to demonstrate how Lancelot's impediment had been acquired. 'Not a real story.'

'It's true,' I protested half-heartedly, 'Lancelot did have an affair with Guinevere.'

'Not like that!'

'It's no more unbelievable than the Greek myths.'

'I will tell the story to my friends and sister ... so funny.'

'Yes, but not finish the story like I did,' I teased, wagging my tongue.

'Maybe with my sister,' she countered wryly, 'we're very close.'

Chapter 7

Crystal clear sunny days and Wordsworth's golden daffodils heralded spring; like the season, I felt my tree of life had blossomed. I was never happier than in Fong's company feeling the warmth of her love in every look and touch. Unfortunately, my weekend absenteeism was already seeding infidelity in Mary's fertile mind.

One Thursday evening towards the end of April, I had finished dinner at the Lotus House and sat reading *The Times* waiting for Fong. It was late and the restaurant was untroubled by other customers until three surly youths entered, their swaggering demeanour ominously portent. They were tanked up on lager from a local pub but in want of more drinks. Fong took their order.

Their rapacious eyes were all over her, the lecherous stares of voyeurs. They tried to detain her with compliments, touching her hands and arms. When she returned to the kitchen, leering comments between gulps of Tsingtao beer sullied the ambience with adolescent slang, every sentence punctuated with 'fuck' or 'fucking', characteristics of the unscholarly, verbally challenged. I'd always thought it a remarkable facility of the English language that f-words can so readily be applied to a host of different connotations yet retain the intended sense.

Fong looked apprehensive sensing trouble from their boisterous unwanted attention. I felt embarrassed by their coarseness and crass behaviour; they were letting the English side down. Empty bottles of Tsingtao stood on the table like skittles at a bowling alley. When Fong leaned across the table to collect the empties and spent dishes, one of the youths pulled her down into the vacant seat beside him. She protested and struggled to get up, fending off his roaming hands. Jimmy was in the kitchen so I felt I had to intervene; I strode to their table and pulled Fong free.

'Sorry guys, she's needed to serve my coffee.'

'Fuck off you prick. Get your own fucking coffee. She's fucking serving us.'

He motioned to get up. With a hand on his shoulder, I restrained him.

'Now don't get excited, she has a regular boyfriend. He would not appreciate your advances.'

'Oh yeah, well bring the fucker on, I'll fucking piss all over him.'

'He's already here,' I announced with a quaver of doubtful conviction.

Despite the booze, they immediately twigged, rising as one and pushing the chairs aside to make space. The mouthpiece swung a right punch; I veered to the left and backed away hoping to avoid a brawl. Fong retreated behind the bar and above the commotion I heard her scream, 'Jimmy!'

I retreated, raised arms fended off his thrusting punches. The other two rushed forward scattering chairs and tables in their wake. I felled the first guy with a straight right before tripping over a table leg. I fell backwards with the largest guy's sweating, flabby body pinning me to the floor. His hail of obscenities filled my lungs with stale boozy breath. I struggled to throw him off, but fists and feet rained down. He suddenly was quiet and limp. I heaved him off and looked up to see Jimmy standing over me braced in a martial arts stance.

'You fucking Chink!' shouted the third lout swinging punches as he lunged at Jimmy.

Jimmy side stepped and his foot found the guy's crotch; he doubled over with the yelp of a kicked dog stifled by a sharp chop to the back of the neck knocking him out. The mouthpiece, wiping blood from a cut lip with the back of his hand, stumbled to his feet and seeing his mates slumped on the floor slowly backed off. I scrambled to my feet, fists at the ready.

'You pay! You go! You not come back!' shouted Jimmy, moving threateningly forwards.

His mates got up, looking fazed and swaying unsteadily, massaging the back of their necks. The mouthpiece threw notes on a table and they sheepishly filed out. Jimmy followed to the door and locked it behind them.

'Did someone phone the police?'

'No police,' replied Jimmy. 'Do not want to lose liquor licence.'

I combed a hand through my hair and straightened my ruffled jacket.

'Are you hurt?' Fong asked nervously.

'No, I'm okay, a bit shook up. Probably a few bruises tomorrow.' I flexed my fingers and rubbed my arms and ribs checking for damage. 'Nothing broken.'

'Your cheek and knuckle are bleeding,' Fong noticed. 'I'll get the first aid kit.'

Jimmy handed me a serviette to dab the blood and with Lucy righted the chairs and cleared up the mess. Fong bathed my hand and cheek and applied plaster dressings and we all sat and drank tea.

'I'm sorry to have been the cause of such a commotion, but Fong needed rescuing.'

'It's okay Chris,' said Jimmy, 'they were looking for trouble ... too many beers.'

'Fong told me you were a martial arts expert.'

'Yes. I'm not a big man so I need protection. I trained with Bruce Lee for the film *Fist of Fury*. A small action part,' he shrugged. 'You go and see; showing in Grimsby next week.'

'I will go with you,' announced Fong. 'I saw it in Hong Kong but would like to see it again.'

No one looked surprised, our relationship apparently common knowledge. In case the louts were waiting outside, Jimmy and I accompanied Fong to her flat and Jimmy chaperoned me to my car. The kiss and cuddle for which I had waited all evening was postponed until Monday.

'Bastards!'

I travelled to Coventry for the weekend and explained my cuts and bruises to Mary as an attempted mugging. With sympathetic concern her headaches were postponed, but I had no enthusiasm, going through the mechanical motions like a programmed automaton.

Mary sensed that I was thoughtfully preoccupied throughout the weekend; I blamed work pressures. A Letter from the solicitor informed the conveyances were proceeding apace leaving me struggling with the approaching decision of my future: Fong or my children?

Now our relationship was common knowledge at the Lotus House, Fong cajoled Mr Zhang to allow her every Wednesday afternoon off. The following Wednesday I reluctantly accompanied her along Cleethorpes Road to the Roxy Cinema to see *Fist of Fury*, with the indestructible Bruce Lee (Lee Jun-fan). Set in 1930s Shanghai under Japanese occupation the story represented a parody of the subjugated Chinese nation obtaining retribution. Fong commented the film's powerful sentiment had Chinese audiences standing in ovation. The action choreography and Lee's athletic Kung Fu skills were amazing; in one encounter, Lee defeats twenty or so armed adversaries including Jimmy.

'Jimmy!' shouted Fong, nudging my arm and pointing at the screen.

The immediate audience looked around accusingly, assuming I to be Jimmy and guilty of a back row groping liberty.

For me, the allure and escapism of the cinema began over twenty years ago with the Saturday morning kid's club screened at the local Odeon. When visiting London with my parents an hour in the Cartoon Cinema at Victoria Station was a high point, with its large screen and glorious colour – our family television had a small black-and-white screen. I was enthralled by the crazy antics of *Tom and Jerry* and the spinach fuelled feats of *Popeye the Sailor Man,* although never a convert to the dark green leaf.

I could not recall television programmes matching the excitement of the heroic rescue of Popeye's girl, Olive Oyl, from the unwanted amorous intentions of rival Bluto. I was too young to know what those intentions were, although remembered Bluto stealing a kiss or two. The older schoolboys joked she remained a "virgin Olive Oyl." Trailing after my parents across Trafalgar Square one day, I spotted a poster on the wall of The National Gallery, "Cartoons by Rafael". You can imagine my disappointment.

With declining audience numbers at the beginning of the 1970s the film industry underwent regeneration. The "Dream Factory" studio system declined, Hollywood moguls stepped down and a new era of adventurous film makers and directors emerged: Coppola, De Palma, Spielberg, Kubrick, Scorsese and Lucas in America, Herzog, Wenders, Bergman, Bertolucci and Fellini in Europe.

The multi-media "blockbuster" was spawned with *Jaws* (1975), followed by *Star Wars* (1978). Relaxed censorship for sex, foul language and violence sanctioned the dystopian *A Clockwork Orange* (1971) and a host of soft porn movies – *Last Tango in Paris* (1972), *Emmanuelle* (1974) and the tit-and-bum fantasies from Russ Mayer. Woody Allen struck gold with *Manhattan* (1979) but *Love Story* (1971) remained the highest grossing film of all time until 2006.

I took Fong to a showing of *Love Story;* twenty-five-year-old Jenny Cavalieri's demise had moistened my eyes upon its release five years earlier. Fong clung to my arm and dampened my shoulder.

As we walked arm in arm along Cleethorpes Road she said, 'Love means never having to say you're sorry. I hope you never say sorry to me Chris.'

I hoped so to, but my marriage and kids made it inevitable I was going to say "sorry" to someone, to break hearts, including mine.

Our next film, *Emmanuelle*, was my choice following expectations raised from the marketing hype. There was a long queue, the cinema packed. We came out disappointed: the naff story, ham acting and tame sex, although I liked Sylvia Kristal with her kit off.

The following morning I arrived at the office to be greeted by Danny; a wry smile replaced his usual scowl.

'What did you get up to last night?'

'Had a Chinese meal and went to see *Emmanuelle* at the Regal. Have you seen it?'

'By coincidence, my wife and I saw it last night.'

He stared at me with a resigned frown inviting admission.

'Okay, so you saw me with her.'

'You jammy bugger. How did you manage to pull her?'

'Now Danny, how could she resist,' I jested, hands outstretched, palms up.

'No, seriously, how did you manage it?'

'Sheer persistence Danny, gradually gaining her confidence my feelings were genuine.'

'What about the boyfriend?'

'Luckily I found out she had no boyfriend, a subterfuge to ward off unwanted attention.'

'Does she know you're married?'

'Not yet. I'll have to tell her sometime. Not looking forward to that,' I added pensively.

'You been granted an entry visa into Chinese territory?'

'I'm saying nothing.' My smile had the coyness of admission.

'You lucky bastard,' he grumbled, shaking his head.

The weeks cruised by and my feelings of guilt gradually increased. Fong's relationship had acquired permanence, a part of my life that could not coexist within my marriage. I was relieved when the estate agent reported the buyer's chain on the Coventry house sale had broken, gaining more time with Fong and the status quo. This sense of being on borrowed time made each episode with Fong precious, occupying as it seemed a parallel universe of love and romance without the everyday chores, hassle and distractions of family life.

Another weekend arrived and I decided to stay over. I phoned Mary with an adenoidal voice pretending a heavy cold which, self interestedly, she accepted as good reason not to invite infection. Fong persuaded Mr Zhang it was imperative she had Saturday off and he reluctantly rearranged the staff rota. I wanted to take Fong to Lincoln to show her the cathedral and neighbouring historical area. Our visit coincided with a concert of classical music and the coda would be a visit to a tea house with a Chinese connection.

Chapter 8

The area around Lincoln Cathedral, known as Uphill, is approached by a cobbled lane appropriately named Steep Hill, lined with quaint, rickety, subsiding houses, some dating from the twelfth century. Fong remarked on the contrast with Hong Kong, where the old is swept away to make way for the vertical new. The Chinese have not the same sentimental attachment to ancient architecture unless of religious or imperial significance.

The cathedral was Fong's first visit to a Christian church. She was struck by the sombre greyness, but impressed by the overall elegance, grandeur and cavernous space – the third largest church in England – compared to the colourful intimacy of many Buddhist temples.

The nave particularly impressed with its slender arched pillars of Purbeck marble and limestone soaring majestically to, unusually, an asymmetric vaulted ceiling. Near the altar a farrago of fragrances loitered innocently: the mustiness of old bibles, whiffs of molten tallow, scents from bouquets of flowers. A polite dust reveals when touching the tactile masonry as we walked the cloisters.

The south transept's large rose window of aged stained glass allowed the afternoon sun to adorn the grey interior with a radiant spectrum. I watched with amusement as Fong playfully avoided the perceived sacrilege of treading on the heavenly beams. To one side a raised tray of sand sown with slender votive candles warmed with its legion of flickering flames; we silently wished as we added to their number. I wished for a resolution to my situation somehow allowing a life with Fong and my children.

We returned to the nave, the makeshift auditorium filling with eagerly expectant patrons whose chatter reverberated off the stone acoustics. We shuffled past annoyed knees to take our seats, austere pews of English oak which may have induced Winston Churchill's observation: "The mind cannot take in more than the seat can endure."

It was Fong's first western classical music concert. A few minutes remained for me to introduce the programme.

'This concert's music is sensually exciting, full of sexual analogy and subtext,' I enthused.

'In a church!' she challenged, with a dubious frown.

'Apparently so. Debussy's *L'Après-midi d'un faune* languidly portrays the après-lunch reverie of a drunken debauched faun with two alluring nymphs. Following Bruch's wonderfully melodic *Violin Concerto No 1*, Ravel's *Bolero* builds to a shattering crescendo as the concert's finale. It's orgasmic!'

With a look of preposterous scepticism, a little fart of a laugh escaped her lips and her nose wrinkled as if trying to sniff out the truth of this assertion. She later admitted to being seduced by the Debussy and mesmerized by the swirling repetitive rhythms and shattering climax of the Ravel.

Being a little after four, I suggested tea be next on the agenda. We eased through the spill of concert goers and sidestepped the tourists preoccupied photographing the bricks and timbers of antiquity. As the crowd thinned we strolled up the narrow street, treading cobblestones worn smooth from centuries of footfall.

A short stretch from the cathedral square, we entered a quaint olde worlde tea shop with leaded windows of rippled olden glass, blackened oak beams and inglenook fireplace. The whitewashed walls were furnished with copper and brass utensils, blue-and-white china plates and antique prints of Lincolnshire aspects. The rustic oak spindle-back chairs suggested a commercial imperative of Churchillian reasoning.

We were met by the frigid gaze of aged regulars politely sipping tea and munching crumpets and scones. The women donned the uniform of woollen twinsets and rinsed perms, their husbands' tweed-jackets and combed over hair. Peering over a parapet of spectacles – a glass wall of class and racial prejudice – they eyed us with the haughty disdain with which their generation viewed inter-racial relationships. Fong sensed the hostile vibes and clung to my arm.

A waitress in black dress, white lace trimmed apron and matching cotton tiara served. We enjoyed a traditional English tea: hot toasted crumpets with lashings of melting butter followed by warm fruit scones with strawberry jam and clotted cream. Swilled down with Tetley's finest, nothing was more ambrosial or agreeably English.

Fong noticed we were ingesting from *Willow Pattern* blue-and-white crockery, with its mythical Chinese landscape shaded by a willow tree. She looked pensively at the plate.

'Does it remind you of home?'

'Nothing like Hong Kong, but reminds me of the meditation garden at our Buddhist temple.'

'Did you know *Willow Pattern* was devised by Thomas Minton and Josiah Spode, two famous British china manufacturers?'

'I knew it was not an original Chinese design although now made in China.'

I turned the plate over. 'This one states "Spode, fine bone china." To help market the *Willow Pattern* the makers created a romantic fable to charm the Victorian public. A wealthy Mandarin's beautiful daughter loved a humble servant but her father arranged marriage to a rich duke. On the eve of the marriage, she eloped with her lover to a remote island. There the couple lived happily for many years, but the Duke sought revenge, discovered their whereabouts and murdered them. The Gods, moved by this injustice, morphed the lovers into swallows, which are pictured flying amorously together.'

'Such a sad story,' said Fong wistfully.

'Come, I have a surprise for you, the real reason for bringing you to Lincoln.'

I clasped her hand and led her through the café to the rear outside door.

'Oh Chris, a Chinese garden. How wonderful.'

'The Victorian owner of the tea shop designed it based on the landscape depicted on the *Willow Pattern* crockery.'

I contentedly watched her explore the miniature walled garden, carefully treading the winding path, pausing to admire each revealed landscape: the pool a great lake overhung with weeping willow; the rockery a mountain range. She crossed an ornamental wooden bridge and peered into the dwarf pavilion. As she wandered, her trailing hand stroked the plants and she bowed to sniff the scented blossom, conscious of the harmony with nature, appreciating the tranquillity the garden's designer intended.

We walked arm in arm to the car park, kissing as we went, before setting course to Grimsby along the A46. Coming to a beckoning country lane I turned off the main road.

'Where are we going?'

'I need a cuddle.'

'One track mind.' She smiled knowingly.

Passing a farmer's entrance to a meadow I screeched to a halt, reversed and turned into the field. After a quick reconnoitre, we adjourned to the back seat. Ravel's *Bolero* thrummed my mind as we reached our shuddering climax. We remained entwined, peacefully absorbed in each other.

'Why do you love me Chris ... for my body?'

'I love the essence of you, everything about you,' I responded with a hug. 'You are cultured, educated, intelligent, beautiful, kind and loving. I have never felt so loved, but I cannot deny being partial to all this flesh.'

We laughed as I hoisted her astride to play with her breasts. I suspected my fetish was probably a desire for maternal consolation having been too soon weaned off the nipple or kept on the breast too long? I never got around to asking mother. Acknowledging my pleasure, Fong had taken to wearing a front opening bra. She wore her breasts with the victorious pride of an old soldier displaying his chest of medals.

Chapter 9

After lunch the following Wednesday, we journeyed to Louth; Fong wanted to see the town where I planned to settle and to visit my digs.

'To picture you when we're apart,' she said persuasively.

We strolled about the town centre. It was market day and the traders spilled from the Victorian market hall into the main street (Eastgate), their lively banter tempting shoppers to colourful displays of local produce and a motley array of household goods and clothing. Fong commented that in Hong Kong most food shopping was daily in street markets, the tradition of fresh food sustained by lack of space and refrigeration. Fong liked the town centre, its small scale layout and quality shops; I guess she considered Louth a potential future home with me.

On the town square we sat under a parasol amidst the bustling and enjoyed afternoon tea and cake waiting for the local bus to Hubbard's Hills. The bus noisily wended its way through the congested Victorian streets past the hallowed precincts of King Edward VI Grammar School – Alfred Lord Tennyson a famed luminary. At the edge of town we alighted by a rickety timber bus shelter and followed the signed public footpath.

The name "Hubbard's Hills" is a misnomer; a valley of outstanding natural beauty with wooded slopes supporting mature deciduous trees filtering the late afternoon sun. The meandering river Lud lazily trickled into Louth on its way to drown in the North Sea. We ambled down the towpath arm-in-arm, hand-in-hand, lips-on-lips, smile-for-smile, chatting contentedly.

On the opposite bank stood a small classical Greek styled stone memorial; the fluted columns supported a plain frieze and triangular entablature. We crossed by a brief wooden bridge to investigate. An engraved plaque revealed the memorial and park to be a conservation area dedicated to the memory of Annie and Auguste Pahud, characters of a tragic love story. Auguste taught French at King Edward VI Grammar School; Annie Grant was the farmer's daughter he loved and married. Tragically, 1899, a few years into the marriage, she fell ill and died. Auguste was devastated and took his life to join her.

'So sad. That's real love,' reflected Fong, 'I want a man to love me as much.' She looked at me with a questioning mien.

'I love you as much, more than words can say.'

We hugged and kissed. I meant those heartfelt words, not knowing one day I would feel as desolate as Auguste Pahud.

Further down the valley a café beckoned. We sat on the grass by an ornamental lake licking ice creams before exiting the park and wandering back to town through the maze of narrow antiquated streets. On Westgate, we stopped to gaze at The Limes, the eighteenth century schoolhouse formerly occupied by the Pahuds; Auguste hung himself with a dressing gown cord from a joist in the kitchen.

We ventured into St James' Church yard. In the shade of a dark yew a listing headstone – stained with lichens from a score of winters – stood witness to my father's abbreviated life. Fong placed a comforting arm about my waist. I was in need of his counsel concerning my predicament of competing loves, although I suspect he would have favoured family unity.

However, in the next grave lay Cecil, his brother, the globe-trotting family rebel. He would have encouraged me to follow my heart, to drop everything – marriage, family, house, country – borrow money and head to the orient.' "Carpe diem" (seize the day) could have been engraved on his headstone.

We left the church and entered The Wheat Sheaf, a traditional pub on Westgate. In a cool courtyard, chilled half pints of cider quenched our thirst and steak and salad and jacket potatoes satisfied our appetites. We cuddled, impatiently waiting for the Sun to set and for Cynthia's whist drive to commence.

Fong was aware of the need to be smuggled across the Howard's prohibited border, evading the patrols of other guests and Mr H. We approached the house from the side to avoid the dining room window, slipped in through the hall and scampered light footed up the stairs without being seen or heard.

The room, double bed and garden view met with Fong's approval.

'You're lucky to have a room to yourself, not to share as I have to in Grimsby and Hong Kong.'

'That's not good; everyone needs their privacy,' I sympathised. 'Perhaps I should go and leave you to enjoy some solitude.' With a straight face, I got up to leave.

'Ha ha,' she scoffed, pushing me back on to the bed and climbing astride.

We had undressed when there was a sharp knock at the door. We froze, staring anxiously at each other.

'Just a minute,' I called out. 'Shush,' I mouthed sotto voce, placing a finger across my lips.

I wrapped Fong in my dressing gown, placed her clothes in the wardrobe and bid she hide behind the hinged side of the door. I replaced my underpants to constrain my erection and wrapped a camouflaging towel about my waist before half opening the door.

To my relief it was Alistair, one of the regular guests.

'Hi Chris, it's my birthday. A couple of us are going down to the pub for a drink; will you join us?'

'Congratulations, but you'll have to excuse me, I'm about to go for a shower and have an early night.'

'We'll be in the Wheat Sheaf if you change your mind.'

'Thanks for asking. See you.'

I closed the door; when Alistair's footsteps fell silent I turned the key in the lock and breathed out the tension.

'Bed, woman,' I said sternly, pointing.

To every movement the wooden bed frame creaked like old floorboards and the obstreperous springs twanged at random in dissonant rebellion as if determined to alert the household to our conspiracy.

Conjoined like Siamese twins we tenderly teased our bodies towards orgasm akin to Tantric converts. The moment came with an uncontrollable rush, her muscles contracting about me with rigor mortis intensity. Her histrionic expression of ecstasy added to the orchestrated medley of the bed creating an atonal cantata for orgasm, bed springs and creaking frame. With glorious relief I gushed over with a moaning coda.

After the cacophony of our reckless abandonment, I half expected hurried footfall on the wooden stairs and accusatory hammering of fists upon the door; but no, all was quiet. After a few minutes of blissful harmony and murmured endearments we reluctantly dressed. It was prudent to vacate the house before Cynthia returned; discovery would be deemed a violation of the moral reputation of her establishment enforced by the "no guests" rule.

Cynthia had met Mary and the kids in January; the family stayed under her roof for a few days whilst we viewed potential houses in Louth. The house decided upon was literally around the corner.

Cynthia's rectitude would consider my transgression indefensible, a crime of immoral lust. I was sure she would demand an immediate vacation of the room and the temptation to act as informant to Mary and Fong would be compelling. On reflection, this adventure had been a reckless risk; perhaps my subconscious willed a declaration of the truth.

Our escape route appeared clear and we stealthily descended the stair into the darkened hall and headed towards the front door. The parlour door swung open and light fell across the hallway picking us out with searchlight precision. Mr H emerged on his way to the cloakroom. He stopped his wheelchair and, with a mix of surprise and confusion, stared at the startled criminals before him. I moved protectively closer to Fong ready for his response. He gazed at Fong and his jaw dropped; his expression took on a look of disbelief as if she were an apparition. He shook his head, as if to clear an image he doesn't believe is before him.

Carefully removing his spectacles and placing them in his lap he said, 'You know Chris; I can't see a blasted thing without these on.'

I encouraged Fong towards the front door.

'Thanks Mr H.'

'I was young once,' he replied wistfully.

On the way to the car, Fong paused. 'Did you see how he looked at me,' she said, with a concerned frown.

'I did. He seemed shocked as if he'd seen a ghost ... as if he recognised you. Is he a customer at the Lotus House?'

'No. I've never seen him before, but ... there's something familiar about his face.'

Chapter 10

After lunch the following Friday as I contentedly sipped coffee, Fong sprung a devastating surprise.

'Are you going to Coventry this weekend?' she said cheerfully.

'Yes,' I hate being away from you but I must go ... things to attend. I wish I could take you with me.'

'Well, this time you can.' Her smile and eyes were alight with enthusiasm.

'What do you mean?' I said anxiously.

'Mr Zhang has given me holiday tonight and tomorrow. I told him it was important I go with you.'

'Oh blimey, wow ... erm ... great,' I spluttered, choking on the coffee.

I coughed and cleared my throat, my grey cells scurrying to find an excuse, a culprit with no alibi. I felt the colour draining from my face. She gave me no time to think.

'What time do we go?' she said eagerly.

'Well ... erm ... I guess about five.'

'Okay, I will be ready. I look forward to seeing your house and to be with you all the weekend,' she enthused.

I paid the tab and got up to go; she touched my arm.

'Are you okay? You look pale.'

'No I'm fine ... in need of fresh air. See you later.'

In a bewildered daze I traipsed back to the office desperately seeking a plausible exit to this self imposed labyrinth. I enlisted Danny to help.

'You've dug a right hole for yourself,' he chuckled. 'Make us a tea lad and we'll think on it.'

We sat and nursed our mugs of sweet tea. I was surprised by Danny's revelation he'd had a mistress a few years back. He was as far removed from your archetypal Lothario as any work of fiction could reasonably imagine.

'In my case we both knew we were in unhappy marriages. Now that's an option. Confess to your marriage. Problem over,' he grins, gesturing with open hands.

'Relationship over as well,' I said dolefully. 'No, that's the last resort.'

'You'll have to tell her sometime, even if you leave the wife,' Danny countered.

'If I had no kids I'd already have left her. I don't love my wife, never did when I think back on it ... but I do love my kids, I wouldn't want to be separated from them. I also love Fong, she lights up my life.'

'She'd be a light in any man's life,' mused Danny.

We sat mulling over alternatives: illness; family bereavement; car breakdown; house sold; having to work the weekend; create an argument and temporarily fall out.

'Take her somewhere more exciting, London for instance.'

'I can't afford a stay in London,' I said, vexed. 'The car breakdown excuse is plausible for staying the weekend in Grimsby to both Fong and Mary, but I'll need a set of wheels to get around over the weekend.'

'Well, we could swop cars.'

'No, I'd have no excuse for not travelling.'

'Yeah, that's true. Tell you what, you follow me home after work, leave your car at my place and take the company van. Tell them you can't go to Coventry in the van, because the company won't let you, but you can use it locally. If either of them queries it, say it's to do with excess mileage ... or insurance cover.'

'I guess they'll buy that, I'll phone the restaurant after I've spoken to Mary.'

Mary already regarded my weekend stays in Grimsby with suspicion and I hadn't planned on another stay so soon. Fong's intervention gave no option, unless I confessed to being married.

With trepidation I lifted the phone to Mary.

'How come it's broken down? The bloody car's new. You only got it in January,' she complained with annoyed scepticism. 'I have a lot planned this weekend, now you've ruined everything!'

'I haven't ruined anything; I can't help it if the damned car has packed up.'

'Why can't a garage fix it and you can come tomorrow morning?'

'They can't get the parts until Monday.'

'Hire a bloody car!'

'I've already tried, there's nothing available; height of the tourist season.'

'Tourists in Grimsby!'

'Not Grimsby. Cleethorpes. It's one conurbation.'

'What about Danny? Ask him to lend you his car.'

'Already asked, his wife needs it for a trip.'

'What about one of the company's vans.'

'Not allowed, insurance restrictions.'

'So why don't you come by train and hire a car here?'

'Oh come on Mary. That's totally impractical. The journey takes too long. I have to change at Sheffield and again at Birmingham. It would be midnight before I got home. I would spend half of Saturday trying to hire a car and lose most of Monday returning it and travelling back to Grimsby. Think of the cost of it all.'

There was an ominous pause. 'I don't believe you. It sounds a lame excuse for not wanting to come home this weekend. Are you having an affair?'

'No. Don't be so melodramatic. The car has broken down, that's all. You can speak to Danny if you want, he will confirm my story.'

I bit my lip; the moment I uttered the "story" line; an unfortunate choice of words.

'Yes, it sounds like a concocted story. A bloody work of fiction!'

I pictured her slamming the receiver down, her face flushed with anger. I gulped a mouthful of tea to rinse away the dryness following Mary's third degree. The guilt weighed heavily as I pictured the kid's disappointment; I would miss them.

The situation was an opportunity to confess my marriage to Fong; otherwise her threat to join me in a trip to Coventry would hang over me like a hangman's noose. But in the knowledge of said eventuality I would not be caught out again and prepare my excuses connected to the house sale, or a weekend sales course at International's head office. Yes, I could conjure up a believable excuse and avoid the need to confess my marriage. I breathed out a sigh of relief and phoned Fong.

In calm contrast to Mary, Fong sounded downhearted but not suspicious. 'At least we will be together Saturday and Sunday. I'm sure Mr Zhang will give me another weekend off.'

I phoned Cynthia who, sympathetic to my car breakdown, agreed to a weekend stay, breakfast only. I parked the car on the driveway at Danny's bungalow and continued to Louth in the company's van. After a shower and a scrumptious evening meal of Lincolnshire pork with apple sauce, roast potatoes and cabbage, Mr H asked to see me.

'Come in Chris, sit down; Cynthia's out and I wanted a word about ... you know ... the other night, your lady friend.

'What about her,' I said defensively.

'Well, I presume she's more than a platonic friend.'

'You presume rightly.'

'Is she from Hong Kong?'

'Yes, she works in a Chinese restaurant in Grimsby, the Lotus House.'

'Oh yes, I know it ... good reputation. Had a feeling she was Cantonese. I served in Hong Kong after the war, a sapper, Royal Engineers, two year tour of duty rebuilding damaged infrastructure after the Japs surrendered in '45. Best posting in the British Army. Hong Kong was teeming with immigrants from the mainland, some of the women stunningly beautiful like your friend. When I said to you the other night I was young once, that was my meaning; I was in love ... been reminiscing ever since.'

He paused with a wistful look of longing and puffed on his pipe.

'Our platoon was repairing a water main in Kowloon and on a nearby street corner a dai pai dong sold hot food. The aromas attracted my attention and I noticed the woman was as gorgeous as your friend; her resemblance startled me the other night ... like an apparition. Anyway, after several days of persuasion she came on a date. I'll show you a photograph.' He reached for a cupboard below the bookshelves, took out a bulky red photo album and thumbed through the stiff black pages. 'Ah, here she is. Don't mention this to Cynthia ... bit of a sore point.'

The photo was of its time, sepia on rigid card with the photographer's Kowloon address stamp in red on the rear: Wang Shu Photographic. A youthful and handsome Mr H wearing khaki shorts and shirt and a broad smile stood with his arm around a petite woman elegantly dressed in a cheongsam. I took a lingering look; she was about Fong's age, of similar physique and bore a distinct facial resemblance. The cut and floral design of the cheongsam looked disturbingly familiar. Could be a popular style, but I remember Fong saying her mother had tailored her cheongsam.

I handed back the photo; he looked at it thoughtfully, breathed out a resigned sigh and carefully reinserted it. I didn't know what to say, I wasn't sure what I was seeing.

He relit his pipe and was enveloped in a cloud of aromatic smoke.

'I loved her; but had to serve out my commission back in England, six months or so. About three months later she wrote she had married,' he said glumly with a shrug. 'I was devastated and married Cynthia on the rebound.'

He leaned forward towards me and his gaze and voice changed from musing nostalgia to fatherly propriety. 'I was single, the wild oats of youth. It's different with you Chris, with your wife and kids. Someone's going to end up hurt if it gets serious.'

'It is serious. I love her.'

'I assume your marriage to be in difficulties.'

I paused to think, bent over, hands clasped between my legs. 'An analogy would be to think of my marriage as a vase of wilted flowers the kids keep topping up with water to prolong the blooms. If it wasn't for the kids the flowers would be dead.'

'Does your wife know of the affair?'

'No, but she's suspicious, keeps insinuating.'

'Does your friend know you're married?'

'Not yet. It's a dilemma I'm struggling with. I love this girl as much as I love my kids. If only I had met her a few years ago, before the kids arrived.' I shook my head despondently. 'I'm due to exchange contracts on the house in the next couple of weeks, so I have to decide my future. You're right; someone will be hurt, including me.'

'Are you sure it's not the sex Chris? Oriental women can be so beguiling. No woman, no matter how good she is in bed, is worth affecting your kid's futures.'

'From the moment I set eyes on her I had the profound emotional connection of soulmates; the sex is great because we love each other. I feel I've been waiting for her all my life, only to turn up a few years too late.'

'Well, think hard about the emotional consequences; consider what sort of life you will end up with if you choose to leave your wife and be separated from your kids. Divorce will also bear heavy financial costs: loss of the matrimonial home and the penalty of alimony to support your children.

'I know.' I nodded agreement.

There was a pensive pause. 'Getting your lady friend pregnant would be an unwelcome complication,' he warned, wagging a raised index finger. 'I suggest you don't bring her to the house again. Your secret is safe with me, but if Cynthia found out she wouldn't be able to hold her tongue.'

'Thanks for your concern. I appreciate the fatherly advice.'

'I have occasion to thank you Chris; I've relived some wonderful memories I thought were buried too deep.'

We shook hands like old friends.

Chapter 11

Saturday mid morning, I drove the van to Grimsby to meet Fong. My thoughts turned to Mr H and his remorse at not being able to pursue his eastern promise; I couldn't bear to think I may not be able to pursue mine; at least it would be my decision.

The similarity of the cheongsam and the facial likeness to Fong in Mr H's photograph were disquieting and I needed to discuss the situation with her.

She opened the door to her flat and joyfully flung her arms around me. 'Room-mate has gone to see a friend and Jimmy and Lucy are working. You can come up for tea.'

'I would prefer an invitation for coffee,' I said, with a knowing smile.

'Coffee? Ah, I know, yes coffee, I see in many films.' She shook her head and waved an admonishing finger. 'One track mind.'

Fong's first floor double bedroom was furnished and decorated in a manner indifferent to style, the legacy of an apathetic landlord and a history of interim tenants with no motivation to refurbish. Passé wallpaper, tired paintwork, worn carpets and drab curtains witnessed many previous impoverished lives.

The room retained a temporary feel despite Fong's homely touches: postcard views of Hong Kong, family photographs and a bunch of fresh flowers (from me). On the window sill a banana intimately cuddled up to two apples in a glass bowl acting as a bookend to a handful of paperback romances, an edition of *Classical Mythology* and a much thumbed *Concise Oxford English Dictionary*.

Two single beds, one on each side of the sash window, were separated by an invisible demarcation line across the carpet. On one side, Fong's neat haven with its few sticks of furniture thoughtfully curated for favourable feng shui. The other side – a shambolic unmade bed with scattered clothing and cosmetics – resembled the aftermath of a burglary.

After the obligatory Jasmine tea Fong's bed also became an unmade shambles. We ended up in a tangle of bedding on the floor, her single bed inadequate for our energetic coffee euphemism. We climbed back into bed; she cuddled in my arms, head on my chest.

From the bedside cabinet I picked up the picture frame containing several family photographs. Fong pointed to her parents, mother Fang Qin and father Jiàn Yi. Fong's younger sister, Mai Ling, looked catwalk model attractive. Half-brother, Zhi Ming, appeared studious with hair swept back and circular glasses.

'How old is he?'

'Twenty six.'

I told Fong about Mr H's revelations of his time in Hong Kong, which explained his sympathetic reaction. While Fong brewed more tea, I picked up the picture frame and again scrutinised the picture of Fong's mother. Although older she had to be the same woman in Mr H's photo.

'You English think all Chinese faces look alike,' Fong chided.

'A stereotype portrayed by old films,' I said indignantly. 'Take a dispassionate look at the coincidences. The two women bear a strong resemblance. The cheongsam looks the same, which you say was tailored by your mother. Your half-brother is a mix of Chinese and white European. Your mother conceiving Zhi Ming corresponds to Mr H's tour of duty in Hong Kong in 1949. The evidence is compelling.'

'I'm not convinced, too many coincidences,' she said thoughtfully. You've been watching too many films.'

'I agree it sounds more like the staple of fiction than life, but the facts indicate its truth.'

'I would need to see Mr H's photo.'

'Okay, I'll try to get hold of it. What does your mother remember about the man she had an affair with?'

'She loved him ... happy times together.'

'No, I mean facts, his name and rank?'

'She called him Bob ... a corporal I think, an engineer in the British Army.'

'Mr H was an engineer. Did your mum sell food as a street vendor?'

'Yes, from a dai pai dong.'

'That's how he said he met his love. I'll find out his Christian name and rank to be certain.'

'Even if true, I'm not sure he will want to know after so long.'

'If it is him, doesn't he deserve to know he has a son?'

'Sometimes memories are best left in the past.'

'Doesn't Zhi Ming want to know his father?'

'Of course.'

'Let's find out for sure, we can then decide what to do about it, if anything.'

'Okay,' she said reluctantly, 'You show me the photo.'

On the ground floor a communal lounge housed easy chairs and a TV. The narrow hall led to a galley kitchen consisting of a couple of pine units over a work surface, cream enamelled sink with dripping tap and several unwashed cups and dishes. A fridge and free-standing cooker looked past their prime. A fluorescent strip flickered and buzzed before reluctantly blazing into life.

Beyond the kitchen a door led to a small bathroom with avocado suite; a shower head was attached to the bath taps by rubber connectors. The windowsill housed toothpaste and brushes, bottles of perfume, shampoo and moisturising lotions. An Ascot wall mounted water heater erupted to life with an ominous report and we refreshed ourselves in its glistening lava before agreeing on lunch.

In 1976, the Barry Marsden chain of seaside fish restaurants established a quality against which others were measured: not for the decor of magnolia emulsion stencilled with images of dolphins and sea horses; not for the tables of wipe clean mock-teak Formica; not for the chairs covered in worn red leatherette; not for the inelegant chubby crockery and cheap cutlery; not for the builders' grade tea the colour of the Formica; and not for the chalky white bread spread with margarine. But noted for the fish: succulent haddock and cod, last caught top of the boat delivered from Grimsby docks every morning, the batter light and crisp with little hint of oil.

'Are fish-and-chips your national dish?'

'Along with roast beef and Yorkshire pudding it has become so, but battered fish was an Andalucían recipe introduced centuries ago by immigrant Sephardic Jews escaping European persecution. We British had the idea of adding chips. It wasn't until 1860 the first fish-and-chip shop opened in the East End of London. Before WWII people in Grimsby could bring their own fish to a shop and have it fried for a penny.'

An overworked waitress brought the tea, the tray plonked on the table with all the finesse of a navvy.

'Today I will drink builder's tea with milk and sugar ... time honoured accompaniment to fish-and-chips.'

Fong checked the brewing, stirred the leaves, perused the colour and ritually poured. She carefully added a dash of milk and two lumps per my wont, stirring until the sugar dissolved the cup and saucer then positioned by my hand. I half expected her to raise the cup to my lips, such was her devotional attention. It could only be a cultural thing, of partial emancipation conditioned to nurturing the needs and comfort of her man.

After enjoying Marsden's fish lunch Fong invited me to see a friend, a waitress in a Chinese restaurant in the centre of Cleethorpes. A sign on the door read *'NO DOGS'* and seeing as we were to dine there later, I was relieved dogs were not on the menu. I do not jest; last year the *Coventry Evening Telegraph* carried a report of a local Chinese takeaway prosecuted by health officials who found a couple of skinned pooches hanging in the kitchen. Fong smiled at my aside but on a more serious note canine dishes became a necessity in China during the great famine created by Mao's failed agricultural policy.

Behind bowed latticed windows the decor and furnishings were kitsch chinoiserie with the obligatory red lanterns enlivening the pale green colour scheme. Several large Chinese paintings inferred an encoded confidence in the quality of the cuisine as much as the owner's penchant for traditional art. A welcome waft of cooling air eddied from four ceiling fans whirring like aeroplane propellers dissipating the lingering aroma of lunches cooked earlier. The cover was greater than the Lotus House but being mid afternoon the staff were untroubled by customers.

Fong's friend, Liu Chuang, was younger, somewhat plain facially but with a cheerful personality. From the kitchen she produced a large flower decorated white teapot of fragrant Jasmine tea and a wicker drum of mixed dim sum and sweetmeats. I politely sipped from dainty porcelain cups and sampled the delectable dumplings, showing off my proficiency with chopsticks.

The two women nattered contentedly in Cantonese and I followed the dialogue from mouth to mouth, like a dog expectant of walkies but with as little understanding. The language seemed to be one of vocal combat than flowing phrases with tone used to convey meaning. Unlike French or Italian, Cantonese is not melodic on the ear.

Although a spectator to their conversation, the recurrent looks in my direction implied I was a frequent topic. I basked in my imagined glory and smiled approvingly to return their glances. After a lengthy hushed discourse from Fong, they both shrieked with laughter; the tale of Sir Lancelot had entered Chinese lore.

Later, following a visit to the beach and an arm in arm stroll along the promenade, we returned to Liu Chuang's restaurant for our evening meal before driving into the countryside. Under the cloak of darkness we christened the van.

Chapter 12

The summer of '76 registered record temperatures with weeks of scorching sun: grasses parched straw blonde; foliage jaded and wilted; earth baked and crazed; rivers and reservoirs dry or depleted.

On Sunday I suggested a picnic high on the Wolds, hopeful for a relieving breeze. I cajoled Cynthia into making sandwiches and packed a bottle of Blue Nun in ice, contained in a makeshift polythene and cardboard cool box.

We motored through Laceby on towards Caistor, homesteads giving way to meadows of cows' chewing-the-cud before hillsides of perpetually grazing sheep. On the crest of the Wolds we parked in a lay-by and with our picnic, blanket and cool box, strolled along the ridge.

After a quarter-mile we encountered one of all too few hardy trees, swept bent like an old man by winter's coastal winds. A mitigating breeze wafted at Fong's hair but the Sun blazed down and we were grateful for the tree's meagre shade beneath which to enjoy our spoils. Despite colonial influences, picnics were yet to be part of the Chinese social calendar.

'Picnics were introduced by the French and quickly adopted as an English pastime,' I informed, 'they even painted picnics into their art.'

Betraying a wry smile I produced a dog-eared postcard depicting Edouard Manet's *Le dejeuner sur l'herbe.* Fong eyed the picture suspiciously, conscious of the implication naked ladies were de rigueur for al fresco fare occasions. She looked askance at me.

'You expect me to take my clothes off?'

'It's traditional for all picnics,' I replied, earnestly trying to keep a straight face.

She smiled coyly, complicit with the ruse. 'I'll take my clothes off if you take your clothes off.'

'Okay,' I conceded, starting to unbuckle my shorts.

'No no, not here, too open, people see,' she chided.

We ate and drank our fill whilst admiring the panoramas. Below us on one side of the ridge, the quaint old town of Caistor nestled amongst grassy inclines, the slate grey houses resembling tombstones on a hillside cemetery, the square dotted with colourful market stalls.

On the other side of the ridge the land as level as the sea to which it stretched: a bucolic patchwork of crop fields, hedgerows, farmsteads, and wandering roads. A tractor furrowed a distant field, the sole intervention to the scenic tranquillity. Scudding cloud shadows stained the ground and the view shimmered from rising air currents.

In the foreground a narrow wooded valley broke the plain, a remnant of this once forested landscape. With our arms about each other we watched the aerobatics of two swallows as they swooped and disappeared into the trees.

'Let's follow,' I said, with the enthusiasm of a boy scout wanting his next badge.

We gathered our belongings and witnessed by a bevy of plump munching sheep descended the hill via a stony, rutted, farm track. A footpath snaked into the welcome coolness beneath the foliage canopy. Wild flower scents greeted our entry and a pigeon cooed in the sublimity of it all. A brook, as inviting as the pool painted by Manet, trickled its meandering way. A Donald Peers refrain – a favourite 1950s singalong of my parents – came to mind:

#In a shady nook,
By a babbling brook,
That's where I fell in love with you.#

There was no doubting our intention; a shady nook found, a blanket laid, we took off our clothes. There's something daringly exhilaratingly about performing love al fresco. To the natural feeling of freedom is the frisson from the unexpected discovery by an audience of roaming ramblers or a wandering gamekeeper. A friend had a related experience in a field one afternoon when, at the crucial moment, a cow came up and licked his bobbing bum. He was lucky it wasn't a bull.

Fong likened us to Adam and Eve after noticing a wild apple tree in our Garden of Eden, although Fong was unlike the waif-like Eve portrayed by Lucas Cranach and other artists down the centuries. Fong's voluptuousness resembled a Rubens or Renoir muse and there was no modesty enabling fig leaf or trailing ivy between her legs, nor between her ears. Looking around this secluded shady glade, I imagined we had fallen through a portal into the distant past; like Adam and Eve we could be the only humans on Earth. I wished we were, to begin mankind afresh.

A roaming breeze rustled the trees; the Sun filtered through the wafting canopy and dappled our bodies with shimmering light. We cuddled, my head pillowed by her breasts, thinking of nothing but each other. After a while I propped myself up with an elbow and Fong turned over.

My hand wandered, caressing graceful calves, the roll of thighs, the wobbly cheeks, the camber of her back, tracing the faint impress of vertebrae to the slender nape of her neck. I beckoned she turned back, and my hand and lips commenced a new pilgrimage, up and over shapely knees, along soft inner thighs to nestle in her silky bush. On across the modest dome of her belly I traced the fluted imprint of ribs before my palm reached the spillage of her breasts, the nipples tensing to firm buds. My touch revealed each nuance with the satisfaction of a blind man reading Braille.

'I love you,' I murmured.

Her kiss of acknowledgement stirred the dawn of another erection, magically growing in her hand like a conjuror's wand. We made love again. Later, I watched her tread gingerly to our babbling brook and dip a toe, withdrawing it quickly.

'Cold,' she complained.

'Must be from an underground spring.'

She tentatively tiptoed back to the blanket and I rejoiced in her bountiful beauty. She stood and stretched her back, the motion lifting her breasts and suggesting their heft. Full drop pearl shaped globes, not overly large, with delicate pink nipples at the centre of large, plum pigmented areolae. I likened her breasts as resembling heraldic emblems installed above the entrance to a family's country seat – the doorway to her inner self wherein a family line could commence. Maybe a love child with Fong would make the decision for me – Fong or my kids – a decision looming like storm clouds on the horizon. How could I possibly resolve two competing loves when I felt I couldn't live without either?

The Sun continued its slow descent and the shadows lengthened reluctantly bringing our idyll to a close. We dressed and trudged back up the hillside track. The sheep munched on; one bleated a mournful farewell.

After the unbridled passion of the first few months, there was a gradual normalisation to our dates, simply enjoying each other's company, paddling in the sea, country walks with pub lunches, afternoon cream teas and reality escapes to the cinema. One afternoon Fong taught me the rudiments of mah-jong and we played a couple of times a week with Jimmy and Lucy when the Lotus House closed for the afternoon.

We were a contentedly comfortable couple, relaxed and happy in our togetherness, chatting aimlessly, smiling and laughing at everything and nothing, at each other. The enjoyment of gentle affection and the sensation of being loved were as meaningful and beautiful as the intimacy between the bed sheets. But to give unconditional love, allowing her happiness, hopes and dreams into my hands was part of knowing and the building of trust. Unfortunately, I had to betray her trust.

Chapter 13

During the last week of June, the point of no return arrived with the sale of the house in Coventry and corresponding purchase in Louth. The status quo of my unbridled relationship with Fong was about to be reined in and I stayed over for another weekend in Grimsby, much to Mary's chagrin and disbelief with the house move imminent.

During a previous weekend return to Coventry an incident caused me to reflect upon my future with the children. Sunday morning after the breakfast fry-up, the children and I drove to Coombe Abbey Park, a twelfth century former Cistercian monastery situated to the east of the city. In the eighteenth century, Lancelot (Capability) Brown landscaped formal gardens and opened up the extensive woodland with rustic trails. An immense lake was introduced as a wild fowl sanctuary, a sort of avian Serengeti.

Sam took out her bag of stale bread and biscuits and paused to feed a group of ducks with fluffy brown fledglings. One duckling was not getting a fair share and in reaching to accommodate Sam overbalanced and completed an ungainly belly-flop into the cold, murky water, dispelling the startled ducks.

She bobbed up spewing out the repugnant water and as I hoisted her out burst into tears, more from shock than anything since she was a capable swimmer. She clung to my chest like a marsupial to its mother which brought home to me how much the kids needed my love and guardian protection. I would always have to be there for them, at least close by in support if, more likely when, Mary and I separated.

I didn't want a life without Fong but realised love for my children had primacy: a blood bond tethered and nourished by an invisible umbilical cord. So I settled upon a self-interested compromise allowing a continued relationship with Fong *and* my family.

With the family in Coventry and my working in Grimsby occasioning weekend visits, I would miss out on much of their growing-up and they would miss my love, protection and guidance; the kids may gradually distance themselves and Mary would probably file for divorce. My visiting rights may be curtailed and I would morph into an outsider, like a distant uncle, as their ordered lives blossomed without me.

There was also the financial consideration, the cost of travelling and continuing with a second accommodation in Louth. The company would eventually baulk at the mileage being run up on the car and discontinue the rent subsidy for the B & B. The stress and humdrum of working all week and travelling backwards and forwards to Coventry at weekends would take its tiring toll and limit my time with both the family and Fong.

If Mary instigated divorce I would lose the family home and with alimony payments unable to afford to buy or rent a suitable property for a life with Fong. Thus I reasoned with the family in Louth I could resume a relatively normal lifestyle and, with some schedule juggling continue my relationship with Fong, providing she was willing after hearing of my marriage. After days of anguished demurral I phoned the solicitor to exchange contracts.

With the imminent arrival of the family in Louth I saw no alternative but to reveal my marital situation to Fong and hope for a sympathetic hearing. I dreaded the confrontation; there was no way to avoid hurting her. I now wished I had come clean on the first date. If I had told her I was mired in a loveless marriage she may have appreciated my honesty and still entered a relationship.

On the last Sunday in June, I suggested a walk to Humberston beach.

'I have something important to tell you.'

'What?' She smiled, intrigued.

'When we get there,' I playfully admonished.

The dunes would be quiet and afford privacy to hide her hurt and express her anger as I begged forgiveness. I tried to rehearse lines to justify my deceit but everything depended on her response.

Hands entwined we strolled along Cleethorpes promenade, passed the gaudy souvenir shops overflowing with kitsch-and-tat and resisting the temptation of the sticky confectionary and ice creams stalls. Ignoring the noisy fruit machine arcades and kids' funfair rides we descended the few steps on to the tarnished golden sand ruffled from a horde of footprints.

We ambled south: away from the splashing, shrieking kids and barking dogs; away from the chatter and clutter of motley beach goers with their picnics, deckchairs and wind breaks; away to the peaceful swell of breaking waves and occasional plaintive call of a cruising seagull. A cocktail of invigorating ozone and the pungent bouquet of seaweed tainted the easterly breeze.

We were both in mufti: shorts, T-shirt and sun hat. Fong had never looked more alluring, almost naked to my eyes because I knew her body so well. As she walked everything wobbled provocatively. The image of her in pared down tight shorts and bra free hugging cotton top would be the centrefold pinup on my eidetic wall. We removed our sandals and playfully paddled the surf, sand squelching between our toes, the tang of seaweed on our skin, a taste of salt when we kissed.

'Is everything okay? You seem preoccupied,' she said, concern colouring her tone.

I could not disguise my divined anxiety, accustomed as she was to my body language. I saw in her look my oblique reassurance added to her apprehension. On any other day I would have had the urge to mimic the torrid love scene between Burt Lancaster and Deborah Kerr in *From Here to Eternity*, rolling in the surf bonded by passion, before basking like exhausted castaways swept onto an island paradise. Making love would have been disingenuously perverse.

We walked on, paddling the surf; the waves lazily heaved and lapped, the Sun's dancing spangles dazzling off the reflected sky. We reached the Haile Fort – a dilapidated concrete monument to two World Wars – standing in the shallows like a kid's giant sand castle about to be washed away by the tide. A few reposeful sunbathers littered the beach like the fallen from battle; with no soldiers to defend Fong's feelings, love and hope would be casualties. I desperately hoped my verbal assault would not degenerate into a war of words.

The loosely shifting sand of the dunes seemed ominously appropriate to the unstable foundation of our relationship. We found a secluded depression amongst the tall grass and sat crossed legged facing each other. A tenor of foreboding engulfed us like a sea mist.

I took hold of her hand. I was about to jeopardize the only true love I had known with words which could never be unsaid. From this juncture she could be an embittered and disenchanted ex-lover rueing the prospect of what might have been. I felt I was petrifying into a monument of guilt. I looked down and shuffled my position in an effort to relax.

She waited patiently, as still as a portrait. I peered into her inquisitive, beautiful, kind eyes in which I had seen so much pleasure and love, now anxiously questioning my motive. I could find no words to soften the blow.

'What do you want to tell me?' Her tone was apprehensive, uncertain she wanted to know.

'Something I should have told you months ago,' I said with a resigned glumness. 'You know I have never loved before as I love you.'

'Me too,' she affirmed, in a tone to be taken for granted.

'You are the love of my life ... but ...'

'But? Your body language today said *but*,' she said despondently. 'Are you married?'

'Yes ... I'm married.' I nodded solemnly.

The sunny radiance of her face flickered and died like a snuffed candle. She withdrew her hand and looked away, staring out to sea. Her eyes drowned. In blinking back the hurt, tears trickled down her cheeks. She stemmed the flow with a handkerchief.

'How married?' she said, with a tremulous sigh.

'An unhappy marriage, I never loved my wife. I *will* leave her. The day I met you was the day I left my wife in every sense other than packing a suitcase.' I retook her hand and squeezed reassuringly.

'Why don't you leave her now?'

'I have two children; they're too young to understand if their Daddy were to leave. I cannot do it, at least not until they are old enough to understand and accept. I love them as much as I love you; a different love, but a binding love.'

I felt tears gather, my jaw quiver as I struggled with the emotion from the hurt I had inflicted. I looked to intercept her gaze, to plead for understanding.

'I thought you might be married,' she said quietly. There were tears in her breaking voice. She turned her sad moist gaze on me.

'I never thought you suspected I might be married. You never intimated ...'

'Afraid to ask,' she interrupted, 'I wanted to know, but didn't want to know. I didn't want what we have to end. Why didn't you tell me before?'

'I wanted to tell you from the outset and several times I had been on the verge of confessing, but I was too scared of losing you. I love you too much. I delayed not wanting to hurt you. I'm so sorry.'

'The first time we made love I told you I thought we belonged,' she reminded.

'We do belong ... but I also belong to my children.'

'I gave you everything; I thought I belonged to you ... no longer fully belonged to myself.'

'I know you did; no one could have given more. You are the person I have waited for all my life. When I'm with you I experience nothing but happiness and I felt you did too.'

'Le ji sheng bei,' she murmured. 'Excessive happiness will lead to sorrow,' she translated, 'two thousand year old Chinese proverb. Today I know it's true. My dream of our life together a flight of fantasy with Icarus wings.' She paused, shaking her head dispiritedly. 'I knew hope, now no hope. I'm only an affair,' she sobbed, her head bowing under the weight of disillusionment.

We gave way to glum silence, forlornly gazing to the horizon, looking without seeing. I wished everything said could be swept out to sea, and like a drowning man frantically waving to those on the shore, we would wave goodbye in blissful ignorance of his predicament.

'I wasn't looking for an extramarital fling, but the moment I saw you my heart was captured,' I protested with helpless innocence. 'Your smile, your eyes, your nature, your body, seduced and addicted my senses. I'm so sorry.'

She turned her dark brown eyes on me. 'Love means never having to say you're sorry,' she said thoughtfully. 'Sorry is never enough.'

I nodded agreement; a glib notion of contrition doesn't erase guilt or make amends. I bowed my head and closed my eyes in an effort to stem the uninvited tears; I blew my nose and dabbed my eyes.

'There is no one I would rather spend my life with. It's my children,' I implored again.

'I understand,' she said, annoyance tainting her tone. 'You're not happy to leave your children ... you'd feel guilty ... always regret. Then you'd regret me.'

'When they are older ... when they understand ...'

'You expect me to wait ... wait for years?'

'I have no right to ask that of you, but in a few years we could be together.'

'I have to return to Hong Kong and will be under pressure to marry. My younger sister already obliged to accept an unhappy arranged marriage. I cannot continue to defy my father's wishes, loyalty to family is paramount.'

'Marriage should be for love,' I said, 'like in films you once said.'

'You married without love, to conform to societal norm. It's not so different to conform to the wishes of family elders in Chinese society.'

I nodded with a frown of reluctant accord, mulling over possible alternatives. 'Tell your father about me, but not I'm married, and plan to come to Hong Kong or for you to return to England. I can send money to you regularly to show your father gestures of commitment.'

'I don't know; He might not look favourably on having an English son-in-law.'

'Your mother loved an Englishman.'

'That's more likely to be held against you. No, he wants me to marry our priest's brother,' she said dolefully. 'You were my hope to marry for love. I never thought you were capable of hurting me, but you have.'

I had no answer except to be sorry. I captured an escaping tear from the downpour inside me as I engaged her sad, rheumy eyes. She dipped her head looking at her hands involuntarily wringing themselves. I had to relieve the tension.

'Let's go for some tea,' was all I could muster, the Englishman's response to a crisis.

She nodded agreement. We stood, I took her damp, limp hand in mine, but I felt she wasn't in touch. We trudged slowly along the shore in silence. The tide was out and I supposed her love for me had been swept out with it.

The Rosy Lee Tea Room was a brash establishment in the centre of Cleethorpes; the locals jokingly referred to it as "The Two Tits," an epithet analogous to the double bow-fronted pink facade and Mrs Emerson, the overly endowed proprietress. Fong stopped as I opened the door.

'I'm not going in there,' she said firmly, shaking her head. 'Chinese.'

'No, it's an English tea shop, I know the owner, I sold her a scale for the kitchen.'

'No. Lee common Chinese name,' Fong insisted, 'I have a friend called Rosy Lee.'

She looked at me with the wide eyed anxiety of a child at the dentist. I understood she would not wish her sorrow to be witnessed by a compatriot.

'Let me explain. In the East End of London there is a community who call themselves cockneys. To confuse the police and outsiders they developed a dialect of rhyming slang to mimic what they want to say. So instead of saying "How about a cup of tea", they will say "How about some Rosy Lee." This well known association with tea has been adopted by lots of tea shops all over the country.

Trust me; this tea room is definitely English.'

'I trusted you before, but you're married,' she rejoined.

A deserved reproach I best ignored. 'On the subject of Rosy Lee, you *can* trust me. My Father was born a cockney. I know. Come on,' I beckoned, ushering her through the doorway.

Fong scanned the interior for countrymen. Beyond the sentimental floral wallpaper, kitsch pictures and gingham covered tables, she saw only a gathering of white middle-aged tourists and Mrs Emerson and her bosom. Mrs Emerson gave me a tentative smile of vague recognition.

Fong chose a table by the window and I took the less confrontational seat beside her. She was not hungry; under the circumstances I abstained from the temptation of the café's renowned spiced toasted teacake. A jolly, mumsy waitress took our order for Earl Grey with lemon. The waitress noticed Fong's red eyes, pale complexion and mournful mien.

'Are you all right dear?' she said in a concerned tone, eyeing me accusingly.

'Thank you, yes,' said Fong with a nod.

'Some unfortunate news,' I interjected. 'Tea will cheer us.'

The aphrodisiac for all troubles promptly arrived in a shiny stainless steel teapot with matching milk jug and sugar bowl. They had no lemon.

Fong looked pensive, staring down at the cooling tea in front of her. She stole a glance at me over the rim of the cup as she sipped the English remedy. A faint pink lip imprint blemished the white teacup. Would such an imprint ever again tinge my lips? She carefully put the cup down with a soft chink, as if its fragility was in question. I didn't know what to say; I considered it best to quietly allow her to come to terms with our new situation.

She peered vacantly into her empty tea cup as if divination from the tea leaves would provide an answer. Perhaps they did. When we were ready to go she stood, paused, her dark liquid eyes lingering on mine, eyes full of sadness but laced with sympathy I did not deserve. Wrapping her pain in the glimmer of a smile, she moved forward, put her arms about my neck and tinted my lips.

'I still love you,' she murmured, 'I always will.'

Relief warmed me like hot tea on a cold day. I hugged, kissed her neck and hair and blinked and sniffed away my joyful relief. The mumsy waitress beamed approvingly.

'No matter what happens, you will always be my true love.'

'Me too,' she whispered, nodding gently and swallowing what may have been her pride, 'me too.'

'You have to believe one day I will be divorced and we will be together. I promise.'

Chapter 14

In bed that night I recalled Fong's initial response: "How married?" I marvelled at the brevity of her question to elicit the situation. Her reaction was exceptional: no recriminations, no jealous tantrums, and no slapped face. Any of these instinctively womanly reactions would have made the encounter horrendous. Her dignified acceptance and confirmation of her continuing love were the stuff of cinematic romances, although like the protagonists of *Brief Encounter*, I may have committed us to a life sentence of regret.

Worrying about her broken heart and nursing mine, sleep remained elusive; in the early hours I decided to retrieve Mr H's Hong Kong photograph. It would provide a distraction and talking point in helping to normalise our relationship again, some cooling of affection would be natural even though she professed her continuing love.

I stood at the top of the stairs listening; the house blackout encouragingly silent. With a burglar's stealth I descended the stairs, although each tread heralded my approach with creaks unnoticed in daytime use. The hinges of the door to Mr H's sanctum gave an announcing whine. The torch beam reflected off the glass fronted bookcase housing the photo album. I thumbed through the pages, found the incriminating photo and tucked it into my dressing gown pocket. I replaced the album and, about to leave, the ceiling light flashed on. Startled, I turned to see Mr H sat in his wheelchair brandishing a revolver.

'Don't move! ... Why Chris, it's you,' he said, lowering the gun. 'What the hell are you doing creeping about in here?'

'Oh dear, sorry Mr H, I must have been sleepwalking.' I yawned and rubbed my eyes.

'Sleepwalking with a torch. Somnambulists don't need a guiding light. You'll have to do better than that.'

'I'm not sure you'll want to know.'

'Try me.'

'Anyway how come you're not in bed?'

'Fell asleep here. Cynthia is staying the night with her sister, a hen party for a friend who's marrying. Anyway, never mind me, what are you doing here in the middle of the night?'

'Answer a couple of questions and I will tell you. Is your Christian name Robert?'

'Yes.'

'Were you a corporal in the army when stationed in Hong Kong?'

'Yes,' he nodded, 'but what's that got to do with anything?'

'I think the woman with whom you had an affair in Hong Kong is Fong's mother.'

'I don't believe you, too much of a coincidence.'

'I agree, a phenomenal coincidence, but I'm sure it's true. When you saw Fong, you looked at her as if you'd seen a ghost, as if you recognised her, but you've never seen her at the Lotus House.'

'I don't deny a similarity in looks, but all Chinese look ...'

'Oh come on Mr H, you know that's bullshit. Was the woman's name Fang Qin?'

He paused, open mouthed with a look of disbelief. 'Fang Qin,' he murmured with a distant look of recognition.

'It was Fang Qin, wasn't it?'

He slowly nodded, open mouth with a look of bewilderment.

'I take it you are unaware you have a son, born 1950.'

'A son,' he gasped, 'no, she would have told me. We exchanged letters after I came back to England.'

'Maybe she knew the story of *Madama Butterfly*, thought her love for you was misguided and didn't think you would return to marry. She was pregnant, her reason for marrying. She didn't know you were the father until the baby was born.'

He slumped forward in his wheelchair, stunned by the revelation. 'Oh God; tell me it's not true; this has to be a nightmare.'

I removed the photo from the pocket of my dressing gown. 'This photo and your recognition of her name provide definite confirmation.'

'Give me the photo Chris. I don't want this to go any further. I have my wife to consider and I'll thank you not to interfere.'

'What about your son? Don't you want to know him? Isn't he entitled to know his father?'

'I've had no role as his father. He's a man, not a boy. It can make no difference now.'

'Isn't that for him to decide?'

'I've decided for him,' he said sharply. 'This matter stays inside this room. Best you find alternative digs as soon as possible.'

'The conveyance on the house has exchanged contracts and completion is next week. I'm sincerely sorry to have upset you; our intention was to determine the facts one way or the other before deciding whether to tell you. Tonight's confrontation left no choice.'

'Well, some things are best left as they were. When I saw your Fong ... such a resemblance ... cherished memories of my time in Hong Kong came flooding back. I was grateful to relive them. Now, the beauty of those memories has been sullied.' He shook his head despondently.

'I'm sorry, but gaining a son ought to be a reason for celebration. Yes you've been a father in absentia, yes her decision may have been misguided, but she took it in the best interests of her unborn child. When you've had time to reflect on her situation I'm sure you'll agree.'

I left him sitting in a glazed trance and returned to my room. I remained concerned as to why he had a revolver to hand.

Next day I lunched at the Lotus House and told Fong of Mr H's aggressive negativity. 'There's no doubt, he is Zhi Ming's father, same name, same rank, and he recognised your mother's name.'

'How incredible! I will write and tell mum.'

'Well, better wait to see if his response changes when he's had time to adjust to what is a devastating revelation.'

A few days later the family moved up from Coventry and I bade farewell to my B & B hosts. I paused and lowered my voice to speak to Mr H.

'Do think on what we discussed last week; if you wish to take it further let me know.'

'I have to admit it has been playing on my mind, feeling depressed by it.' He hesitated with a frown of uncertainty. 'Erm ... does Fong have a photo of the boy?'

'Yes, I'll ask her for it and drop in to show you. Better still, I'll ask her to show you and tell you about him.'

'Okay, but ring first to make sure Cynthia is not around. Wednesday evening's best as you know.'

I was encouraged by his change of heart and we shook hands as friends.

The following Wednesday I told Mary I had to entertain International's district manager to a working dinner. After work and an early meal in the Lotus House I collected Fong and we drove to Louth. Alistair let us into the hall and I knocked on Mr H's door. Fong's presence was emotionally too much; he gazed at her and with a heave of the shoulders tears ran down his pained face. Fong placed a comforting arm on his shoulder.

'I'm sorry my dear,' he croaked, clasping her hand, 'but you resemble Fang Qin ... too much to bear.'

He reached for the Kleenex, blew his nose and dried his eyes. A tear escaped Fong's eye, she also took a tissue. I squeezed her hand in support. We listened as this crumpled man poured out his sorrow.

'I loved your mother, but I couldn't stay in Hong Kong. My tour of duty finished and the regiment returned to England. I had to complete my service before I could leave the army and asked her to wait for me. About three months after leaving Hong Kong I received a letter from her telling me she had married.

I was devastated. I couldn't understand why she wouldn't wait for a few more months. I promised faithfully to return, find work and we would be together. I guess she thought I was another Lieutenant Pinkerton; I also fathered a son ... a bloody tragedy of operatic proportion,' he scowled. He bent over shaking his head, his hands covering his face. 'I was sure she loved me. She should have told me she was pregnant.'

'My mum did love you. Unfortunately, she was in a parallel relationship with a taxi driver. After you returned to England she realized she was pregnant but not sure of the father. She took the more certain option of a marriage proposal for the sake of the child. You will remember times were hard for her. She'd fled China when relatives were murdered by Mao's red guards; she had next to nothing. Marriage offered a degree of security for her and the child, a pragmatic decision overriding her true feelings.' She smiled sympathetically. 'Here's a photo of your son.'

He held the black and white print: a three-quarters portrait of a gently smiling young man smartly dressed for business in a dark suit, neat hair combed back and wearing scholarly looking circular rimmed glasses.

'He's a fine looking young man,' he said, studying the print, 'has my mouth and jaw line.'

'The photo was taken last year. He's twenty-six and works as an estate agent.'

'Is he married? Does he speak English?'

'He has a regular girl friend. English is necessary for his work.'

'Your mother spoke hardly any English. I knew a few words and phrases in Cantonese, but it wasn't much help; she spoke a Shanghai dialect. Somehow we connected and understood each other. In the beginning she told me she had a boyfriend, but I persisted.'

'A family trait,' I remarked, smiling knowingly at Fong.

'I took her to a mess dance. She wore a pink cheongsam. She was a sensation; I had to protect her all evening from amorous advances by most of the company.'

'Fong wore the same cheongsam for me. I recognised it in your photo of Fang Qin.'

'I saw her whenever I could get leave, must have been for half-a-year or more. One night she took me back to her tiny studio room in a block of flats in Kowloon, a bedroom cum lounge cum kitchen; the bathroom was shared down the hall. An elderly relative was there but I guess she told him to vamoose; he reluctantly shuffled out and didn't come back. We made love all night. She intimated she had some protection, but I don't know what it was, or even if it was true. I didn't care, I loved her.'

He paused in reflection, with a glazed look of nostalgia to his eyes. His comments made me ponder my situation with Fong.

'Cynthia was not able to have children. I never loved Cynthia;

my heart was always in Hong Kong. My life could have been so different; easy to find work in Hong Kong with my civil engineering experience, the colony undergoing regeneration with rebuilding and infrastructure projects everywhere. I often wondered what she made of her life. Tell me about her Fong.'

'When she married she gave up the dai pai dong and rented a grocery shop on Hennessey Road, but it's due to close next year for redevelopment. When Zhi Ming was born and not Chinese, my father left her, but our priest mediated and I was born the following year. I have a younger sister, Mai Ling; she's working in Watford this year. Zhi Ming wants to come to England for a holiday. You will meet him, yes?'

'No! Definitely not. I wouldn't want him to see me like this, old, fat and crippled. I don't want Fang Qin to know anything about me. Her memories are best left undisturbed as I now wish mine had been.' He paused in thought. 'No, this must be our secret, she must never know how unhappy I have been, how I never stopped loving her. She would be hurt and it would serve no purpose. I know you two meant well, but unfortunately you have defiled the precious memories I had of her, knowing she was pregnant with my child, knowing she was sleeping with someone else. When she knew it was my child, she should have written to tell me, given me the option to participate in his upbringing. If I'd known I would have returned to Hong Kong.'

'I'm sorry we have caused you pain,' Fong said gently, 'but mum always loved you. I hope that's a comfort.'

'In some ways it makes matters worse.' He paused, looking despondent. 'Now I would like to be alone. Thank you for coming; I hope you and Chris work things out. I will not see you again my dear.'

As we drove to Grimsby we debated the situation and decided to abide by Mr H's wishes. I now regretted pursuing his link to

Fong's family which appears to have brought sorrow to the man by contaminating the integrity of his memories.

Saddened by his response, Fong reminded me of her foreboding, 'I did suggest some things were best left in the past.'

As I drove through Louth on my way home, I passed the Highholme B & B; a police car and ambulance were parked outside, blue lights flashing ominously. I stopped to enquire the reason. A medic exited the house carrying an equipment case.

'What's happened here?' I said nervously.

'Are you a relative?'

'No, a close friend and neighbour.'

'There's been a fatality ... gun shot.'

'Oh no. Not Robert Howard.'

'Yes.'

'An accident?'

'No, it appears he took his own life. He left a note.'

I stood in the street enveloped by a pall of grief. I remembered his parting phrase to Fong, "I will not see you again." I now realized he had decided his intent before we left. My mind wracked with guilt several hours passed before sleep prevailed.

I didn't tell Mary; it may only be a matter of days before she heard from neighbours or read about it in the local paper, but I reasoned distancing the news from my visit with Fong would be less likely to attract a connection. The situation would have been okay if Fong hadn't been seen by Alistair and I feared a link would be established from Cynthia's post-mortem, a proverbial ticking bomb.

Chapter 15

I had yet to tell Fong Mary and the kids were installed in Louth because on the occasional weekend I could not see Fong – when Mary had events arranged for the kids – it was convenient Fong assumed I travelled to Coventry. I hated the ever deepening hole of deception I was digging for myself but withholding the truth assisted the life balance between Fong and family. This non-disclosure proved to be a ticking bomb of nuclear capability.

The prospect of Mary discovering our affair had dramatically increased following Mr H's demise and I felt the tension building. My game was in extra time and, unbelievably, I was to score an own goal.

Seeing Fong other than at the Lotus House required resourcefulness. The "working late at the office" excuse would not normally hold water – for centuries overused by straying husbands and played out in countless movies – except evening and weekend sales calls were a legitimate bane of my reps life and acted as co-conspirators.

Additionally, the company did not deal in second-hand scales, so Danny and I covertly satisfied this demand. Danny attended to the mechanics and Weights and Measures stamping; I spruced up the bodywork, cleaning, repairing and respraying. It helped to keep the competition at bay, an assertion the company did not accept. Discovery would result in summary dismissal, but all the reps did it. The managers were ex-reps but viewed the situation with a Nelson's eye as long as quotas for new sales were exceeded.

Danny was enlisted to alibi the pretence of working on second-hand scales after hours and Sundays. Bogus sales courses, new product launches, regional manager entertaining, and staff stag nights were all enlisted to the cause. Despite these plausible excuses for absenteeism, Mary noticed an emerging pattern and her suspicion of infidelity was about to acquire tangible evidence.

No doubt she had searched my clothes, wallet and briefcase for some scrap of indictable evidence and been found wanting. I could not be accused by one of the more conventional film script acts of complicity: lipstick on the collar, a telltale receipt, an errant piece of jewellery, telephone bill, and so forth. Unfortunately I was my Judas, betrayed by erotic nocturnal murmurings.

Friday, 7 am. After cancelling the alarm clock, a second more clamorous bell reverberated ominously through my head from the hammer strike of Mary's accusation.

'Who is Fong?' she said sternly.

Silhouetted against the morning light, arms folded defiantly, she cast a menacing shadow over the bed. I vaguely remembered waking in the night calling Fong's name and drowsily reaching out only to find Mary coldly rebuffing my overture. Fong was the default setting for my dreams; the details were fading but the narrative had been unmistakably wet. I pretended bewilderment but wondered if my face betrayed guilt as prominently as a smudge of lipstick.

'I'm sorry, you've lost me. What do you mean, who is Fong?'

'It sounds like a woman's name. Some bloody oriental. Who is she?' Her decibel level rose ominously. 'You were dreaming. You groped me moaning the name Fong!' The name spat out like the detestation of Angostura bitters. She yanked the bedclothes from my body. 'Look, you've got a hard-on.'

'You know I often wake up with a stiffy. It must have been a dream, to do with a film perhaps. I don't remember.'

I pulled the bedclothes back to cover the erectile contraction resulting from this confrontation and sat up leaning against the bed head.

'You're lying. You're having an affair.'

I engaged her stare. 'I am not having an affair, it's a dream. Forget it.'

Forget it she would not, storming out and slamming the door. My contemplation of this unexpected situation was distracted by a spider abseiling down the curtain towards a perplexed bluebottle head butting the window pane; the fly could see out, see where it wanted to go, but was inexplicably restrained. The analogy with my situation did not escape me; I knew where I wanted to go, but was confined by the restraints of familial love and responsibility. I put the fly out of its misery and denied the spider a last meal.

Mary returned to the bedroom repeating her allegation. I pushed by to the landing; she followed in tow blurting further indicts until I took refuge in the bathroom. She hammered on the locked door.

'Lying Bastard!'

I stared into the mirror and considered the gravity of this new situation, Mary's first tangible evidence. It was only hearsay, not proof and I decided to stay calm and bluff it out. After a tensely quiet breakfast – with the children and cat aware of the strained atmosphere – I was relieved to shut the front door and commence the commute to Grimsby. The Lotus House provided lunch but I had no opportunity to tell Fong of Mr H's demise or Mary's accusations.

Saturday afternoon, whilst in the rear garden playing with the children, Cynthia Howard strode up the drive. She stood on the doorstep talking to Mary before being invited inside. I nervously busied myself at the bottom of the garden, but a few minutes later Mary called out Cynthia wanted to talk. A bomb was about to detonate.

As I reluctantly entered the house Mary whispered, 'Mr Howard has killed himself. I'll make some tea.'

Cynthia stood arms crossed; her defiant stance and determined pout radiated the self-importance of the harridan headmistress of her past. Robert's shock demise appeared to have aged her by a decade of late nights, the once handsome woman withering on the vine of life. Even when younger I imagined she had the frigidly anaphrodisiac effect of a sexless maiden aunt. Poor Robert; after his oriental fantasy, consummating his irrational decision to marry Cynthia must have been depressingly disappointing.

'Hello Cynthia, I am sorry to hear about Robert. What on earth happened?'

'He shot himself ... his old service revolver.'

'Do you know why?'

'I thought you'd be able to tell me,' she said coolly. 'Alistair told me you visited Robert with a Chinese woman the same evening.'

'What makes you think the visit had anything to do with Robert taking his life?'

'He left a note.' From her handbag she withdrew a folded sheet of blue Basildon Bond paper. 'Here, read it.'

Dear Cynthia,

Forgive me for what I am about to do. My past has
caught up with me and I cannot face the future.

Robert.

The brevity of the black cursive writing was chilling. I handed it back feeling decidedly uncomfortable. Worse, Mary arrived with tea and biscuits to join the conversation.

Cynthia's steely eyes, like the barrels of a shotgun, demanded attention.

'Why did you visit Robert the same night with a Chinese woman?'

'What!'

'Hold on a minute Mary,' I remonstrated, raising my hands. 'It was an issue Robert wished kept confidential Cynthia. I feel bound to respect his wish.'

Like a headmistress confronted by a recalcitrant pupil, she grimaced and wagged a dismissive finger. 'That's not good enough. I'm his wife; I'm entitled to know why after you turn up at our house with a Chinese woman Robert blows his brains out!' Her stony glare was worthy of Medusa.

'I'm entitled to know as well,' Mary chimed, glowering with manic inquisition.

'I'm sorry, but I must respect Robert's bidding. If he wanted you to know Cynthia, he would have given his reason in the note he left. I have nothing more to add.' I got up to leave.

'If you don't reveal what's behind all this I shall go to the police. You and this Chinese woman as good as murdered my husband!'

The three of us, for a moment of eternity, froze in the motionless silence of a tableau.

'Chris?' prompted Mary.

The name hung in the air like a hangman's noose awaiting my neck. I saw no way out but to relate the story of Mr H's Hong Kong days and age Fong thirty years in an attempt to limit Mary's concerns. I shrugged my shoulders and adopted a resigned frown.

'All right Cynthia, no need for melodramatic threats. If you insist on knowing ...'

'I have to know,' she interrupted, 'I can't spend the rest of my life wondering.'

'You may regret knowing.'

'For God's sake tell me!' she shouted, flapping her arms.

'I presume you knew Robert served a couple of years in Hong

Kong with the army after the war?'

'Yes. He had photos of his time there but never spoke of it.'

'Well ... during his stay he had an affair with a Chinese woman and unbeknown to Robert, he ... erm ... fathered a son.'

'A bastard son with a Chinese whore! Oh my God. So that's what all this is about.'

She flopped onto the sofa. A scowl contorted her ashen face. I dared to glance at Mary; she returned my look with a menacing glare.

'What induced Robert to take his life over a prostitute's bastard? It probably wasn't his anyway,' scoffed Cynthia.

'I did warn you Cynthia you were better off not knowing. Her name is Leung Fang Qin, the love of Robert's life; she is not a street girl and the child is his. After his commission completed he intended to leave the army and return to Hong Kong to marry her. She never told Robert of the pregnancy because of not being certain Robert was the father. She feared Robert would not return to Hong Kong and for the sake of the child she married a Chinese man she thought could also have made her pregnant. On hearing news of the marriage, Robert was devastated and fell into marriage with you.

The other night when Robert met Fang Qin's sister – the two are facially alike – all the memories flooded back and to learn he had fathered a love child I guess proved too much to bear. His son planned to visit England this autumn and Robert didn't want his son to see him old, spent and wheelchair bound and for that image to get back to his mother.'

Cynthia bent forward staring at the carpet. Mary looked at her and poured the tea. 'Do you take sugar,' she asked tentatively. Cynthia ignored her.

'I think you must shoulder much of the blame for Robert's death,' Cynthia barked accusingly. 'How did you become involved?'

'That's what I was wondering,' said Mary ominously.

'I lunch regularly at the Chinese restaurant in Grimsby where the sister works. Over a period of several months I got to know the staff and her predicament came up in conversation. From photos and army service records they had identified Robert as the father but were unsure of how to approach him. As I said, it was pure coincidence I knew Robert and she asked me to act as go-between.

Robert knew about his son, now a man of twenty six, some weeks ago, but last week I accompanied the sister to show Robert a photo. Neither I nor the sister can accept any blame for Robert's action; we acted in good faith. Robert had a right to know he had a son and the son to know his father. No one could have foreseen Robert's unfortunate response.'

'I knew he was preoccupied with something for the last few weeks,' said Cynthia thoughtfully, 'but I had no idea ... Are these Chinese after compensation?'

'No; the sole intention was to unite father and son.'

'This Chinese woman ... is her name Fong?' said Mary accusingly.

My brazen off-the-cuff storyline to Cynthia had passed muster, but remembering my nocturnal advances Mary remained suspicious. I admitted friendship with a woman called Fong but reiterated my claim she was a married, motherly, over sixty and the twin sister of Mr H's lover. I blamed the tense situation with Mr H and the discovery of his illegitimate son as to why I dreamt about Fong. Mary remained unconvinced; she had no contrary proof, although that was shortly to change.

Fong's next Wednesday off was another blisteringly hot day, although thankfully tempered by an easterly breeze off the North Sea.

I suggested a trip to Cleethorpes beach. 'I have something important to tell you.'

Fong remembered the previous beach trip preceded by the same phrase.

'You want to stop seeing me?' she said anxiously.

I shook my head and hugged her with a full lips kiss. It was too hot to relax on the beach and we sought the shade of a promenade café. Ice cream cornets melted more quickly than we could gorge and we resorted to iced tea to keep cool.

'What have you to tell me?' she said warily.

'Some sad news ... Mr Howard is dead, took his own life.'

'Oh Chris, no. What have we done? The poor man.'

'In retrospect you were right, some things are best left in the past,' I said dolefully. Tears filled her eyes; I took her hand with a consoling squeeze. 'I had an awkward confrontation with his wife who accused us of causing his death.'

'We must have done,' said Fong remorsefully.

'I don't think so. The fact he confronted me with a loaded revolver when I tried to get the photograph made me think we merely prompted what he had intended. We acted with the best of motives; he deserved to know he had a son and your mother loved him despite marrying someone else. He had no other children, a wife he didn't love and the sedentary existence of an invalid. Knowing he had a son with the prospect of meeting and getting to know him should have been life affirming.'

Fong frowned thoughtfully and slowly nodded agreement.

'I think it best you keep the nature of his death from your mother and Zhi Ming. No need to cause them unnecessary grief ... our secret.'

There was no invitation for Mary and me to attend Robert's funeral. Fong and I visited St James' Churchyard a couple of weeks later; the wreaths and sprays of flowers had begun to wither like our memories of him.

Chapter 16

The Lotus House continued to be my venue for lunches and occasional early evening dinners and Fong afforded as much attention as work commitments permitted. Mr Zhang allowed some flexibility to her rota and Fong's flat mate co-operated allowing invites for "coffee" every so often. Danny provided intermittent alibi's for working on second hand scales enabling some long Sunday afternoons with Fong. To add credence to these forays Danny came to the house one Sunday to work on a platform scale acquired from a local farmer. Mary remained suspicious and on one occasion telephoned the branch office to check. She got no answer.

'We don't answer the phone on Sundays because we're not supposed to be there. Ring Danny if you don't believe me.'

In July I contracted gastric flu. I phoned the Lotus House leaving a message with Jimmy I would not see Fong for a few days. Unfortunately my recovery dragged on through the week and Fong became concerned by my absence. On Sunday afternoon she travelled to Louth by bus and walked to the Highholme Guest House where she assumed I was still resident.

Cynthia took her chance for revenge, gave Fong my address and accompanied by a torrent of abuse sent Fong running down the street in tearful alarm. She sat on a park bench to compose herself before entering a corner newsagent to ask directions.

The detached house of a design typical of estate builds from the 1960s, had large windows, Marley tiled floors and spacious rooms. The front garden laid to grass with floral borders was secluded from the road by a high evergreen hedge. A driveway to the side of the house ended beneath a carport. The front door, on the side elevation, opened to the dining area with separate kitchen beyond. The lounge faced the front with a window overlooking the garden and driveway. Ensconced in an armchair reading, with more horror than delight I saw Fong approach.

'Oh fuck!'

Like Popeye having swallowed his spinach I leapt from the armchair and dashed to the front door to intercept Fong before she rung the doorbell. I hurried outside, quietly closing the door behind me. Her broad grin showed how pleased she was to see me. I clasped her hands.

'Why have you come? How did you know my address?' I said nervously, 'my wife is here.'

'You were ill; I worried about you. Woman at the guest house gave me your address. You didn't tell me you had moved and your wife was here,' she protested.

'We can't stay here. Come on.'

Hand in hand we hurried down the driveway, entered the street and stood behind the boundary hedge out of site of the house.

'It's so good to see you. I missed you,' I said, between hugs and kisses.

I explained my absence from work and the family situation. Fortunately, Mary was upstairs with the children. Unfortunately, Samantha had seen me scurrying down the drive with an unknown woman and informed her mother. Mary appeared at the end of the drive and caught us in an embrace.

'So this is your bloody wet dream whore!' She moved menacingly towards us. 'You're Fong aren't you? Motherly. Sixty. You lying bastard!'

In response, all I can bluster are the old film script clichés. 'This is not what it seems Mary. I can explain everything.'

I ushered Fong behind me; she placed her hands on my waist and nervously peered around my body. With my arms defensively outstretched we shuffled backwards in unison as Mary advanced. A disgusting hail of expletives poured from her distorted mouth like unstoppable vomit, her ruddy contorted face seething with humiliation, jealousy and hatred. Looking around for a weapon she snatched a stick from the hedgerow and arm raised lunged forward to strike.

'Run,' I instinctively shouted to Fong.

Grabbing Fong's hand we set off full pelt up the street as I felt a glancing whack of the stick across my back. Mary's screams and pounding feet filled our ears. We rounded the corner into Highholme Road and sped towards the entrance to the recreation ground. Mary gave up the chase with a final abusive holler, hurling the stick clattering down the road after us. The scene was pure pantomime certain to set the neighbours' tongues wagging. Even with her mind raging I later surmised she remembered the unattended children back at the house.

We sat on a wooden park bench, breathing heavily from the run. Fong was visibly shaken, pale and tearful, but looked beautiful draped in a pale green and red floral patterned summer dress, darker green cardigan and, fortunately, sensible shoes for running.

'I'm sorry my coming will make trouble, but I worry about you.'

'Its okay, my fault, I kept meaning to tell you I had moved and my wife had arrived. It's called Sod's Law. I'm impressed you traipsed over from Grimsby on your day off. I have missed your smile, your touch, your voice, everything.'

'After she gave me your address, the woman at the guest house was nasty, called me a slut and a murderer! I was frightened she would hit me and ran away, came to sit in this park.'

'Robert's widow, Cynthia, maliciously creating mischief because she thinks we were responsible for Robert's suicide. She knew my wife was here. I nearly had a heart attack when you walked up the drive. I hate to think what might have happened if my wife had answered the door.'

'What will happen when you go home?'

'Big argument I suppose,' I said, with a shrug of the shoulders. 'Not to worry, I'll be okay, back at work tomorrow so I'll see you for lunch at the Lotus House.' Fong's frown of concern declared she was unconvinced. 'We better walk into town and get you back to Grimsby. There aren't many buses on a Sunday.'

With no sign of Mary, we left the park and filtered through the Victorian backstreets to the town centre. There was a half hour wait for the next bus and we bided time with tea and fruit cake in a café adjacent to the market hall. With a final hug she boarded the bus and I walked down the main street in trepidation of facing Mary's wrath. As the bus swept by I saw Fong seated by the window. I waved but her head was drooped like the bloom of a rain burdened flower, a handkerchief to her eyes. With clenched teeth I resolutely fought back my tears; her hurt was my hurt.

What of the hurt caused to Mary by this unfortunate emergence of the truth? If Samantha hadn't seen Fong I could have gotten away with it. Mary's feelings and hurt pride would have been spared and Fong would have avoided the invidious shock-and-awe of Mary's rage. With the cover story involving the sister of Mr H's lover blown, we all faced an uncertain future.

I walked slowly back to the house, trying to gather my thoughts for a credible explanation, but they swirled around like autumn leaves in a gusting wind. As I neared the house, chest tight, throat parched, stomach churning, legs leaden, I started to hyperventilate from the rising tension. Turning into the driveway I half expected to see my belongings in an inglorious heap on the front lawn, but no, all was peaceful and undisturbed, that ominously expectant stillness in jungle war films moments before the patrol is ambushed.

Chapter 17

I took a deep breath and opened the front door; Mary and the children sat quietly at table having supper. The cat munched from a bowl on the floor. They all turned to look.

'You fucking bastard!' yelled Mary, leaping to her feet. A half empty bottle of milk whistled past my head as I instinctively raised an arm and ducked. The bottle smashed against the wall beside me, splattering glass and milk. The children were aghast and gaped in fearful astonishment. The cat stood to investigate the spilt milk.

'Bloody rotten two-timing bastard,' she screamed.

Grabbing a knife from the table she lurched forward, arm raised to stab me. I grabbed her arm and wrestled the knife away but in doing so slashed my left hand. The manoeuvre exposed my groin and her right knee found its vulnerable target. I yelped like a kicked dog, doubling over wincing with pain.

Her fists rained hammer blows across my shoulders. I thrust her across the room. She fell against the wall but rebounded with adrenalin fuelled strength, a mad virago of flaying arms and kicking feet, spitting rancorous bile on gusts of stale breath. Her eyes blazed with hate; if looks could kill I would already be dead.

The cat became a victim of the struggle, shrieked a strangulated miaow and scooted out through the open front door. The children remained rooted to their seats but screaming in alarm, witnesses to the unfolding horror.

I fended off the blows loudly imploring her to stop before shoving her away again and raising my fists in warning. She hesitated and I moved across behind the children to offer comfort and, I admit, as shields.

'It's all right,' I assured, bending to hug them as they nervously clung to me. 'Mummy's angry, but it's over now.' I glared at Mary, 'It's over now isn't it!' I emphasised with raised voice.

Mary realised the children's distress and retreated to the kitchen, slammed the door and was heard to wail. My left hand stung and there was blood on my shirt front from the oozing wound. I clutched a wad of tissues to stem the flow. My balls ached and I pushed my right hand down my trousers to check for damage.

I was astounded by Mary's vicious reaction and obscene language; she had become a hysterical vixen of unwomanly strength and common in the vulgarity of her anger. She was usually so demure, refined and cultured, a school teacher for Christ's sake!

Milk dribbled down the wall into the splashed pool on the tiled floor. The cat ventured back and licked at the milk; I shooed him away from the splintered glass and poured a cup of lukewarm tea, added sugar and drank without milk. I gripped the cup with both hands trying to hide and stem the trembling. Confrontations are not my métier.

The children gradually calmed but remained anxious. Simon had my blood on his T-shirt. I cuddled them; they clung to me like barnacles to an old hull. It hurt to see them crying and distressed.

'Okay guys, everything is back to normal, no more excitement. Finish your supper and go upstairs and wash and get ready for bed.'

'Mummy is angry about the woman who came to the house, isn't she?' Samantha said with adult concern.

'Yes, Mummy doesn't like her.'

'Why? She's your friend isn't she?'

'Yes, she's my friend, but Mummy would prefer I have male friends.'

'Why? Does she think you're gay?'

'No I don't think that's the reason,' I chuckled, surprised by the logic.

'Why? Mummy has lady friends.'

'Some types of lady friends aren't allowed.'

'Why aren't they allowed?'

'Believe me; you need to be older to understand.'

'Maybe I will understand if you tell me. I want to know now.'

'I'm sorry; it's difficult to explain until you are older.'

'Oh Daddy, you're always saying "when I'm older." I will never learn anything.'

'You could ask your teacher tomorrow. Maybe she will explain.'

I smiled internally as I pictured Miss Clarke grappling with Sam's thirst for grown-up knowledge and how it might enliven the next parent-teacher meeting.

'Mummy's a teacher.'

'I think Miss Clarke more advisable; but you mustn't repeat the swear words mummy used, they're not nice. Mummy was upset.'

'I've heard all those rude words at school,' she chimed sagely, 'but there's usually other words in between.'

'Well, even if you've heard those words before, you are not to repeat them; they're vulgar and for grown-up use.'

'Does it mean mummy doesn't love you anymore?'

'Maybe not today. Now it's time you were both getting ready for bed,' I reminded with more insistence. 'Simon, put your shirt to wash.'

'We still love you daddy, don't we Simon.'

Simon nodded, mouth open, still aghast.

After the children retired I joined Mary in the lounge. She sat on the end of the sofa staring vacantly out of the window through which I had seen Fong arrive. I eased into the furthest armchair with a resigned sigh. I felt guilt for the drama of the day but not regret for the affair. Mary's frigid silence invited my confessional.

'I am truly sorry about today. Most unfortunate the way things turned out.'

She glared contemptuously. 'You're only sorry you've been found out, you bastard. You've made Cynthia a widow and I feel like a widow in this marriage.'

'No one could have predicted Robert's unfortunate response. As explained to Cynthia, I acted in good faith with the best of intentions and I will not accept blame for Robert's demise. As for us, I didn't want you to be hurt ...'

'What hurts is how you turned away from me and the children.'

'I haven't turned away from the kids or ...'

'You have,' she interrupted. 'Don't you see, you've ruined our marriage and destroyed our family unity, and for what ... a few sordid fucks with a Chinese whore.'

Her facial contortions wouldn't have been less had she accidentally eaten something from the cat's litter tray. The cat is sensibly keeping a low profile, curled up trying to sleep but sensing the tension and hardly daring to close his eyes. I thought Mary's feelings would forever be corrupted by a vindictive prejudice against the Chinese race, every woman branded a whore. Chinese food was not likely to feature on the family's future menu.

'She's no more a whore than you are, so don't keep denigrating the relationship, it's not helpful.'

'Oh! So it's a relationship is it? More than a few filthy fucks.'

'It just happened; I wasn't looking for an affair.'

Although it didn't ring true; subconsciously I had probably been open to an affair with the opportunity the job move to Grimsby afforded. I was lonely separated from the family and Fong's oriental grass temptingly lush on the other side of the cliché. In loving Fong I realised the loneliness was within my marriage; Mary and I lived apart together, living our lives through the children. It's what many parents do, but the inevitable refocusing of energy and affection excised a toll.

'Affairs don't *just* happen; I didn't go and fuck someone while you were away,' she retorted. 'Fidelity is a matter of inviolable trust. Once broken trust can never be restored. She's a burglar, broke into our marriage and stole my husband and trust.'

'No one has stolen anything ... a ridiculous analogy.'

'Yes, you're right. She didn't steal you; you gave yourself away. All the lies and deceit, all those weekends you stayed in Grimsby so you could fuck *her*. You're contemptible.'

'I'm sorry. I took advantage of our temporary separation but I think long term marital monogamy was always going to be an unrealistic expectation. Most of the men I know have had affairs. All around us relationships are in a state of fission: your sister's husband, Peter; our former neighbours Bob and Irene, and Danny Parker of all people. They've all had affairs but their marriages survived.'

'Their marriages could never be the same,' she said scornfully. 'You could glue the broken milk bottle back together, but the cracks would remain; the loss of trust, respect and love can never be repaired.'

'It was just sex,' I lied. 'Love and sex are different Mary. Sex is biologically driven.'

'You're pathetic, like all men, blood drains from your brains into your cocks.' Her look of utter contempt categorised me as representative of an inferior species.

'I've been faithful for six years of marriage. After the previous decade acting a Lothario I'm deserving of some credit.'

'Credit,' she scoffed, 'remember your marriage vows: "Forsaking all others, until death us do part." You've shown a total disregard for the commitment of marriage and consequences for us as a family.'

'Monogamy is an artefact of religious doctrine and cultural conditioning,' I said wearily, 'totally unrealistic for the Church to impose morally binding decisions on behalf of my future self. I am someone other than I was when I stood at the altar six years ago. Character traits are not preserved in aspic.'

'No, but marriage vows are,' she retorted.

We sat in funereal reflection. I hadn't the heart to tell her I never truly loved her, the marriage vows were a lie, a ceremonial theatrical sham. I should not have married her or anyone else. I was too young and married to satisfy peer and family pressure to conform, to buy a house and start a family, commit to the mortgage treadmill and ennui of monogamy. It was what you did in the sixties unless you wore flowers in your hair.

The joyous pageantry and expectation of Mendelssohn's *Wedding March* disappointed when it came to the honeymoon bed, which was no midsummer night's dream. The pulsating thrill of all night passion with Fong was never kindled with Mary, because there was no deep love between us.

After the premature death of my father, mother vowed never to enter the House of God, and as I left the church a husband, she stood among the mildewed graven images beyond the spill of confetti, an omen to her caveat: "She's not the one for you."

I had not the courage to wait for the Fong of my life. Fong had realised in me a different person, to question and reveal the pretence of my marriage. Love for Samantha and Simon were the only preventatives to immediate divorce.

Mary broke the mournful silence. 'So what future do you envisage for us? Are you moving out?'

'Whether you and I stay together depends a lot on you. You're not an innocent party as to why the affair happened.'

'Bloody ridiculous.'

'I beg to differ. The affair was symptomatic something in the marriage was wrong. After the kids were born your affection towards me changed; from being a woman you mutated into a mother. Sex has become a reluctant conjugal duty; not once can I remember you making the first move. So I felt entitled to have an affair.' She shook her head but didn't respond. 'Let's face reality; the children are the most important part of our marriage, not my fidelity. In my view we should continue to maintain our family environment. We can review our situation when they are old enough to understand. I love the kids; I want to be with them, to be part of their growing up. They need me ... both of us. I don't want this to affect their lives.

So far there's been no permanent impact on them, but there would be consequences if we were to split up ... Look, we can put this behind us,' I extended my arms, palms upwards. 'We have to move on for the benefit of the kids. We can't change the past but if you can forget, or at least forgive, it will not mar the future.'

'I'll never be able to forget this Chris, your lies, your fraudulent sentiments, sex with me when you wished you were fucking *her*. I'll never be able to put your filthy cock into my mouth again.' She shuddered with distaste at the memory, wiping her lips with the back of her hand. Abruptly her eyes widened, her jaw dropped. She sat bolt upright like a Cobra preparing to strike. 'Did you fuck her in this house? Did you defile our marital bed?'

I stood to adopt a more defensive posture. The cat reacted to the ominously raised tone, angrily waving its tail as it slunk off to seek quietude.

'She has never been here until today,' I said emphatically. Cynthia told her the address.

'She'll blab the scandal to all the neighbours,' she said

despondently.

'You didn't help chasing us up the street hollering obscenities.'

'I presume Danny Parker has been part of your conspiracy, pretending to mend second-hand scales. I'll never be able to show my face there again.'

'Danny knows about Fong; he saw us at a cinema one evening.'

She paused, staring vacantly out of the window. 'Are you going to see this Chinese bitch again?'

'The affair is over Mary. I may have the occasional lunch at the restaurant but her visa expires soon and she will return to Hong Kong.'

'You tell her if I ever see her again I'll kill her!' The words were spat out with the religious fervour of a zealous preacher.

I supposed it to be cathartic for her to vent her spleen with repugnant remarks. Her mind set was inaccessible to reason or reassurance, everything turned around as evidence against me. Despite her jealous reaction, I am sure it was dented pride more than strength of feelings for me. I avoided eye contact, her resentment gently simmering, threatening to boil over at the slightest provocation. We sat in chastened silence like two bereaved relatives in a mortuary. After a while she stood and I flinched defensively.

'I'm going to bed. I don't want you there. Get your things and sleep somewhere else.'

Chapter 18

I collected a bundle of bedding and sat on the sofa upon which I slept. The clamour in my mind slowly subsided as I mulled over the day's unfortunate events. The image of Fong crying on the bus broke me: my body heaved, my jaw quivered, my eyes welled up. As twilight shaded to darkness, I reflected on the circumstances that led up to a marriage I should never have entered.

My life had been determined by a series of chance encounters, each triggering profoundly life changing events. The seemingly inconsequential meeting of two people who didn't know each other introduced me to Mary and marriage; a few seconds difference and they may never have met.

I was enjoying a decidedly physical affair with Vanessa, a blue-blooded graduate from Roedean School working as a supply teacher. Vanessa had an aversion to sleeping alone. Her steady boyfriend was back on home turf in Brighton and travelled up to Coventry at weekends. It fell to me to keep her bed warm weekdays. So far so good. Then one day a misdirection of fate occurred. Whilst shopping in Coventry, Vanessa passed Mary in the street; they wore the same Birmingham Teachers' Training College scarves and struck up a conversation – both primary school teachers. Surfing a wave of giggling chatter they arrived at the café where I patiently awaited Vanessa's pleasure.

My initial meeting with Vanessa was also pure chance when one afternoon I joined the same blurred bus queue of ordinary people in which she stood out in sharp focus, ticking all the B's: beautiful, beguiling, blonde, blue eyes, and boobs. I gazed longingly, hopeful of a half smile to elicit conversation. My eyes dropped to the distraction of her cleavage.

'You had your fill yet,' she said with a wry smile.

'Two full cups,' I chuckled, 'almost overflowing.'

'Talking of cups, do you fancy a coffee?'

Her voice had the cut-glass timbre of the county set; she proved to be witty, cultured, intelligent and a passionate lover of sex – one chaste kiss and her flat was littered with jettisoned clothes. We performed everything in every position with mutual insatiable inexhaustibility. Michael Douglas could have been referring to Vanessa when he later said of Sharon Stone's character in *Basic Instinct*, "She is the fuck of the century." Unfortunately, when school term ended, Vanessa went back to Brighton and married the damn boyfriend.

Mary was an attractive brown eyed brunette but, unlike Vanessa, not instantly sexually provocative. Public school educated, cultured in music and art, her wide hips and ample bosom heralded good mothering stock. In the absence of Vanessa, convivial evenings with Mary often enough ended in bed and our casual association gradually developed frequency, advancing to habitual and an unstated assumption of permanence. Thus it was I ended up at the altar.

There were two problems marrying Mary, neither of which surfaced until after the knot was tied. As a teacher Mary was unable to leave her disciplinarian hat on the classroom coat rack. After a day modifying the behaviour of thirty or so brats I was an older version in need of behavioural redirection. I became her clay maquette to be pummelled and reconfigured.

Mary's mother was the second problem, a matriarch forever finding fault and imposing *suggestions* based on some unrealistic idealism of manhood she had so evidently failed to marry and convert. She had a tyrant's ability to enforce her will based on the fear of a god-awful set-to and I was no heroic revolutionary.

Love gives you permission to be your own person, not to be reformed with a different persona. I don't think Mary loved me other than to satisfy her societal status of marriage and motherhood. I never witnessed the heart pounding deep gaze of unconditional love seen in Fong's eyes.

Perhaps the strength of Mary's jealousy indicated she sensed a real threat, even more than the perceived reputation of oriental women between the sheets. Mary never found me provocatively attractive and domesticated my ardour, relegating sex to an occasionally allocated slot between headaches and the routine of home life.

Meeting Fong was also a chance encounter. Cynthia provided packed sandwich lunches for all her lodgers and one day I forgot to take it and ended up at the Lotus House. By chance Fong had recently arrived from Hong Kong and had no boyfriend, despite many admirers. Fate's fortuitous introduction had been laced with deceptiveness; having brought us together it intended to keep us apart.

My train of thought was interrupted by the cat wandering into the lounge and jumping onto my lap for a welcome cuddle, purring contentedly. Eventually we both fell asleep on the sofa, the door barricaded with a wedged chair. After Mary's knife wielding violence, caution seemed prudent. Reports in the Sunday press were not uncommon of the horror of women creeping up on their partners in the dead of night armed with garden shears or carving knives and amputating the culprit of infidelity. The cat no doubt remembered Mary was responsible for the loss of his manhood at the Blue Cross surgery.

On Monday morning Danny found my retelling of the fallout hilarious. 'A bloody pantomime,' he sniggered. 'The neighbours must have loved it. So you getting divorced or what?'

'Depends on Mary; I don't want to be separated from the kids and I doubt she wants to become a one parent family.'

'Yeah, but how can you not wake up each morning next to this Chinese bird?'

'If you had young kids, Danny, you'd realize how.'

'How does she feel about you now she's met your wife?'

'She loves me unconditionally. She's like no other woman I've known. I feel her love with every look and touch.'

'Isn't it too much to sacrifice?'

'It is; but I can't sacrifice my kids either. Now Mary knows the situation has to be resolved.'

'One of those so-called open marriages perhaps?'

'I can't see Mary going for that. She's already threatened to top Fong if she sees her again. Anyway, Fong is here on a finite visa and will return to Hong Kong.'

'So her departure will resolve matters for you,' he said with a shrug.

'I suppose so. I'll either go with her or stay with my kids and grin-and-bear-it with Mary.'

I left the office and sat in my car thinking on what Danny had said; Fong's return to Hong Kong would resolve the situation. Until now there had been no reality to her leaving my life, possibly forever.

Upon reflection, my true happiness with Fong had been possible because the mundane reality of daily life had been suspended. Our affair had been an adventure of the senses with neither time nor opportunity to drift towards the ennui harmony of domesticity, the persistent draining incessancy that dulls desire.

Paradoxically I couldn't help regretting we hadn't slept nightly in our own bed, to wake in the darkness and hold each other, to feel the joy of belonging. I lamented the lack of constant togetherness and shared activities of living under the same roof: a coffee whilst reading the Sunday papers, shopping for groceries, dining with friends, cuddling up watching a film on television.

Fong was relieved to see me at lunchtime. I kept my left hand out of sight – in my pocket, behind my back or beneath the table – but she eventually espied the bandage.

'What happened to your hand?' she said, caressing the victim, her expression oozing sympathy.

'Oh it's nothing ... cut myself shaving.'

'Don't Joke. Your wife did this.'

'Yes, but not intentionally,' I fibbed.

'I don't believe you,' she said, shaking her head. 'Chinese have saying, "A spark of love hides a fire of jealousy."'

'Jealousy definitely, but not love. Don't worry; the worst is over.'

Fong remained unconvinced. 'The bandage needs changing; I'll get the First Aid kit.'

Over the next few days a succession of neighbours came to borrow the proverbial cup-of-sugar fishing for details of Sunday's theatricals. Each ring of the doorbell reignited Mary's animosity accompanied by retreats behind slammed doors. Conjugal services of ironing and laundering and some meals were curtailed. Her demeanour gradually changed to a period of righteous indignation, the raging silence of I'm not speaking to you, I'm ignoring you phase, but her silences were weaponised, primed to return fire at the slightest provocation.

I slept on a camp bed in the third bedroom; the door locked from the inside. The kids felt the tension.

'Why are you and mummy not talking?' Sam probed.

'We *are* talking. We don't have anything to say at the moment,' I replied.

'Why are you sleeping in the small bedroom?'

'I talk in my sleep and it keeps mummy awake.'

'Daddy,' she exclaimed, with the scepticism of a voter questioning a politician.

With political adroitness I evaded further questions.

Mary's anger and hostility gradually played out to render an uneasy peace for the benefit of the children. Nevertheless, the occasional opportunity to obliquely express her resentment was not allowed to pass. The physical minutiae of my shortcomings manifested into the customary retorts and nagging familiar to couples locked into joyless marriages.

Before getting the company car I owned a blue Triumph Dolomite, the comfortable leather upholstery and polished wood facia smelled of a luxury above its marque. The car became a member of the family, like the cat, and I was sorry to part with it. It's why I noticed a blue Dolomite parked up the street from the office. It's why I noticed the same Dolomite parked adjacent to the café in Brigg High Street where I munched a sandwich lunch. It's why I noticed the same car back in Cleethorpes Road as I walked to the Lotus House for an early evening meal. Someone was following me. The next day I mentioned it to Danny.

'Nah, not the company. You're putting in good sales figures and if they suspected anything they'd come to the branch and turn up at your house. It has to be your wife mate. Shouldn't go playing away from home.'

'You did,' I reminded him.

'Yeah, but I didn't get caught,' he smirked, his fist playfully bumping my shoulder.

The Dolomite remained my shadow and I slipped out through the back entrance, walked around the block and approached the car from the rear. The driver sat reading a newspaper and supping tea from a thermos flask. The driver's side window was down and I reached in and grabbed the keys from the ignition.

'Hey! What the fuck are you doing? Give me those keys!' He attempted to open the door.

'Now don't get excited,' I cautioned, my knee pressing against the door, 'I used to own a Dolomite, same colour. Just want a chat; don't want you rushing off, okay.'

I walked around the bonnet and opened the passenger door. The guy removed his packed lunch from the seat and folded his newspaper. He was a puny bespectacled specimen more suited to a desk job, not your archetypal film noir tough private dick – a Sam Spade or a Philip Marlowe – where I would need a Colt .38 to prod his ribs. I sat half turned to face him.

'What do want to talk about?' he said guardedly.

'Well, how about why you've been tailing me for the last couple of days and who you're working for?'

'I don't know what you mean.'

'You don't, eh? Well you see the drain along the road, your car keys could accidentally drop into it when I leave the car.'

We glared at each other, frozen as if caught in a tableau.

'I can't divulge my client's confidentiality,' he said nervously.

'Okay, well at least you've confirmed you're following me. Now, what if I told *you* who your client was?'

He hesitated, looking straight ahead. I sensed the cogs whirring behind his furrowed brow: how to extricate from this unprecedented situation?

'Hmm,' I frowned. 'Well I guess you'll have to get the bus home.'

I opened the passenger door.

'Wait,' he said in alarm, a restraining hand on my arm. 'If you were to mention a correct name,' he said tentatively.

'Okay, so you tell Mrs Patterson you've been rumbled with nothing to report and I'll give you your keys back.'

I stood on the kerb and watched the Dolomite pull away, the familiar engine sound and exhaust pop triggering my nostalgia. So, Mary was still suspicious; but of course.

After packing the kids off to bed, we sat in the lounge waiting for a TV film to start.

'Why are you having me followed?'

'You're still seeing that bitch. I know where she works,' she said threateningly.

'As your private dickhead no doubt informed, I lunch at her restaurant as I've regularly done; she serves me and I enjoy the food.'

'Services you more likely.'

'Oh, please Mary; your jealous rants undermine any credence to putting this behind us. Yes I had an affair, but it's over, and now you need to get over it too for the sake of the children.'

'I shall never get over it. How can I ever forget your treachery and the humiliation of her coming to this house?' Tears welled up to quench the fire in her eyes.

'I told you, she's in England on a visa and will soon be returning to Hong Kong.'

How prescient these words proved to be.

Chapter 19

On Fong's next afternoon off we drove to Cleethorpes and basked in the August sunshine outside a seafront café, holding hands, chatting aimlessly, sipping tea, watching the world go by, simply glad to be together. But I sensed a restrained sadness, something troubling her; the alarming thought she might be pregnant crossed my mind.

'What's wrong? You don't seem your cheery self today.'

'This will explain,' she said glumly, taking a letter from her handbag.

The letter from the Home Office stated her visa to stay in Britain would not be renewed. A dismal gloom engulfed me as I mourned her loss now prescribed in black and white: 31 August 1976.

'Oh Fong, I'm so sad' I said forlornly, we only have three weeks. I don't want you to go. I love you so much.'

'Me too,' she said tearfully. 'I have one week in Grimsby before I stay with my sister, Mai Ling, in Watford. You will come and see me and meet Mai Ling wont you?'

'Yes, of course.'

We cuddled in grim silence, staring vacantly out across the sea of grey emptiness reflecting our mood.

'Can you appeal against the decision and extend the visa?'

She shook her head. 'No. I already tried with help of Mr Zhang.

He wants me to stay, says I'm good for business.'

'You certainly are. Will you apply for another visa and come back to England?'

'Fare too expensive,' she said sadly.

'I will pay your fare, and I'm sure Mr Zhang would give you your job back.'

'It's not what I want ... I don't like waitressing and I don't like Grimsby. You use fare to come and see me in Hong Kong, yes?'

'One day, I promise.'

There appeared to be no way to avoid her deportation. Even if I was to instigate divorce proceedings and promise to marry, she would still have to leave and may not be eligible for another visa.

I could not conceive of a greater love or eroticism than experienced with Fong, but on reflection, our relationship other than as temporary lovers had been doomed from the start.

Throughout the week the sadness of her imminent departure tainted each meeting. In the afternoon of her last day in Grimsby – Wednesday 18th August – we made love: melancholy, tender, tearful love.

Later, arm in arm we strolled Freeman Street to jewellers H. Samuel; I wanted to reaffirm the enduring strength of my love with an eternity ring. She chose a yellow and white gold band, engraved and embossed with roses; in the centre of each rose the sparkle of a tiny diamond. I placed the ring on her finger.

'This ring is a symbol of my unending love; my heart will always beat for you,' I said in a hushed tone.

'Me too,' she murmured, squeezing my arm.

Fong insisted on reciprocating the gesture. I resisted, after all I would not be able to wear it in Mary's presence, but she persuaded and I chose a plain gold cygnet ring with small offset single diamond set into a black onyx disc. With our eyes moist from emotion we clung to each other in the street.

Late afternoon we stopped for tea and cake in a café overlooking the market. I saw her admiring glances at the ring, revolving it around her finger, feeling the contours of the design. She could not have been more moved had it been an engagement ring.

We returned to her room and made love again, with a mix of joyful and soulful emotions as the sand of her time in Grimsby ran out.

In the evening Mr Zhang closed the restaurant early, a "private function" notice displayed on the door. The occasion, a farewell feast in honour of Fong's service. My invitation recognised our relationship. Jimmy and Mr Zhang were not party to my marital situation; in their eyes, Fong's relationship with me had changed from colonial stigma to favourable prospect of marriage. Prestige is paramount with the Chinese and it was testimony to the strength of her love Fong remained loyal after I revealed my marriage. Lucy noticed Fong's ring and the two of them huddled in explanation.

A variety of Cantonese specialities graced the table: fried spring rolls, marinated pork spare ribs, deep fried prawns on toast, crispy seaweed, a large bowl of Wanton noodle soup – with dumplings of pork and shrimp – and pots of jasmine tea. Everyone ladled a generous portion of soup and supped with ornate ceramic spoons.

Mr Zhang was a patriarchal figure and commanded respect; when he spoke others listened. I posed a question.

'How did Chinese food become so popular in Britain?'

'Post war rationing was in place until 1953, the food monotonous and bland. In the 1950s there was an appetite for exotic spicy food to which many service men and civil servants had become accustomed from postings to Hong Kong, India and Japan. Chinese restaurants were informal and inexpensive meaning restaurant dining was no longer the preserve of the wealthy. We Chinese democratised dining out.'

He paused with a nostalgic smile. 'I knew Johnny Koon, owner of the Lotus House in Bayswater; I named this restaurant after his. Soon after Koon opened in 1958, the restaurant became so popular people were often unable to get a table and wanted to take the food away to eat at home. News of his success spread quickly and many Chinese immigrants came from Hong Kong, including me.' He laughed proudly, placing an open hand against his chest.

'Chinese food is regional – Peking, Shanghai, Sichuan, Hunan – all different. Canton and Hong Kong ports opened up to foreign trade and the influence of different ingredients produced a greater variety of dishes and Cantonese became synonymous with Chinese food in Britain. However, its integrity has been damaged by the dubious quality of cheap takeaways, with clumsy imitations of traditional dishes over sweetened or sodden with soy and laced with sodium glutamate.'

He grimaced with distaste as if he'd eaten something unpleasant in other establishments. He paused and gave a heavy sigh.

'Our food here is not authentic; recipes anglicized, ingredients changed, dishes neutered of their cultural and social custom. It's the same with Indian cuisine, both nationalities adapted to please the British palate; it's why chips were introduced, to compete with fish-and-chip shops.' He gestured his disdain, raising both hands in mock surrender.

'We Chinese live to eat; food is central to our social life, binding families and friends in joyful union; happiness is tea and food. You British eat to live. Your happiness is alcohol and sex.'

I sensed Fong's embarrassment and condemnation as she dipped her head and looked away; I thought better than to challenge Mr Zhang's assertion, conceding it was not without foundation.

The mood lightened when Jimmy triumphantly produced two whole crispy ducks. With two forks he shredded the flesh with mechanical efficiency. From a wicker drum ultra thin pancakes were bathed in Hoi Sin sauce using the back of a spoon, the duck flesh rolled in with spring onion shoots and diced cucumber.

Later, Fong collected a small bowl of dim sum from the kitchen. 'Dim sum special for you Chris; not usually eaten at dinner.' In Chinese, dim sum means "to touch the heart." You touched my heart Chris.'

'You captured my heart,' I whispered, 'If things were different, if only I had met you a few years ago.'

The emotion welled up and I struggled to stem tears of love and guilt, happiness and sorrow urging to flow. Under the table, I squeezed her hand; her answering pressure returned my feelings.

Steaming hot dishes of stir fried beef and vegetables in oyster sauce and egg fried rice followed before the dessert of lychees and milky, warm rice wine plus medallion sized roundels of moon cakes sprinkled with ground coconut.

'What are moon cakes made from?'

'Moon cakes are moist pastry filled with an egg yolk and flavoured with adzuki bean paste,' said Mr Zhang. 'The cakes have an unusual history, used by revolutionaries in imperial China to smuggle imbedded messages written on edible rice paper. After reading, the messages were eaten to avoid detection. If the cakes fell into wrong hands they were innocently consumed along with the messages.'

Fong selected a cake for my plate.

'This one has a message for you.'

I split open the cake and carefully unravelled the rice paper message, "I will always love you." I looked across at Fong and breathed heavily. With moist eyes and nodding gently I adopted her signature phrase, 'Me too.'

'What does the message say?' taunted Jimmy with a rare transforming smile.

'Forever a secret,' I said, placing the rice paper into my mouth and chewing.

Everyone laughed.

'Now Mr Zhang, I have another question. China has been the source of many scientific discoveries and inventions, including paper making and printing, silk and porcelain, gunpowder and fireworks, and most importantly for us British, tea and the umbrella. So why are China's great minds defeated when it comes to eating food using wooden sticks?'

'Ancient tradition Chris, from the writings of Kongzi (Confucius). Meat and vegetables are never cut at table, always diced in the kitchen, so there is no need of a knife. For poor people and travellers it was easy to get wood or bamboo to make quick chopsticks anywhere, eat with and throw away. No washing-up! Method in design, yes?' he chuckled.

'Avoiding washing-up is certainly an advantage Mr Zhang.'

Later in the evening Jimmy photographed the gathering before Mr Zhang and the others tactfully removed to the bar leaving Fong and me at table. With the traditional respect of both hands, Fong presented a small parcel wrapped in red tissue paper and tied with a gold ribbon.

'It's a keepsake,' she explained, 'to always think of me.'

Inside the wrapping was a leather bound volume entitled *Chin P'ing Mei* (Lotus Blossom).

'A book from a lover is kept under the pillow to dream on,' she said.

'What a beautiful idea.'

On the flyleaf written in English and Cantonese, "Love you always. Fong xx."

She explained the book was an English translation of a condensed version of a famous Chinese novel from the seventeenth century Ming Dynasty – illustrated with delicately painted artworks of explicit sexual acts. The eponymous Lotus

Blossom was the sexy mistress who kept her master satisfied. The book was the first Chinese narrative to focus on ordinary people and everyday life, as opposed to mythical heroes or dynastic wars. Apparently the story was as notorious in China as *Lady Chatterley's Lover* in Britain, banned by Mao but available in Hong Kong. As I thumbed the pages I noticed the prose cloaked in poetical similes and metaphorical allusions making charming reading.

'It's a beautiful gift, I will always keep. I also have a keepsake for you,' I said, producing a slim rectangular royal blue box.

She opened it with a child's look of awe. 'Oh Chris, thank you; it's lovely.'

'Wear it on your wrist and when you look at the time, think of me.'

She strapped it on, clasped my hand and love flowed between us.

I walked Fong back to her flat and we agreed a time to collect her the next morning to drive her to Grimsby Town station for her journey to Watford.

Fong had two suitcases of clothes and effects; to ease her journey, I suggested I keep the larger case and deliver it Friday week to Mai Ling's house. With train changes at Sheffield and Birmingham, having only one case of essentials will ease her tiring five-and-a-half hour journey.

British Rail generously allowed us an additional twelve minutes hugging and kissing before the train rumbled into platform three. Fong was worried about missing her connection at Sheffield but I assured her there were plenty of trains and her ticket would be valid. With impending sadness I waved her out of the station.

Chapter 20

The working week dragged interminably and I sensed the depressive loneliness of life without her. Lunches at the Lotus House were particularly mournful and the staff recognised my sadness. Jimmy paused to chat.

'What are you and Fong going to do?'

'I am going to see her at her sister's next weekend.'

'You know what I mean,' he said, with a knowing frown.

'Yes, I know what you mean. With Fong having to return to Hong Kong, I don't know.'

'You should marry otherwise you'll always regret it. Her father wants her married, like her sister.'

'I know Jimmy. It's a difficult situation for us. I'll keep you posted,' I fibbed.

I took Friday as holiday from work and motored down to Watford under the pretence of a new job interview and staying over to visit my cousin in St Albans. Job interviews often took place at hotels and at weekends as I had experienced some years previously when applying for a genuine sales position. I had reserved a double room in a modest hotel for two nights and paid cash on arrival.

It was late Friday afternoon when I drew up in front of Mai Ling's rented house, a greyish-yellow brick, splayed bay mid-terraced a mile or so from the centre of Watford. Casio Bridge Road was typical of a Victorian working class street – treeless and devoid of front gardens – where previous generations of wives knelt to scrub their front doorsteps. My arrival was seen from the lounge window; Mai Ling greeted with a broad smile and appraising look.

'You are most welcome Chris. Fong has told me *all* about you,' she said smiling.

She shook my hand and bowed slightly before pulling Fong's suitcase across the threshold and calling upstairs to announce my arrival to Fong.

I was ushered into the lounge with the promise of tea. The room was decorated in tired magnolia, rectangular blemishes betraying where paintings once hung. A solitary oval mirror hung over an oak sideboard adorned with framed family photographs. The upholstered armchair suite looked third-hand but comfortable. I sat and waited. A young girl and two elderly adults stood motionless in the open doorway, peering with curiosity at their alien visitor.

'Hello. What's your name?' I smiled at the little girl.

Cute with pigtails and Bambi eyes she shyly hid behind the skirt and inscrutable expression of the old woman, a grandmother with at least three score years of hard labour etched into her features.

'Her name is Wei Ling, she's three years old,' said Fong as she entered.

To my relief, a burst of Cantonese dispelled the voyeurs. We embraced and cheek kissed with an air of polite formality; the Chinese do not favour a display of affection in front of family.

'So good to see you.' I whispered. 'Missed you.'

'Me too,' she replied, squeezing my arm before easing from my embrace.

Jasmine tea promptly arrived with morsels of sweet rice cake. Fong and Mai chatted in Cantonese. Betrayed by looks and smiles I was the main subject of their conversation; I hid my mix of discomfort and pride behind sips of tea.

Taller than Fong with a model's sylph figure, Mai was attractive compared to Fong's classification of beautiful: her hairstyle, generous mouth, neat nose, dark almond eyes and breast swell attested to her sisterly genes.

Mai and her husband worked in a Chinese restaurant in the centre of Watford as waitress and chef. Mai's husband was currently in Hong Kong preparing for the family's return later in the year. The old couple were Mai's in-laws. Tea supped we were ready to depart and Mai needed to leave for the evening waitressing. Fong swung a blue travel bag over her shoulder and said farewell to the family.

At Fong's suggestion we drove to a nearby park with lake and café. A large weeping willow bowed to caresses the dark brown water, stippled with sun spangles and reflections; ducks lingered expectantly. After an arm in arm stroll around the lake we sat cuddling on a park bench. We didn't say much; we simply needed to reconnect. Such periods of empathetic togetherness were its own language, more expressive than words and as meaningful as the thrusting of loins.

We dined at Mai's restaurant. Dining with Fong – instead of being waited on – was a sensual pleasure, an overture to our night of passion. As I devoured the spare ribs, I mentioned the ribald tavern scene in *Tom Jones.*

'I remember,' said Fong with a laugh, 'Albert Finney munched a chicken leg like he wanted to eat his date.'

'Lobster, oysters and fruit as well,' I commented. 'The erotic symbolism of foreplay was never more vividly portrayed in the cinema.'

Sexual allegories of food had been painted and chronicled for centuries although eroticism linked to food first caught my attention in the 1960s with the double entendre "Unzip a Banana" adverts, whence the schoolboy euphemism for sex was born: the male banana inserted into the female fruit salad. When the dim sum and vegetable rolls arrived, my arrangement of the pieces to a genital representation induced a knowing frown and familiar reprimand.

'Food is more than flavours on the palate,' I excused, 'it's the foreplay to life's most sensual duet.'

After coffee, I produced a cherry brandy liqueur chocolate and, trying to keep a straight face, informed Fong of a British foreplay tradition. Placing the chocolate in her mouth, via lips and tongues we carefully transferred the slowly melting chocolate backwards and forwards between us. After a few transfers the chocolate melted and the liqueur spilled out in a confectionary orgasm as we vied for the nectar as if eating each other.

We bid fond farewell to Mai and by 10 pm were inside the hotel room; I had insisted on room eight. After the foreplay of the meal, I was eager to make memorable love, but there was an unexpected problem.

'It's the wrong week,' she said shyly. 'I bleed; I must be padded up.'

'Oh no,' I groaned with dismay, 'not tonight of all nights.'

'We still make love,' she assured, continuing to undo my clothes, 'but I will have to use my mouth.'

I agreed, inflecting my voice with feigned disappointment, whilst secretly relishing the prospect of the offered surrogate.

'So you are a musician,' I said, with a mischievous smile.

'What do you mean a musician?'

'Let me read you a paragraph from my pillow book.' I rummaged through the clothes of my travel bag and took out my keepsake. I climbed into bed beside her and thumbed through the pages. 'Ah, here it is.

Golden Lotus played the flute exquisitely, but that was not the instrument she placed between her lips. For a long time she played softly, his pleasures gradually becoming unendurable. At last, deft fingering tormented a cascade of music from the pipe, and he dissolved in bliss.'

Fong must have had music lessons so expertly did she compose an irresistible tune and inexorable coda. This was no beginner's composition and I felt a pang of jealousy towards previous beneficiaries.

'There is no greater act of love, no greater intimacy than fellatio,' I said in admiration.

'I want to please you, love you; maybe our last time.'

'Not our last time, I will come back next weekend.'

She looked down on a job well done with a proud expression of empowerment. She commented on the duality of my member: a strong, upright and dominant young warrior now reduced to a flaccid and wrinkled old man. With a satisfied smile she sat astride proffering her breasts to my mouth as if daring my warrior to rise again in combat. I drifted off to sleep in her arms to the distant drone of vehicles waxing-and-waning as they passed in the night.

I awoke as Fong drew back the curtains; the daylight silhouetted her figure through the flimsy negligee.

'It's raining,' she observed.

'The weather is crying for us; our separation is like bereavement.'

'Nice thought.' She slipped back between the sheets for a cuddle. 'Oh, oh,' she said ominously, 'what's happened here?'

I shared her appreciative gaze. The wrinkled old man of a few hours ago had mutated to a fine upstanding soldier, smartly attired with freshly pressed livery and shiny helmet. I didn't let on I often woke in the mornings with a stiffy without any obvious arousal, a metabolic phenomenon.

'We must see what we can do about *that,'* she chastened. 'It's a fine willy Chris.'

'Willy will miss your passionate attention,' I sighed.

'Why you call him Willy?'

'It's customary to name the little warrior by a first name, a polite personification: cock is too vernacular, penis too clinical, manhood too prosaic.'

'Okay, but Willy is not your name.'

'William is too formal,' I jested.

'Ha ha,' she mocked, taking it between her lips with the enthusiasm of a child sucking a lollipop.

To my moans of euphoric sensory overload her hands moved up-and-down the shaft to milk every morsel of pleasure. No milkmaid ever drained the phallic udder drier. Like a nurse attending a wounded soldier she gently wiped the concertinaed casualty with a tissue.

A reviving cup of tea was her next task. As I lay in her arms the over filled kettle seemed to encore an analogy: gradually simmering, becoming more agitated and urgent as the temperature slowly rose before uncontrollably boiling over, spitting and spilling its excited liquid from the nozzle before coming to rest.

Another battle was won outside; the dawn conquered the night gloom, the dull early light became brighter as the rain eased and the triumphal Sun moved the morning on. After a few precious minutes cuddling, we washed and dressed and took breakfast downstairs in the hotel dining room. Fong was quiet and from her hesitant looks I felt she had an issue to broach.

'You look a little uneasy. Is there something you want to tell me?'

'Not tell, ask. It's difficult. I don't know how to begin, how you will react,' she said cautiously.

'After last night, there can be nothing unspoken between us.'

'It's not us; it's my sister, Mai.'

'Oh, what about her?'

'You like her, yes?'

'Yes, she made me feel welcome. She's good looking; I could tell she was your sister.'

'She likes you. I tell her *all* about you.'

'Not everything I hope.'

'Yes, *everything*. What a good lover you are. No secrets.'

'Oh my. I'll be embarrassed when next we meet.'

'Thing is ... husband is no good in bed: quickie, in, bang, out, sleep. She has never had an orgasm with him.'

I started to have an uncomfortable feeling as to where this conversation was leading.

'Didn't she have sex with him before they married?'

'Father pushed her into marriage ... family ties, no love.'

'Perhaps she should take a lover.'

'Would you be her lover?'

'Me! No. I love *you*,' I remonstrated, hugging her hand with both mine.

'Mai has never been loved properly, no orgasm. 'You love her, for me.'

'Oh no. No. I don't think so. I'm not a gigolo.'

'Not pay you! Do because you love me, I love Mai, and I ask because I'm not available. Mai will deputise.' She grinned, pleased with her logic.

'Are you suggesting she join us at the hotel for a threesome?' I said with more enthusiasm.

'No! Mai would be embarrassed if I was there.'

'I might fall in love with her.'

'No.' She shook her head and smiled confidently. 'You love me; Mai will only be sex and soon she returns to Hong Kong.'

'What about her working at the restaurant? I have to go back to Louth tomorrow.'

'She will say she's unwell and not work tonight. Please Chris, for me.'

So these conniving sisters have it all worked out. No wonder Mai Ling was so welcoming. Pity about the threesome, but I admitted to not having the moral fibre to refuse the generous offer of an attractive no strings stand-in. I wasn't keen on performing to order and bursting her bubble could not be guaranteed.

'Hmm ... well ... okay ... if you're sure but remember, I do this for you because I love you,' I said firmly.

'I allow because I love you and love Mai,' she said resolutely.

This liberated logic seemed somewhat at odds with Chinese family values but self interestedly I wasn't going to question their emancipated persuasion. In some perverse way I looked upon the solicitation as acceptance into the Leung family of future benefit.

We perused the town centre and high street shops, Fong looking for presents for her family and friends in Hong Kong. An intimate lunch in a small Italian restaurant followed and after more shopping, we searched for a café for afternoon tea.

'There you are. What did I tell you,' I said, pointing.

'Okay,' she conceded, smiling as she read the "Rosy Lee" signage.

We entered and are met by a Chinese waitress! Fong doubled up in a wave of laughter.

'Unbelievable.' I smiled abashed, shaking my head.

Fortunately the amber nectar and fruit scones were traditional English fare.

We drove back to Casio Bridge Road. Mai Ling opened the front door looking shy and uneasy.

'Fong and I wondered if you would join us for dinner tonight at the hotel.'

'Thank you Chris, I am delighted to accept your kind invitation. Fong will make tea while I get ready.'

At the hotel, room eight was again noted as a propitious number. The bed and en suite were inspected as thoroughly as a surgeon's operating theatre and I was apprehensive of the clinical efficiency of the preparations. Whilst Mai used the toilet I spoke earnestly to

Fong.

'What will you do while Mai and I ... you know?'

'I have a novel to read,' she replied dismissively.

'Are you sure about this? Won't you be jealous? I don't want it to affect our feelings for each other, for you to regret it afterwards, hold it against me for seeming to give in so readily.'

'You do this for me. I do this for her. You make her come, we both love you.'

'Okay,' I shrugged, bemused by her dismissive simplism, 'as long as you're sure. Does she have protection? It would not do for her to become pregnant with me.'

'She's on the pill. She doesn't want more children with her husband.'

'Are you still on the pill?'

'I finished last pack two weeks ago, no time to renew at clinic. I will not need in Hong Kong unless you come to see me.'

We dined convivially; a bottle of Merlot helped thaw the ice of apprehension although by the time coffee arrived I sensed Mai's anticipation shaded in anxiety. With kisses and encouraging cuddles, Fong took her leave.

I held Mai's hand. 'I am as nervous as you,' I admitted with a sympathetic smile. 'Being married, I realize what a big decision this is for you.'

'Yes, difficult ... I never loved him, didn't want to marry ... father insisted.'

'I understand, so you shouldn't feel guilty. We will create something beautiful tonight. All we need to do is relax, take our time and enjoy our bodies. Did Fong tell you about the British tradition of sharing a liqueur chocolate after a meal?'

She nodded, her face creased with a knowing smile.

'Well, I happen to have another chocolate with me.'

The chocolate ritual replaced our nervousness with enthusiasm.

The more we kissed and the more our tongues parried, the more we knew we should be in bed. I intended to close my eyes and pretend her body to be Fong, after all they were sisters and not dissimilar in looks, but Mai had her own personality and responses and feel seducing me to think only of her; I felt pangs of guilt at my ardour.

Around midnight we heard a discrete knock on the door. Mai Ling donned a dressing gown and opened to a joyous sisterly hug and excited chatter. Mai Ling stayed the night; no raunchy threesome, merely a cuddling, snoozing bundle of three contented bodies.

Chapter 21

With the excuse to Mary of a second job interview I returned to Watford the following Saturday, arriving late afternoon. On the drive down my mind still contested the dilemma: Fong or my children? In all conscience I knew the decision was made; the morally right decision, the financially viable decision, but the decision I feared I would forever regret.

I wished I was blessed with Uncle Cecil's adventurous spirit to up-sticks and relocate halfway round the world to an alien culture, with no job prospects and little hope of speaking the lingo. I had not the bravura to give up my home, the comfortable life, the blood love of my kids. I couldn't muster the irresponsibility, the courage. I had to play it safe, go on mowing the front lawn and cleaning the car every weekend.

It was a strange sensation meeting both sisters with whom I had been so intimate, and Mai Ling seemed embarrassed at my presence in front of her husband who had returned from Hong Kong. Both women trod warily in his presence and I took an instant dislike to the guy and his abrupt nature. It was obvious he disapproved of my relationship with Fong. I felt genuine sadness for Mai Ling, trapped in a wretched marriage of her parent's behest.

Fong and I took our leave and had dinner at the hotel, a sombre affair feeling the impending separation of our lives. We discussed

Mai Ling's situation but divorce was not an option, family ties and loss of face the overriding factors.

The hotel room and bed had a comforting familiarity. After the obligatory tea and chatter, we enjoyed each other's warm nakedness, the gentle sensuality of touch and kisses. Amongst the endearments came the arousal of humour.

'You're like a drug. You've made me an addict,' she jested. 'I fear cold turkey when there are no more willy injections.'

Despite the underlying cheerlessness I had to smile. 'What shall we call this drug?'

'Sexstasy,' she proposed. We laughed. With a more serious expression she said, 'I think it's time for an injection.'

After the syringe emptied, the heat of passion abated to a warm glow, like the ashes of a smouldering fire, its embers burnt and collapsed; but the fire rekindled before we drifted blissfully to sleep.

I woke in the early hours, conscious she was awake in the darkness. I put my arm across her breasts, she rolled against me and I felt wetness on her cheek. Wounded hearts don't spill blood, they weep tears; I can offer no coagulant to stem the flow. I caressed away the salty drops. Her quiet weeping degenerated to shuddering sobs. She clung to me and buried her face in the crook of my neck. Without uttering the words, she pleaded with me to up sticks and fly east away from the sunset of separation, but my name was not Cecil. I sniffed and with the back of my hand wiped away my irritating wetness.

After a while, in a quivering, mournful murmur she said, 'I'm so sad; our last time together.'

'I wish it could not be so; but you understand.'

'Yes.' She nodded.

Eventually sleep overtook her. I lay awake listening to the raging silence of the night, tormented by the guilt of her hurt. At the first hint of daylight I eased from the bed. The rhythm of her breathing had the gentle purring of slumber. I drew the sheet over her against the chill of the dawn and crossed to the window, nudging the curtains slightly apart. A dismal shaft of light fell across the room. Our last dawn was as ordinary as any other; the stars had turned-off and the subdued shades of night faded to reveal the natural colours of the urban landscape.

I slumped into a chair and watched Fong doze on, her breasts gently rising and falling. No man could want more than to wake up each morning with such a body beautiful in his bed. That man could have been me, if only I had met her a few years ago. Life's a bitch.

Once again I raised the question to which I had the answer. As Mr H declared, a father doesn't leave his children for a woman because she's good in bed, except with Fong it was so much more. I had become lost, totally immersed and absorbed in her. She was the one who could make me forget all others, to quell my hunger for greener grass on the other side of the cliché. It's all I ever wanted, the one to give me the peace of physical and mental fidelity, the happiness born of the contentment of unconditional love.

I slipped back to bed. She drowsily stirred as I enfolded her in my arms. After a few minutes kissing and cuddling she was astride and emptying the syringe with the recklessness of a junkie desperate for another fix. She collapsed on me with a gasp as if the injection had been lethal.

There was no time for an encore, no time for a last breakfast; Fong had a plane to catch. I watched her dress, experiencing a palpable sense of fear and sadness as I harboured doubts of life without her.

'Best we say goodbye here; family will come to the airport,' she said despondently.

I nodded agreement, but unable to suppress my feelings and tears welled up.

'I will think of you always, love you forever. You have given me the most treasured memories of my life.' My voice trembled with emotion. 'If I was free, you know ... '

She placed her fingers on my lips. 'I know,' she nodded, 'I know.'

'Resist your father's pressure to enter an arranged marriage. Tell him we are engaged, the ring should convince him my intentions are genuine. I promise we will be together, I just need time.'

'I will try to persuade him,' she said hopefully.

'Write to me at the office address.'

'I will. You write to me at this address,' she said, handing a slip of paper.

'Wear your ring and wristwatch to always remind you of me.'

She looked down at the ring and twirled it on her finger.

'I love you Chris, I always will. I must go now, have to finish packing.'

'Here, take a taxi.' I handed her a £5 note.

We stood and hugged, our cheeks wet with tears; we had both run out of words. She eased from my embrace, picked up her shoulder bag and opened the door. With a last sentimental look wistfully voicing her sadness she turned away and was gone. The hotel door clicked shut, a closure to the most memorable period of my life, but a door I would always long to reopen.

The crumpled, stained sheets and squashed pillows were evidence to the end she had been the faithful lover attending to my every need and pleasure. I will miss the joyous sex and being unconditionally loved. She had unselfishly given her everything, but it was not enough. She understood, made no demands for the future and no recriminations for the past. It's over, but will never truly be over because she will be alive in memories to taunt and haunt like the yearnings of a drug addict.

As I drove up the A1 on the long commute to conformity, I

thought of her at the airport. *Casablanca* came to mind with Ilsa's lament to Rick a parody of our situation as she's about to board her flight:

Fong: "But what about us?"

Chris: "We'll always have Grimsby ... Here's looking at you, kid."

I managed a smile. On reflection, perhaps grimy, smelly, weather beaten Grimsby wasn't such a bad place after all, like Rick's Paris, a city of love and treasured memories.

A Leo Sayer ballad on the car radio, *Raining in My Heart,* triggered an emotional out pouring. I pulled over into a lay-by. Outside the rain was teeming. The windscreen wipers hypnotically oscillated from side to side as I stared into the gloom. The wipers couldn't clear my vision. Sayer's song became the soundtrack of my life yearning for Fong.

Fong and I had joined the ranks of millions of separated lovers through history. I remembered a visit to Cimetiere du Père Lachaise in Paris and admiring the grave of a beautiful young Russian woman, Tatyana Rachevskaya. When separated from her Romanian lover she committed suicide. Sculptured by another Romanian, Constantin Brâncusi, he erected a headstone in memoriam: "To all unknown couples of the world who loved each other before suffering the agonies of separation."

The emotional *Brief Encounter* had uncanny parallels with our situation: a couple meet by chance, fall in love, but after a few months separate with aching hearts. He goes off abroad to bring finality to their affair. The audience are rooting for them to stay together but she is married with a young son, moral commitments proving too great an obstacle.

Fong and I acted out our own brief encounter; like the film ours is a moral but unhappy ending. Fong would forever be the leitmotif of my life; with hope for the future, our script was still being written.

Chapter 22

The headline news, September 9th 1976, was of Mao Tse-tung's death with public outpourings of grief – more likely relief – on the Chinese mainland. In Hong Kong people danced in the streets and attended all-night parties in celebration. At the Lotus House I joined the festivity; even Jimmy and Lucy raised smiles toasting the future. How desperately I missed Fong as I thought of her enjoying the revelry with family and friends.

Like the leaves of autumn Fong had coloured my life, but the dying foliage and bereft trees mirrored my gloomy insistent sadness. I lingered at the office each morning awaiting the postman, thumbing through the drab manila for an eagerly awaited airmail blue. The memory of the lonely Russian girl, who committed suicide in preference to a life without her lover, played on my mind. An unsettling six weeks dragged by before the relief of her first missive.

Pocketing the envelope I adjourned to the privacy of the car, unfolding the fragile paper with all the reverence of a discovered ancient manuscript. I felt the handling should have been with white cotton gloves, so precious did it seem. The photograph I had taken with her camera at the Laceby hotel dropped out. She looked out at me, her gorgeous smile breaking to a toothy grin; I smiled back.

The cursive writing was as black as her hair; my eyes detoured to the lyricism of her closing endearments: "I love you, miss you", the ciphered kisses and our "cold turkey" in-joke. My eyes moistened at the sentiments. I read the page over and over with all the awe of a schoolboy with his first love letter.

Fong informed a change of address, a flat on the Pak Tin Estate, Kowloon; I copied it into the back of my diary. I later learned the estate was a public housing complex, the Hong Kong equivalent of the British council flat. There were no details with whom she lived and no telephone number.

She described the large gathering of friends and family celebrating Mao's demise and said the heavy rainfall, far from dampening peoples' spirits, was regarded as a symbolic cleansing. However, Fong had surviving relatives on the mainland and like many compatriots was concerned Mao's widow, Jiang Qing – leader of the so-called "Gang of Four" – would win the succession power struggle resulting in no change.

She apologised for the delay in writing and related how busy she had been moving address, catching up with friends and looking for work. A new film, *Robin and Marian* – starring Sean Connery and Audrey Hepburn – triggered a remembrance of my story of King Arthur and his Knights. She suggested my version could be applied to the Robin Hood and Marian legend, with Robin away on a Crusade. I smiled at her insight. Her family, her friends, the culture and the food contributed to her happiness being back in Hong Kong, our separation her only regret.

She related the frightening experience of Typhoon Iris (Toyang) which plagued the colony for the last two weeks of September, the wind slamming against the block of flats where she lived with such force the building swayed alarmingly. Roads around the harbour became rivers of seawater. There were several casualties but she was safe.

Two further letters arrived before Christmas, their underlying tone less upbeat, their content frustratingly mundane, like two people voicing inane pleasantries preceding the real purpose of their meet. Perhaps I was wrong to expect more emotion after our unhappy separation.

She informed her block of flats in Kowloon had been scheduled for demolition, she to be re-housed in Tai Po, a town under development in the New Territories. Tai Po was less crowded, the air less polluted and boasted tree lined avenues, parks and a river promenade. The housing was newly built with air conditioning, the rents cheaper than Kowloon. I replied how pleased I was for her.

In a later letter she confessed to working in a garment factory, learning the sewing trade. The news tortured like a masochist suffering penitence, for I feared I had sentenced her to a life of drudgery in a sweat shop akin to a Victorian workhouse of a Charles Dickens novel.

To everyone's relief, Mao's widow and her cohorts had been arrested and charged with an attempted coup. Premier Hua Kuo-feng, took over as leader, a leap into the unknown Fong wrote. Each letter was a comfort and confirmation she was thinking of me and our love remained intact. I asked after the situation with her father regarding pressure to marry and how our pact to convince him of my intentions had played out. With the obscuration of a politician she equivocated.

My feelings transcended the limitations of the written word but writing to Fong was a cathartic necessity. I wrote in the most heartfelt way, delving into my fund of happy memories affording joy in their reminiscence. There was nothing of a personal nature I could write she did not already know; nothing new to change our situation or provide fresh hope. My missives were simply a desperate attempt to prevent the pilot light of our romance from extinguishing. I told her I remained hopeful she will come back to

England and I had opened a Building Society savings account – funded by the sale of second hand scales – to pay her airfare.

Autumn departed with the leaves and the chill of winter echoed in the mood changes of her monthly letters. All was not right. I had no proper foundation for the inference, simply a between the lines presentiment. I felt there was a subtext to her narratives to which I was not privy. Her affectionate codas had cooled, but I dared not ask if she had a new lover, I didn't want the pain of knowing.

Over tea one morning, I mentioned my concerns to Danny. 'Why don't you have her handwriting analysed,' he suggested. 'I know this woman, a psychological profiler and forensic graphologist with South Humberside Police. She does freelance work; you could have a chat with her and see what she thinks.'

Barbara Bowen lived with her mother in a detached 1930s bungalow on the outskirts of Barton-upon-Humber. In her mid thirties, unmarried, outsize plump, shoulder length brunette and wearing little make-up, she had the cheerless look, appropriately, of a person "helping the police with their enquiries." Whilst I admired the view of the Humber Bridge from the French windows, she produced tea and fruitcake from the kitchen. She listened attentively as I related the situation with Fong, without revealing my marriage; I needed Barbara's sympathetic help.

'My concerns relate to the tenor of her writings. In trying to read between the lines, I feel she is suppressing her feelings; her writing has taken on a character unlike her affectionate personality. I'm sure there is something wrong, a preoccupation not being divulged.'

'Reading the lines, instead of between them, will be more enlightening,' quipped Barbara.

'I understand graphology can identify a person's handwriting but also reveal much about their character, health and mental state.

I have to admit to some scepticism as to how reliable an analysis could be without you having met the writer. She's Chinese, from Hong Kong.' I plucked Fong's photo from the lining of my wallet. 'Before I knew her name, I called her Aphrodite, goddess of love renowned for her beauty.'

'Oh my, yes she's beautiful. Makes me wish I was a lesbian,' chuckled Barbara. 'Interestingly, it was the Chinese who first developed the study of handwriting and its analysis a millennium ago.'

'Part of my scepticism is because my handwriting varies considerably according to my mood, how quickly written, and the style of pen.'

'Okay Chris, well let me clear up a few misapprehensions about graphology. A person's character, temperament, health and emotional wellbeing can be disguised when face to face by their look and behaviour, by what they say and how they say it. Their handwriting reveals their true body language on the page, the underworld of their subconscious, an expression of their state of mind. More tea?'

'Yes, thank you. It's delicious cake.'

'Home-made, my mother's recipe. Do have another slice, I'm going to. As regards different styles of writing from the same person, this is common to everyone, but the key character and emotional indicators will remain the same; style is merely a superficial variation. Let me give you an analogy. At the end of the working day you go home, take off your suit and relax in casual clothes; a cosmetic change, but you are still the same person.'

'Doesn't the way I write depend on how I was taught as a kid?'

'Not at all. As a child you were taught to write by your teacher, probably neatly between two ruled lines. You don't write that way now; the fact that you don't can be used to interpret your personality traits and mental wellbeing. You have to understand handwriting is virtually subconscious, we think about what we are writing not how we write it. Bypassing the consciousness reveals the true state of mind.

Writing is like a jigsaw, the elements piece together to form an overall picture of the person's character and mental state at the time of writing. So if you want me to look at her writing, I would need several examples over a period, originals not photocopies.'

'I have them here.' I said, reaching for my brief case. 'Perhaps I should explain some of the references and tell you about her personality?'

'Not necessary; my interest is in the writing style, the nuances and foibles of her hand will lead to conclusions. As for her personality, I will tell you what sort of character I think she is. If it corresponds to your opinion it will give you confidence in my findings. I need to know if she is left or right handed and her age?'

'She's twenty-five and always wrote my restaurant selections with her right hand.'

'You will need to leave the letters with me and come back next week. Ring me first to make sure I'm not in court and I've had time to examine them.'

'Your fee?'

She leafed through the blue flimsy sheets.

'Let's say £30 cash.'

The following Wednesday I was again served tea, this time with a Victoria sponge. The fruit cake was better.

'So, what have you deduced from the letters?'

'I've made photocopies for you and written my observations in red ink. I would say from the initial letters she has a sense of value and modesty, is affectionate and good natured with a gentle disposition.'

'Yes, I would agree with those conclusions.'

'As the letters progress date wise I see a troubled persona, emotional confusion, desperation; she is struggling with an inner turmoil. Her writing has a hesitancy indicating uncertainty about the future. Even allowing for the flimsiness of the paper, the heavy pressure is a sign of stress and anxiety.'

'That's worrying. Any idea of the cause?'

'It could be family pressure coercing her to marry; negation of self for the honour or wellbeing of the family is deeply ingrained in the Chinese psyche. Chinese women tend to marry later than us, but at twenty-five she's in the frame. Arranged marriages are still common in China, admittedly less so in Hong Kong where British rule fosters westernised values and romantic literature and films connect marriage with love.'

'Her younger sister was compelled to accept an arranged marriage,' I said with a resigned frown.

'It could be she is ill,' continued Barbara, 'something serious like cancer or a heart condition, but if I had to speculate ... she could be pregnant.'

'Pregnant! How can you draw that conclusion?'

'Well Chris, forensically correlating the dates of the letters to the observable psychological changes could correspond to the timescale of realising she's pregnant and coming under pressure to do something about it, such as marry the father. Unmarried mothers are bad news in Chinese society where family honour is paramount. Does she have a boyfriend?'

'She's not mentioned one.'

'Did you have unprotected sex?'

'Yes, for six months.'

'Did she take any precautions?'

'Yes, she went to an NHS Family Planning Clinic for the pill, but ran out a couple of weeks before returning to Hong Kong. She definitely had her period a week or so before she left England.'

'And you had sex shortly before she left?'

'Yes, a couple of times.'

'Mmm ... well it would be within her optimum period for conceiving. Do you know if you're capable of having children?'

'I have no reason not to think so, but what you say seems highly speculative.'

'Well, as I said, the pregnancy scenario correlates to the forensic timescale and tenor of the letters. There is a funny side to this Chris; you named her Aphrodite and it's usually the nature of couplings in mythology the woman is lumbered with a chic-in-the-coop. Aphrodite bore several children by different fathers, but joking apart, I am confident your Aphrodite is struggling with a dilemma which she is concealing from you. I can't think of other plausible reasons she would not readily divulge to you. If it was a question of illness, unless something embarrassing or sexual, there would be no reason not to tell you. If pressure to marry she would tell you; after all, you may want to marry her. Did you discuss marriage with her?'

'We did, but it was not an option.'

'I take it because you're already married.'

'How ... how did you know?' I said, taken aback.

'I didn't. I suspected last week; her photo hidden in the lining of your wallet. A beautiful oriental on the arm of an Englishman implies the colonial custom of a mistress.'

'You're perceptive.'

'Goes with the job. Do you have children?'

'Two, the reason Fong and I are not together.'

I thanked Barbara for her analysis and headed back to Louth to compose a letter to Fong expressing my concerns. Two weeks later, her next letter confirmed one of Barbara's speculative notions.

Chapter 23

I stared in disbelief, completely disillusioned it had happened so soon and without warning. A depressive gloom invaded my body like a virulent virus; she had betrayed me, but worse betrayed herself.

The letter included two photographs: one showed the bride and groom, the second the bride. The couple posed stiffly, like carved wooden dolls, the bride with a look of joyless resignation, the groom with a smile of conceited self-satisfaction.

There was undeniable irony to her white wedding dress: in the West a symbol of sexual purity, in China also the colour of mourning. The sleeveless flowing gown dropped from an embroidered bodice hugging her breasts. She held a posy of flowers.

The groom donned a grey morning suit with white bow tie. As squat as a barrel, his statuesque head perched upon a short stout neck; a bulbous nose sprouted between two plump cheeks squeezing his eyes to myopic slits. Lines dropped from the corners of his mouth giving the impression of a ventriloquist's dummy. He was shorter than his bride and twenty or more years older.

My ominous prescience and Barbara's evaluation were proven. Like Mai Ling before her in a misguided obligation to the family, her father had pressured Fong into an arranged marriage. Having experienced love with me, perhaps she considered it time for duty. The letter revealed her spouse to be a taxi driver, a friend of her father and brother of her priest. Ah yes, the guy Fong referred to on our date of wet bums.

As I stared at her image, I noticed her eternity ring. Her groom might be paying the rent but had no lease on her heart. She wanted the love and romance of the cinema in marriage and I bore the guilt of denying her. I thought she had put on weight; an impression from the loose fitting style of gown perhaps, or too much home cooking and sticky congee breakfasts. Barbara suggested she could be pregnant; I'm not sure I wanted to know.

Those two photos tormented my life. I realised how desolate Mr H felt upon receiving similar devastating news. I felt the sorrow in her words as she implored me to keep writing, to role play our pact of love; she needed to know I was there for her. However, her husband had a working knowledge of English so I must not write as I have in the past; the endearments and memories were compromising to her as a married woman. I am relegated to pen pal status.

Thereafter I was stalked by a recurring nightmare. Sat in a cinema, the curtains draw back and the silver screen projects a pornographic film from the darkest recess of my imagination. I am an unwilling voyeur watching this randy taxi driver prising Fong open night on night, fucking her every which way, cackling with lust as he mauls and defiles her body beautiful.

She rises from the bed like a spectre, her belly stretched and bloated, her breasts distended and dripping milk forever ruined as a lover's toys. A devilish putto erupts from her belly screaming defiantly like a bizarre alien, splashing down between her legs amidst a deluge of blood and gore. Fong's outstretched arm points an incriminating finger, eyes blazing with accusation.

This harrowing nightmare, like a hideous Greek tragedy, jolted me awake every night, sweating with distress, a subconscious unwelcome penance. I questioned the dream as a foreboding equating it to the situation of Fong's mother; she married because pregnant and kept it secret from Mr H out of love and social pragmatism. If Fong was pregnant by me, would Fong's mother have given the same advice? Had she admitted to being pregnant with my child what the hell would I have done? I didn't dare question Fong; I couldn't bear thinking about the consequences although now married there appeared to be no consequences.

I continued to lunch at the Lotus House a couple of times a week. The muzak fades as the memories consume. I found myself staring at the swing door to the kitchen daydreaming one day she will walk through as she did that first unforgettable day. Those lunchtime visits were oddly calming and the familiar surroundings illustrated my nostalgia. Jimmy heard about Fong's marriage from Mr Zhang.

'I'm sorry for you Chris, but I did warn you her father wanted her married.'

'You did Jimmy, but it wasn't to be.'

'Why Chris? I thought you loved her.'

'I did ... I still do, but she didn't want to live here and I didn't want to live in Hong Kong.'

He seemed unconvinced and I decided to forego future visits to the Lotus House. Eventually my marital status would emerge and the deception embarrassing.

The months scrolled by and the nightmares gradually subsided along with my disquiet. My marriage limped on ably supported by the love and distraction of the children, although Mary continued to wallow in a Jacuzzi of woe, acrimony bubbling to the surface at the slightest provocation. Her feminine instinct probably surmised the affair was more than a sexual dalliance, a realization that kept her wounded pride bleeding.

Time is a relative palliative and I hinted to Mary conjugal relations should be resumed – judged to be helpful in healing her wounded ego and more entertaining than pleasuring myself. Mary's initial rebuff was anatomically impossible. However, as the weeks slipped by her aggression gradually moderated into a kind of combative harmony, eventually hoisting the white flag with an invitation to join her in the bath.

I sat behind her, she between my legs, my hands directed to her breasts. With her back to me, astride my automatic erection, she could have been a blow-up doll for all the emotion generated. However the warm bathwater thawed her innate ice and thereafter I was invited back into the marital bed with sex an occasional reward, although I felt like an offender doing community service.

The joyous festivities of Christmas with the kids were a distraction and united the family. The excitement of the kids decorating the Christmas tree, giving Father Christmas their wish list and hanging up their stockings a pleasure to behold. Christmas Eve proved to be the one night of the year when they displayed an enthusiasm to sleep, more quickly to bring on the onset of morning. Samantha's belief in Father Christmas had been shot through at school by older children but shrewdly decided more was to be gained by "believing" than not believing.

Fong's infrequent letters sustained my maudlin yearning and aching regret. She never mentioned her marriage and I didn't enquire. She emphasised how she looked forward to my missives. However, the fragile paper chain linking our enduring love was about to be broken causing momentous consequences to all our lives.

In the summer of 1980 I changed employers, leaving Grimsby and International for an independent scale company in Cambridge.

During the house move Mary accidentally discovered Fong's letters and photos, interpreted as continuing infidelity. The incriminating evidence was ceremoniously burnt in a perverse act of finality to the Fong episode. With the children bewildered witnesses, she buried the ashes at the bottom of the garden; a wooden cross mockingly marked the grave.

Her brutal desecration and triumphal boasting lit my blue touchpaper. My anger uncontrollably surged like a rocket leaving its milk bottle. An image of a second grave at the bottom of the garden flashed enticingly across my mind. I had to get out of the house and out of the marriage before I strangled her, such was my fury. With fear in her eyes, she ran to the bathroom and locked the door. The children looked on in dumbfounded amazement.

I swallowed my pride and carefully dug up the earth to recover forensic evidence of the crime, the scraps of charred remains reverentially salvaged to a small plastic bag. Without the letters I did not have Fong's address.

I started to pack a suitcase of essentials, loyalty to the family irrationally discarded in the turmoil of rage. Mary ventured from the bathroom and looked on with astonishment and perhaps a hint of regret her bonfire had triggered such a decided response. She insisted I was to blame. I cursed her despicable behaviour, she rejoined with righteous indignation and insults shunted back and forth like beads on an abacus.

I summoned the kids to come upstairs. 'Get out Mary I want to talk to them alone.'

They sat on the bed, hands in lap, nervously apprehensive, as if expecting a scolding. I pulled up a chair and sat close in front of them.

'Why are you crying daddy?' said Samantha.

'I'm not crying I have something in my eye.'

'In both eyes?' she countered.

'Yes, in both eyes. Now listen up guys. I have to go away so will not see you every day.'

'Why are you leaving us Daddy?' said Samantha mournfully.

'I'm not leaving you guys. I'm leaving your mother. I will always love and support you, but I have to live somewhere else.'

'Don't go Daddy,' they chime in unison. 'Please don't go.'

'I have to. Mummy and I can't live together any longer. When you're older you will understand. I'll be living close by and we'll have days out and maybe you will be able to come and stay. You remember when you were in Coventry and I was away in Louth. Well it's similar, except I will see you more often.'

'It's all because of your Chinese friend isn't it,' said Samantha. 'Is it because she's Chinese?'

'Nothing to do with her being Chinese. She's a special friend with whom I want to keep in contact. She lives the other side of the world in a place called Hong Kong. We write to each other, but with your mother burning the letters I can no longer write which makes me sad and angry. I cannot forgive your mother and she cannot accept my wanting to keep the friendship going. So we have to separate. It's a grown-up thing and important to both of us in different ways.'

We hugged and Samantha cried. Simon looked confused, uncertain of the reasoning and consequences. Mary followed me downstairs to the front door.

'If you leave, there will be no coming back. I will file for divorce and custody of the children.'

'You can have your divorce, but you won't stop me from seeing the kids.'

I moved to a small hotel on the outskirts of Cambridge and started searching for a room to rent. It was my turn to write to Fong but could not remember her address. I checked the poste restante almost daily, impatiently awaiting another letter, to be able to explain why I had not written and to reveal my separation from Mary. After a six week eternity her letter arrived, with no return address!

'Oh Fong, how can you send an airmail letter with no return address,' I scolded. 'How am I going to re-establish contact?'

I anxiously trawled my memory but the Chinese names would not resurface. In desperation I wrote her name, her age and the city of Tai Po hoping the local Postal Service would trace her. Three weeks later the letter returned, the envelope rubber stamped "Incomplete address".

I visited the Cambridge library and found the Grimsby volume of Yellow Pages and phoned the Lotus House.

'Hello Chris. What do you want,' said Jimmy in an ominous tone.

'Jimmy, I have accidently lost Fong's address, do you have it?'

'Me, no. I'll ask Mr Zhang.' A couple of minutes later Jimmy returned to the phone. 'He will not give you her address. He says you raped Fong with your lies. You treated her like Tsip Sze for sex. If we had known you were married we would not have helped you.'

'That's not how it was Jimmy. We loved each other and genuine love does not need the sanctity of marriage.'

'That's not how it's viewed in Hong Kong. The good name of her family has been tarnished. Mr Zhang said you deceived everyone.'

'Let me talk to Mr Zhang Jimmy.'

'He will not talk to you. You are not welcome here.'

The dialling tone purred in my ear; I slowly replaced the handset, dismayed by Jimmy's unexpected response.

I wrote to Mai Ling at 36 Casio Bridge Road. No response. I telephoned the Watford Chinese restaurant where Mai Ling had worked. The past tense of time had taken its toll; Mai Ling and her husband had returned to Hong Kong, address unknown. I remembered I had written Fong's early temporary address in the back of my 1976 diary. Fong told me the block was due for demolition, the reason for her being rehoused in Tai Po, but I wrote anyway, hopeful someone still lived there and would forward the letter. No response.

Over the next year three more letters arrived, each one a more heart breaking plaintive lamentation than the one before: "You say you always love me. Why do you not write? Don't desert me." The narrative of disillusionment and hurt was palpable; in her eyes my not writing had betrayed the love I claimed to be eternal. Each letter bore the watermarks of her tears and the blemishes of mine as I became more distraught. Then her letters ceased.

Chapter 24

Divorce from Mary finalised in the summer of 1981, the discarded shackles of marriage replaced by the financial handcuffs of alimony. The petition cited the old chestnut "irreconcilable differences", but the Family Court considered me the errant partner, I who packed a suitcase. The children ensured Mary was awarded the house, most of the furniture and the cat.

My only restrictions to seeing the children proved to be location and financial. Mary sold the house in Cambridge and moved the family back to Coventry to be near her sister and ageing parents. The house was in joint names but I could not reasonably withhold permission for her to relocate near her family, especially as my mother also lived in Coventry. I would be entitled to a half-share in the Coventry house once the children had flown the coup.

I was working and living in London, having to do a second job to make ends meet. I had changed career ladders, representative for a finance company based in Mayfair. The company arranged mortgages for clients who would not normally qualify for a loan from the banks or building societies. For example, one day an accountant referred a beautiful woman in her mid twenties whose principal assets were covered by the couture clothes she elegantly modelled. Her profession: an *entertainer* of overseas corporate clients. She had no regular salary, but in excess of £50,000 had entered her bank account in each of the last three self-employed years. She had a beguiling nature; I approved her mortgage and was invited to the flat warming party.

Each afternoon after work I walked across Hyde Park to spend most evenings behind the bar in a Kensington pub. The cash-in-hand payment avoided liability for tax and alimony. Serving customers afforded company from regulars and staff plus the opportunity to chat-up a few women; there was less time to feel sorry for myself in the rented, abject basement room I now called home.

The pub landlady resembled a pantomime dame: a dyed blond aging doll with rouged cheeks and blood red lips who peered out from behind false eye lashes and a camouflage of foundation applied with a mortician's generosity. She was an amalgam of exterior titanium hardness and a heart of malleable gold. My hard luck story ensured her gold took a shine to me and she threw in an invaluable cooked meal halfway through the evening.

Using the company car, I motored up to Coventry to spend time with the children one weekend a month. Mary's hostile attitude cast me as an unwelcome intruder upon their ordered lives. I was not allowed over the threshold and had to take the kids out, buy meals and stay overnight in a B & B. I cannot afford the expense and thus cannot visit them as often as they or I would like. Over the next few years the children morphed into young adults and became progressively distant, building a life without me. I saw the blame in their eyes, felt their lack of enthusiasm; my visits changed from joy to duty.

The accident happened on the notorious A45 dual carriageway on the outskirts of Coventry, the year 1985. My manager, Bill Sampson, called me to his office. A woman police constable sat next to his desk. They both stood as I entered.

'Hello Chris. Please sit down,' he said, gesturing to a vacant chair. 'This is constable Williams from the Metropolitan Police.'

Had I unknowingly committed a crime? A driving offence perhaps? Was a mortgage I'd approved fraudulent? I had no inkling.

'Hi,' I said. 'I have an alibi.'

They both glanced awkwardly at each other and I wanted to withdraw the quip.

'Chris, the police have been asked to find you by the Walsgrave Hospital in Coventry. I'm afraid there's been a serious car accident involving your ex-wife and ... children.'

'How serious?' I said nervously. They both looked at each other, as if embarrassed. 'Do you know how serious?' I asked again, looking to constable Williams.

'Your daughter and her mother are in hospital ... I'm afraid your son's injuries were fatal,' she said quietly.

'Oh my God!' I spluttered, jaw quivering, eyes brimful of tears. 'How ... what happened?'

'The driver of an HGV lost control, forcing their car off the road to collide with a tree. The driver has been arrested and charged with dangerous driving and involuntary manslaughter. He was trying to read a map at the time. I'm sorry for your loss. If you need counselling or support we can arrange ...'

'No, I'll be okay,' I interrupted, dabbing my eyes and blowing my nose. 'Such a shock. I need to see them, be there with my ... daughter.'

'Take a few days paid leave Chris. Pass any outstanding business over to me.'

'Thanks Bill.'

I couldn't face the drive from London and took the intercity from Euston and a bus out to the hospital. At the reception a nurse informed I could not see either patient or my son's body until the next day. I insisted on seeing the Doctor in charge of their care.

He was tall, slim, dark and handsome, bespectacled and spoke in highly accented English. In looks he reminded me of a waiter in my local tandoori.

'Hello Mr Patterson, Dr Patel, consultant registrar.' We shook hands. 'Please accept my condolences regarding your son. The ambulance crew were unable to save him and he died from head injuries before reaching hospital.' He paused with a sympathetic frown. 'Samantha suffered a concussive head trauma, internal abdominal and spinal injuries from the impact. She underwent surgery yesterday to stop internal bleeding and is in an induced temporary post-operative coma to aid her recovery.'

'Are her injuries life threatening?' I said nervously.

'No. Her condition is serious but stable. She will remain in intensive care for the next few days pending further surgery.'

'Will there be any permanent brain damage or physical deformities?'

'Probably some locomotion impairment to her legs from the spinal injury.'

'Can I see her tomorrow?'

'Yes, but she can't communicate.'

'What about her mother's condition?'

'She has multiple external injuries, from the impact and flying glass, contusions from the seatbelt and airbag but nothing permanent.'

He paused, as if allowing time for me to process the information. Hesitantly he said, 'You are divorced from their mother Mary Patterson I understand.'

'Yes,' I nodded, 'but what's the relevance?'

'Well ... you are the father of Simon Patterson ... but do you know the whereabouts of Samantha Patterson's father? The seriousness of her injuries oblige we inform him.'

'I'm not sure what you mean. I'm her father,' I confirmed with a frown of confusion.

He raised his eyebrows indicating a slight look of surprise, shuffled awkwardly and adjusted his glasses.

'I'm sorry to bring this up at such an unfortunate time ... I didn't know you were unaware you are not her biological father ... her blue eyes ... a genetic impossibility.'

I gazed in disbelief. 'There must be some mistake.'

'No mistake,' he said, with a shake of the head.

'Are you certain?'

'Absolutely. You are not her biological father.'

'I'll discuss it with her mother,' I said slowly, as if recalling the words from a distant past.

'Yes, well, I'll leave that with you,' he said, ill at ease. 'You will need to formerly identify Simon's body tomorrow and arrange collection by an undertaker.'

I nodded agreement.

In a waiting room on the ground floor I sat slumped, head in hands, engulfed by feelings of betrayal and anger, loss and bewilderment. Inconceivable Mary had taken a lover during the first couple of years of marriage. The hypocrite! Who was the bastard? Someone I knew? How did they meet? Where did they do it? Were they still at it? Does Mary know Samantha isn't my child? Does the bastard know Samantha is his? Does Samantha know I'm not her father? If I'd known I would not have lost Fong. I had lost a son, now a daughter too. I never felt so dejected, so alone.

I took a bus into town and another bus to mother's maisonette. She knew about the accident and Simon's demise from the police. We hugged and tears flowed. I decided not to reveal Samantha's parentage revelation. I needed to talk to Mary and hear her explanation before deciding what to do. Mother made tea and served up an omelette; I was not hungry but swallowed it to please her. Mother made up my bed in the second bedroom; mentally and physically exhausted, I retired early and slept soundly.

Next day I entered Mary's ward and granted a few minutes visit. Mary was propped up with pillows, the top half of the bed angled up at about thirty degrees. Swathed in bandages to her head and chest, tubes snaked into her nose and under the bedclothes like alien tentacles. I sat and looked at her, wondering what to say.

'Simon,' she croaked. Speaking seemed an effort. She fought back the tears.

'Yes, I know. They told me.'

'Have you seen Sam?'

'Not yet, maybe later. They've put her in a temporary coma.'

A deafening silence overtook us. I looked questioningly at her.

'What?' she mumbled.

I paused and after a deep breath said, 'Who is Samantha's father?'

She looked nonplussed, as if I had spoken a foreign language.

'I don't understand,' she replied hoarsely.

'It's a simple question Mary. Who is Sam's father?'

'You're her father.'

'No. Not me Mary ... her blue eyes. According to the doctor, a genetic impossibility.'

A red light illuminated on the panel above her bed; she had pressed her hand held call button. I stood.

'Answer me you hypocritical bitch! Who did you fuck after we were married? Who was it?' I said loudly.

The entire ward was transfixed, hanging on every word. A burley matron of the Hattie Jacques mould hurried forward like a scene from *Carry On Nurse.*

'Mr Patterson! I must ask you to leave.' She imposed herself between us. 'You are distressing your wife and other patients on the ward. We will not tolerate such raucous behaviour. Leave now or I will call security.'

'This adulterous, hypocritical bitch is not my wife,' I said firmly. Mary begun to cry.

'Leave now Mr Patterson,' matron insisted sternly, shepherding me away with outstretched arms.

'I'm not paying alimony for someone else's brat,' I shouted over matron's shoulder. 'I'll find out Mary, even if I have to go to court.'

I went to the refectory and drank coffee. I needed to calm down before going to the intensive care ward to see Samantha. Did I still want to see her? I did. She lay motionless, as if gently snoozing, heavily bandaged with tubes disappearing into her arm and nose like plumber's snakes. She was hooked up to a saline drip and a monitor recorded her heart rhythm and other data.

All my anger drained away. After thirteen years of loving, I couldn't turn off the flow like a water tap. She was not to blame; she was still the same little person I had cherished. It broke my heart to see her bandaged and damaged; she could be scarred for life, possibly paraplegic. She would need my love and support. I held her hand and the tears flowed.

Housed in the basement the hospital morgue was cold and clinical, white tiled to all surfaces and harshly lit by fluorescents. An ominous bank of rectangular stainless steel doors lined one wall. The attendant sat in a warm adjoining office and completed a couple of forms as I answered mandatory questions before ushering me slowly, respectfully, towards the wall of metal. He opened a door and pulled the stretcher out like a giant rumbling filing cabinet drawer. He checked the label tied to a big toe – an artifice I thought from old black-and-white crime movies – and folded back the covering sheet.

'Are you able to confirm this to be Simon Ashley Patterson?' the attendant asked quietly.

'Yes.' I nodded.

The expression 'deathly pale' was apt. I touched his arm and kissed his forehead; so cold, I felt robbed of the opportunity to experience the last of his warmth.

I remembered his first warmth. Mary's contractions started about eight in the evening. By ten she was installed at this hospital. The nurse told me to wait in a room down the hall. I would be called in time to witness the birth.

'Have I got time for a cup of coffee?' I said to the nurse, 'I don't want to miss the birth.'

'Oh yes, I think so. There's a machine in the next block.'

I rushed for the coffee and waited another eight hours surrounded by as many empty cups before the little bugger deigned to put in an appearance. He delivered the customary red and pink but gradually turned slate blue; he wasn't breathing. The nurses worked to clear his airways with ever increasing urgency. He turned purple, like a dark evening sky. I saw the panic button pressed and a doctor charged in and took control. When I heard him cry I joined him in tearful relief; I had never been so frightened. I held him and felt his warmth.

Simon glided away and the door closed with a hollow metallic clang. The morgue attendant handed me a form and told me to record the death with the registrar at the Town Hall.

I sat on a bench in the corridor leading from the morgue. I was weighed down with guilt and shame that I wasn't there for them, to defend and protect their lives. If I hadn't left them, the family would not have moved to Coventry and the accident would not have happened. Maybe if I had been driving, the accident could have been avoided. I felt I was drowning in a sea of remorse and loneliness at no longer being a father. If the dispensary issued a suicide pill I would have taken it.

I dried my eyes and took the lift to the fourth floor. As I entered the corridor to the ward the hefty matron barred my way, arms outstretched.

'Sorry Mr Patterson, better you not visit your wife ... ex-wife.'

'I came to apologise matron, to you and Mary. My behaviour was unacceptable and it will not happen again. Please ask Mary if I may talk to her now I've seen our daughter ... things to say, to make amends.'

'Wait here,' she said sternly, 'I'll see what she says.' She turned and barged through two swing doors into the ward. I peered through the porthole door window. After a brief discussion with Mary she returned. 'Okay Mr Patterson. Sit in the chair I've positioned for you. Do *not* get any closer. You've got ten minutes. I *will* be watching.'

'Thank you matron. I'll be no trouble.' I walked sheepishly across the ward to Mary's bed. 'Hi. Sorry I over reacted. It won't happen again.'

'I didn't know about Samantha,' she croaked weakly. 'Raped ... Peter.'

'Peter?' I gasped. 'Peter Markham, your brother-in-law.'

'Yes. Came to the house. You were away on a sales course. I had showered ... in my dressing gown. Forced himself on me ... too strong. He'd been drinking. My sister loves him; I didn't want to destroy her marriage. Too frightened to tell you.'

'I had no idea. I'm sorry I accused you. Does he know he is Sam's father?'

She shook her head. I paused in thought, bent over, hands between my legs. I decided to pay Peter a visit. He was a big guy and I'd need a baseball bat. I looked up at Mary. 'Look, I've seen Samantha; the colour of her eyes makes no difference. She's our daughter and I love her. Best she never knows.'

Mary nodded agreement. 'Is she still in a coma?'

'Yes.' I nodded solemnly. 'The doctor says her brain scan has revealed a clot they need to remove but she has a spinal fracture and may suffer paralysis to her legs. She's to undergo further surgery.' With tissues we dabbed our eyes.

Mary was discharged at the end of the week and convalesced at her parent's bungalow. The following week Samantha had an operation to remove a blood clot on her brain and was released from the induced coma a couple of days later. She remembered little about the accident.

'Everything happened so quickly. The lorry slammed into the side of the car and pushed us off the road. We had no chance. Next thing I know I'm in here.'

'You weren't wearing a seatbelt?'

'No, I was in the back,' she said sheepishly, attempting to excuse the misdemeanour.

With a resigned frown I shook my head. Hugging her hand I gazed into her blue eyes; it was as if I had not known.

Chapter 25

Simon's funeral took place on a bleak windy day at Coventry's Crematorium, located at Canley Cemetery, off the infamous A45 as you drive out of the city. As I drove up to the entrance I saw Peter's gleaming silver grey Mercedes ahead and noted the licence plate number. Near the gates two surly looking youths sat on a low wall smoking and drinking canned beer. I walked mother to the chapel entrance and made an excuse I'd left something in the car. I walked back to the entrance via the car to speak to the youths.

'Hi Guys, I don't suppose you want to earn £50 for a few minutes work?'

'What sort of work?' replied the taller.

'Beat up a car for me, tyres, paintwork, windscreen, headlamps.'

'Fifty quid you said.'

'Yeah, fifty.'

'Okay, you're on. Which car?'

I shelled out the money with a warning. 'Now don't go running off without doing the job, 'cause me and my mates will find you and break both your legs,' I said menacingly, waving a fist. I was pleased with my tough guy theatrics.

'What were you talking to those youths about?' mother said when I returned.

'I didn't like them hanging around the entrance drinking beer ...

inappropriate to the funeral ceremony. I asked them to leave.'

Mary and her mother had conducted the arrangements, chosen the service and eulogies. There was a good turnout from Mary's side of the family, plus several school friends, Simon's form teacher and the school's headmaster. Apart from my mother, no Patterson bothered to make the trip. Samantha remained in hospital not well enough to attend. As I accompanied mother into the chapel I noticed Janet in the pews. She smiled warmly; I nodded acknowledgement.

I struggled through the panegyric to my eleven year old son, jaw quivering, eyes watering, relating the tragedy of a life barely lived; what a splendid little fellow he was ... had been. I recited the expected praise and admiration, finishing with a humorous incident related to me by an elderly neighbour.

'Simon was about four at the time, playing in the front garden when the lady walked by and struck up a conversation. I had popped out to the local VG Food Store to get some crumpets and cakes for tea.

"Hello Simon. All by yourself. Where's Samantha?"

"She's helping mummy in the kitchen."

"And where's your daddy?"

"Oh, he's gone to the local VD shop to pick up some crumpet."'

A ripple of polite laughter. I also recalled an example of his wonderful child logic.

'I had forgotten to get Mary a card for mother's day. The school had prepared the kids for the event with their handmade artistic examples. I was berated by Simon. "You wait; you won't get a card when it's mother's day for fathers."'

To the refrain of *Auld Lang Syne,* the coffin chuntered on its way like a suitcase on a baggage carousel. The congregation filed solemnly out and in the remembrance garden I suffered Peter's shallow sentiments with a Cheshire cat smile visualising the wrecked Mercedes I hoped awaited him. I wanted to hit him but the demolition of his coveted car would hurt more.

Janet approached; we clasped hands. 'Sorry for your loss Chris, a dreadful accident; I read about it in the paper.'

'So nice of you to come, lovely to see you, it's been too long.'

We hugged and cheek kissed.

'You're looking good,' I complimented.

'You too.'

We gazed at each other with nostalgic longing. She broke the hesitant pause.

'How is Samantha?'

'Not so good, some permanent paralysis from the waist down.'

'Oh Chris how awful, such a tragedy.' I frowned and nodded. 'I see Mary over there, but gather you're divorced. Are you living in Coventry?'

'Not yet. I'm working in London for a finance company, but planning to move back here to be nearer Samantha and mother. Rents are cheaper and I have friends here. Are you still married?'

She shook her head. 'Harry died a couple of years ago ... drank too much, cirrhosis of the liver, developed hepatitis.'

'I'm sorry.'

'Don't be. You know it wasn't a good marriage, the reason you and I got together for a year. I'm now free to be the best version of myself.'

'You're not lonely?'

'The only time I've been lonely was in my marriage.'

'What about Terry?'

'He's working in Switzerland for FIFA. Like his father, always mad on football. I now have the house to myself.' She smiled knowingly. 'I could do dinner.'

'Sounds good. I'll talk to you later.'

As I stood in the remembrance garden chatting to mourners

the distant sound of a car's alarm bleated like a demented sheep. I smiled inwardly, the sweet smile of satisfaction only revenge can muster. The lads had vamoosed after giving their all using rocks from the cemetery garden. I will never forget the rage and incredulity on Peter's face discovering his beat-up Mercedes. I feigned outrage. Mary tugged at my arm.

'Do you know anything about this?' she said quietly.

'Me,' I said, hand on my heart. 'I was in the chapel with you.'

Mary looked unconvinced but probably thought justice had been served. We left Peter fuming and waiting for the police and garage tow truck.

After dinner I shared Janet's bed. We made love with the hunger of extended abstinence but with the comfort and familiarity of long term bedfellows. She was a good cook and enthusiastic lover. Over the next few months Janet proved to be the life belt fate threw to rescue me from the sea of depression and remorse at Simon's loss and Samantha's invalidity.

I resigned my financial advisor's position in the autumn of 1985 and moved my meagre possessions to Coventry, staying at mother's maisonette for the first few weeks until I found a rented apartment. It could never be long term with mother, who insisted on parenting me as if the arrival of adulthood had been permanently delayed. I loved her dearly; she had been a caring, supportive single parent, but our mindsets and values were from different eras.

By the time I was sixteen our incompatibility of age and moral code led to constant disagreements and I moved to a house with three other male students. Post mother's cooking I soon tired of baked beans, scrambled eggs or cheese on toast and applied myself to the culinary arts.

Regular weekend parties provided occasional lays, the path to bed lubricated by copious quantities of beer brewed in a dustbin in the kitchen; as often as not the beer gave everyone diarrhoea a few hours later. Those student days – the beer, women and song days – were happy and carefree. Life was a peach.

Despite the distractions posed by the opposite sex I managed a degree in chemistry. I worked on various projects at Courtaulds – including the revolutionary production of carbon fibres – before being seduced by the suave suits and swish cars of the sales reps eventually leading to Grimsby and Fong.

Along the way I made the mistake of marriage clipping my wings of any tendency to take flight. I had a restless spirit – but not an adventurous one – and allowed the years to uneventfully slip by except for the miracles of births and joys of fatherhood. Seeing the children born were vividly emotional experiences and the only times I came close to feeling love for Mary.

After leaving London for Coventry my sales and mortgage experience secured a position as sales negotiator in an estate agency. Mary continued to teach a new militant breed of cosmopolitan brats. Samantha was confined to a wheelchair and pursued a protracted compensation claim against the haulage company and driver. Eventually the High Court awarded her sufficient capital to purchase her own flat and relative independence, in both meanings of *relative.*

Despite increasing portliness from restricted activity, she married another wheelchair user but was unable to have children. I was not invited to the wedding, a fait accompli from Mary. Her requitals had no end date. Samantha's independence obliged Mary to sell the house in our joint names and my share enabled the purchase of a one bedroom flat.

Janet and I preserved our independence, living apart but being together most of the time and sleeping over regularly. For all the delights of friendship and satisfying sex with Janet, love and emotional tumult were not what I knew with her. She understood my yearning passion for Fong and lamented she had never known such fervency. Our arrangement worked well for the next twenty years, with neither of us feeling the need for additional partners.

Chapter 26

My life slipped by, tolerably, comfortably, largely uneventful until midnight, 30 June 1997, when another pink outpost of British colonial imperialism changed colour in the atlas, this time ominously red. Next day over breakfast, I watched the commemoration on television, the thunder, lightning and cascading stars of the fireworks illuminating the harbour, despite the heavy rain. The mood was more wake than party, the advent of a communist landlord forced upon this glittering centre of capitalism ushering in an unpredictable era.

It was raining in my heart as I pined for Fong. I forlornly looked for her face in crowded street scenes recording the footage on the VHS. Was she thinking of me as I of her? I doubted it after the cessation of my letters.

The concept of one true eternal love – each person part of one divided soul – is probably a figment of mine and Plato's imagination. However, my mind – like the minds of countless lovers down the centuries – relentlessly dreams of its truth. How else to account for Fong being the recurring theme in the symphony of my life? For two decades she stalked my memories, I being unable and unwilling to give them the slip. Time is a great healer except when the mind remembers what the heart cannot forget.

Almost twenty years ago I gave up on finding Fong's address

when the obvious leads of restaurant staff and her sister proved negative. She had married and I harboured doubts of ever seeing her again. I was penniless, living in a squalid rented room with no viable future to offer even if I was able to re-establish contact. Now, with my improved financial circumstances and concerned by the colony's change of regime, I experienced a desperate new wave of longing to find her. I carried the heavy burden of guilt of the loss of her address and of the bewildering hurt inflicted by my unexplained silence. I had to try to make amends, to explain and beg forgiveness, to know how her life had panned out.

So, how to find this pearl in Hong Kong's seven million oysters? I collated what I knew and started with the address written in the back of my 1976 diary. I had written previously but without reply and the apartment block had since been demolished. The address was a Public Housing flat, so I wrote to the Housing Authority to see if Fong or her husband were listed as tenants at any other public housing address, but data protection regulations intervened.

Fong's husband was a taxi driver, one of more than eighteen thousand cabbies serving the Hong Kong region. The Department of Transport confirmed his licence but refused to divulge further details. I couldn't help feeling disappointment her elderly husband had yet to be visited by the Grim Reaper.

I ploughed up the halcyon verdant fields of my nostalgia with a visit to Louth; much was changed, none for the better. The usual suspects had commercialized the town centre and caused the demise of several independent traders of my 1970s remembrance. Cynthia's B & B had reverted to a private house. I tended my father's and uncle Cecil's graves, scraping lichens from the headstones and cutting the grass. I said "hello" to Mr H.

Grimsby remained a town without grand intentions, the east coast's answer to a question nobody dared ask and wasn't about to answer my questions. Cleethorpes Road had not changed character or even acquired some, although the red light area had gone along with the glowing red lanterns of the Lotus House – replaced by the harsh fluorescent lighting of an office of accountants.

The Lotus House was no longer listed in Yellow Pages so I assumed had not relocated. Mr Zhang was not on the electoral register. He was elderly in 1976 so may no longer be alive or more likely had returned to Hong Kong enacting the Chinese proverb: "Falling leaves return to their roots."

The International showroom's graveyard had been deconsecrated and moved to a nearby industrial estate. A mechanic said Danny Parker had his tombstone in Cleethorpes Cemetery.

I dined at the Cleethorpes Chinese restaurant where Fong had so proudly shown me off to her friend Chuang Liu, but she had long since returned to Hong Kong. No one had her address or any knowledge of Fong. The lapse of time would always be my nemesis.

Fong's husband was the brother of a Buddhist priest. There were several hundred temples and monasteries throughout the territory and I had no idea at which temple the priest officiated, or if he was still alive.

I wrote to the Hong Kong Government Births, Marriages and Deaths Registry requesting Fong's marriage certificate. I was told I would need to present myself in person and justify the need for a copy. Without a date of birth, they would not conduct a records search.

The Home Office in London informed any release of information would be subject to compliance with the Data Protection Act 1998 and records more than ten years old were not kept. In requesting information about her visa I had hoped to obtain the vital date of birth and maybe a lead via a different address.

All avenues of approach to find her ended in cul-de-sacs of bureaucracy and frustration; under a cloud of depression I gave up the task as a lost cause.

* * *

Thirteen years later, 2011, I started to have dreams and an unsettling feeling Fong was calling out to me to come and find her – akin to the *butterfly effect.* Like gentle but persistent snowflakes floating onto my landscape of time, this feeling unnervingly gathered momentum, turning into a full scale blizzard. Time was running out before the snowflakes would cover her tracks or before the faint footprints would lead only to a cemetery.

The rise of the internet and social media sites presented new avenues of potential research, reaching back into the past to change the future. I was also in a position to afford to travel to Hong Kong to pursue promising leads and so commenced another determined effort to find her.

Fortunately, Chinese tradition ensured married women kept their family name. I registered accounts with *Facebook* and *Friends Reunited.* Both sites listed several Leung Yuk Fong members but eliminated by their photographs or age. These sites also afforded an avenue of approach for Fong to contact me, although why would she want to.

Why would she want to? The hurt of my silence would be indelible, our pact of love and trust broken, her love for me crushed. If I could get the chance to explain the circumstances and how I had suffered, and suffered for her, there must be a chance of forgiveness, of rekindling her feelings, of reconciliation.

I revisited the Hong Kong Government Births Marriages and Deaths Registry website. In a change from thirteen years previously, online copies of marriage and death certificates could be requested – for a fee of HK$140 (about £15) paid by bankers' draft (there was no credit card facility). Unfortunately, the online system will not accept my application without a date of birth! After an exchange of several emails the registry agreed to accept a postal application for a physical search based on the limited information

I could provide. I sent off the application form with a renewed confidence the certificate would afford the essential date of birth, details of her husband and an address – albeit nearly thirty-five years old – to start a definite trace.

A month passed before I received a reply. The registry was unable to trace the Marriage! How was it possible? I know she married; she sent photographs. All hope had again been dashed and I was enveloped by a pall of depression. In desperation I appealed to God for help, lighting a votive candle in Coventry Cathedral.

After a few weeks moping about, I regained my determination and decided to sound out one of the many professional tracing agencies available on the internet. Having trawled through possible contenders I telephoned the James Lau Detective Agency late afternoon – morning in Hong Kong – and briefed a young man who thankfully spoke fluent, if accented, English.

'One of the problems with Chinese surnames is despite the number of Chinese – about 1.4 billion and counting – there are only three thousand surnames, and ninety per cent of Chinese use a mere one-hundred surnames. An example is the ninety-five million named 'Li', the world's most common surname.'

'Oh, I thought Smith the most common.'

'You are correct in one respect sir. Smith is the most common name in the English speaking world. For comparison, there are a mere three-and-a-half million persons with the name Smith, about half million resident in the UK. Unfortunately, Leung is also a common surname, some fifty-five million worldwide. A date of birth is essential for narrowing down the search.'

'Do you have any suggestions as to why the registration of her marriage could not be found, which would have provided her date of birth?'

'Leung is the Romanized spelling of the Chinese character "Liang." If she reverted to the Chinese "Liang" her name would not show up in database searches for Leung. The other possibility is she married outside of Hong Kong's Administrative region, if she or her husband had relatives in mainland China.'

'She came to England towards the end of 1975 which means she probably applied for a visa and passport the same year. Are you able to check those records?'

'Not so far back. The British Home Office and the Hong Kong Administrative destroy records after ten years. A date of birth is vital to filtering down the Leung surname possibilities, because the forenames Yuk and Fong are also popular. To illustrate the problem you face, while we've been talking I've done a search for the Leung surname in Hong Kong's seven-and-a-half million inhabitants. There are over eighty-thousand females listed.'

'Wow, so many. Can you narrow the number down to those with given names Yuk Fong and with a birthday in January 1952?'

'I'm afraid not; the census database doesn't have the facility and to produce a specific database by trawling through the census would take months.' He paused. 'There are other options to finding people. Lawyers trying to locate lost relatives who are beneficiaries of a deceased's estate advertise in the press.'

'Sounds a good idea. Which newspaper is most likely to be read by the Chinese populace?'

'*Headline Daily,* a free Chinese language paper covering news, sport, lifestyle and entertainment would be a good bet. *Ming Pao*, a Chinese daily with news, culture and leisure sections is also widely read. They both accept adverts. You can compare rates and circulation numbers on the internet.'

I thanked him for his kind advice and placed adverts in both publications, in Cantonese – courtesy of the waitress in my local Chinese restaurant – offering a reward of HK$500 (about £60) for information on her whereabouts. I ran the advert twice, in both papers, on different days of two consecutive months and waited expectantly. No response. My last avenue of hope had turned into another cul-de-sac of despair.

I took her photograph from my desk drawer and my eyes watered as she smiled at me. I placed it back carefully, image down to reduce fading and, as I closed the drawer, the red address stamp on the reverse signalled 'stop' like a traffic light: Wang Shu Photographic, 43A Hankow Road, Tsim Sha Tsui. The name seemed vaguely familiar. Eureka! The name on the back of Mr H's photograph of Fong's mother. Could there be a family connection? The internet revealed the shop's continuing existence with a picture of the facade loaded with cameras and advertising photo printing.

I had a copy of Fong's photograph reproduced – including their address stamp – and sent it with a covering letter (in English and Cantonese), requesting any information they could provide. I enclosed a HK$50 bill (about £6) to cover their cost of reply.

On a grey uninspiring December morning as I despondently munched through a bowl of soggy breakfast cereal, I heard the clatter of the letterbox and watched the postman hurry on his way. The blue airmail sticker and Hong Kong stamp stared up from the coir accelerating my heart in anticipation. On the reverse of the envelope was Wang Shu Photographic. At lunch time I rushed to the local Chinese takeaway for a translation:

Wang Shu Photographic
43A Hankow Road, Tsim Sha Tsui, Hong Kong
6 December 2011
Dear Sir,
Thank you for your letter. We do know Leung Yuk Fong, the niece of my former partner, now retired. I have told her of your enquiry, but she does not wish to communicate with you and does not want her address divulged. I am sorry I cannot be more helpful.
Respectfully,
Zhou Nian Zhen.

At last; a footprint in the snowfall of time. She was alive and I was alive with excitement. Tears of happiness clouded my vision as I imagined the emotion of our meeting and the renewed joy of getting to know her again. It was understandable she would withhold her address after the hurt caused by the cessation of my letters. When she knew of the circumstances, knew I had never stopped loving, reconciliation must be possible. I still had to find her and when I arrived in Hong Kong I would cajole or bribe Mr Zhou to reveal her address; everyone has their price.

Chapter 27

Before I could arrange the flight and hotel, my mother passed away and I was charged with finalising her affairs as executor and principal beneficiary of her will. Mother's demise was not unexpected and I sat at her bedside with the district nurse as she wheezed her last. At eighty-six she appeared to give up the uneven struggle for life from one-too-many afflictions.

A secular ceremony at Eastbourne Crematorium, attended by a couple of neighbours and a nurse, were witness to the loner she had become since my father's premature death half a century before. None of the Patterson clan made an effort to attend.

A few years previously she had removed to Eastbourne having inherited a bungalow from her sister and I had been a regular visitor to the south coast resort to keep an eye on her welfare. I liked Eastbourne; a reasonably sized well appointed town with a hospital, several theatres, international art gallery, and a tolerable ninety minutes from London by train.

In 2012, I qualified for a free bus pass, retired from the estate agency in Coventry and decamped to Eastbourne to inhabit the bungalow. I no longer had definite ties to Coventry apart from a few disposable friends acquired through common endeavours. The Coventry flat was rented to provide an income since I had no pension other than provided by the state.

My best friend of forty years, Janet, aka "Mrs Robinson", had succumbed to pneumonia the previous winter. Over the years I witnessed the beauty of this woman gradually fade, like the wilting bloom of an end of season flower. I missed her love, her companionship, her understanding and her cooking. Her property passed to her son, Terry, who was decidedly frosty at the funeral having somehow learned of my adolescent relationship with his mother.

Mary never remarried, retired from teaching at fifty-five and devoted her years caring for Samantha, but in 2014 Samantha suffered a brain haemorrhage and her ashes took up residence next to Simon's.

On the flight to Hong Kong I watched an old black and white classic, *The Lavender Hill Mob.* Stanley Holloway's character, Pendlebury, reflects on his failed life with the words of American poet John Greenleaf Whittier: *"Of all sad words of tongue or pen, the saddest of these – it might have been."*

Those words took me back to the stolen days in Grimsby and the intense storm of emotions which could have led to an alternative life: the infamous *what if* dilemma? Taken separately these two small words are insignificant, but combined they assumed the threatening power to haunt and torment an entire life, my life. I lived to regret the *what if* moment of my life – the uncle Cecil moment – which I let pass. My nurtured fragments of memories were a constant aphrodisiac to the fantasy notion of realising *what if* three decades late if I could find Fong.

I had noticed the unbridled decay of many older Chinese women; compared to their Western counterparts they did not age well. However the alchemy of past passion worked its fantasy formula of denial and my imagination refused to conjure up any semblance of an image as to how Fong's beauty will inevitably be impaired by the ravages of time, toil and disappointment. It was a conspiracy supported by her Laceby Hotel photograph, her young image remaining firmly unchanged in my mind's eye. I was unable to accept the radiant bloom I had known in Grimsby might now be a frail wilted flower.

As much as I tried I couldn't stop such unsavoury images intruding upon my thoughts. In her mid-sixties, she could be stooped with the shuffling gait and languorous locomotion of a grandmother. The welcoming toothy grin could be false, her face as wizened as a prune and her slender neck crinkled like the bark of a mature oak. Her breasts, which had so aroused my libido, may be drooping to her waist, their sex toy roles but a memory. Her raven's wing hair may be a tarnished halo of greying split ends and the once toned legs disfigured with swollen varicose veins. All images too ghastly to be willingly conceived.

Instead I surmised she had lived the charmed life of the nouveau rich, her husband commanding a fleet of taxis. The good life would have preserved the youthful quality seen among people with money, even without the occasional nip and tuck.

I thought of the many beautiful ageing actresses who weathered the decades, looking younger than their biological ages: Catherine Deneuve, Ann-Margret, Claudia Cardinale, Sophia Loren and Jane Fonda. In this vein, Fong remained in my mind's eye as preserved and dignified as these seasoned screen idols. I was aware of the deception but clung to the notion real beauty remained beautiful, as evidenced by those alluring veteran actresses; the form of beauty changes with age, but it is beauty nonetheless.

Fong's beauty was not purely physical. My wish was her heart of gold had not tarnished with time, and she remained the most gracious, kindest, loving, undemanding person ever met and whatever misfortunes life had thrown at her she had stayed true to herself. Whatever her journey through life I wanted, I needed, to know the route.

Denying me her address indicated she hadn't carried a candle for me over the decades after I lost contact, the hurt and bewilderment too great. I needed to tell her of the many unanswered candles lit for her in churches all over Britain, exalting the notion of piety when it suited my secular wish to find her. Such appeals to the Deity may have been hypocritical, but I was giving God His chance of a reprieve. On the evidence so far, you can't make deals with God; there is no quid pro quo. If the photo was God's way of leading me to her, why did He wait so long?

The overnight Cathay Pacific flight 731 arrived late afternoon and I looked in awe at the cascade of illuminations and skyscrapers set against the dramatic mountain backdrop as we came into land at Chek Lap Kok airport off Lantau Island. The airport impresses – third largest in the world – but also disappoints, the other worldly orient exotic lost to a contemporary western design. I've arrived in Hong Kong, but I could be somewhere else.

I followed the signs and boarded the A21 city bus to Tsim Sha Tsui claiming a top deck seat for the views. The drive from Lantau Island passed over the Tsing Ma suspension bridge with distant views of the edifices of Kowloon and Hong Kong Island dwarfed by the backdrop of mountains of The New Territories. The bus plunged into the Ma Wan tunnel and emerged to the spectacular lighting display that is Kowloon.

The four star Parkside Hotel, situated opposite Kowloon Park on Nathan Road, towered above most of the entertainment and business district of Tsim Sha Tsui. My reservation was for two weeks. After I had settled in and taken a refreshing shower, I ventured out to eat.

The lower section of Nathan Road approaching the waterfront is known in the tourist trade as "The Golden Mile" although a more appropriate epithet would be "Neon Mile" such is the dazzling rainbow of illuminated signage. The myriad lights merged to a cohesive whole like the dots of colour of a Pointillist painting.

It was raining, but the pavements thronged with visitors and locals, umbrellas everywhere but only protesting against the weather. I waited out the downpour with a Starbucks coffee before venturing into a side street. The areas off Nathan Road were a soulless tourists' ghetto: shops, bazaars, malls, markets, restaurants, clubs and bars. Young women outside the louche honey trap hostess bars enticingly tossed out life belts into the sea of neon reflections to rescue my Hong Kong dollars. Although I presumed she still lived in Tai Po I couldn't help but forlornly look for Fong's face everywhere, although there were many establishments where I would hope not to find her.

In Hankow Road I sought out the Wang Shu Photographic shop, a brightly lit compact retail unit sharing a common door with a tailor and garment repair service. The window of glass shelves was crowded with cameras, sales offers claiming never to be beaten on price. Inside, shielded by a counter, were two printing machines and a photocopier. A young woman waiting to serve smiled invitingly and beckoned I enter. I returned her smile but moved on. I would seek out Mr Zhou come the morning.

My sole intention was to eat local fare and sleep off the jet lag. I came across a buffet style restaurant with wide white marble steps leading down to an underground auditorium the size of an aircraft hangar. The cover, for at least a thousand bums on seats, was three-quarters full of mostly young chattering Chinese, a good recommendation. To one side the dishes and delicacies were displayed on long, heated, self service counters, continually restocked by a company of chefs slaving over steaming woks and chopping boards. The descriptions were in Cantonese. For me, the advantage was seeing the culinary delights before choosing although some dishes defied identification.

Dim sum trolleys roamed the floor, your choosing a scribbled addition to the bill at table. Jasmine tea was included and I noticed when other diners wanted a refill they left the lid off the teapot; an obliging wandering waiter deftly refilled at arm length from a kettle with a metre long spout, never spilling a drop, a veritable cabaret act.

Hong Kong is a city which doesn't sleep and for what seemed an age the excitement of being there kept me awake. I was unable to clear my mind of the apprehension of being on the verge of meeting Fong again, providing Mr Zhou would play ball. It was into the early hours before the jet lag prevailed.

Chapter 28

Over breakfast I decided that cajoling Mr Zhou into revealing Fong's address was implausible and bribery demeaning to my character and an affront to his integrity. I would have to resort to subterfuge.

I left the hotel and walked back along Nathan Road to one of the many electronics shops previously noted and purchased a tracking device, the small button sized transmitter operated by an app. The shop attendant downloaded the app onto my mobile and demonstrated the screen functions. I found a florist a couple of blocks away and bought a large bouquet of flowers, attached the tracking device amongst the stems, completed the greetings card and headed off to the Wang Shu Photographic shop.

He was my height but slightly stooped, slim, late fifties, black hair combed back, rimless glasses, dressed in a dark suit probably stitched by the tailor next door.

'Mr Zhou?'

'Yes, may I help you?'

'My name is Chris Patterson, I wrote to you from England several months ago regarding Leung Yuk Fong.'

'Yes, I remember,' he said guardedly. 'I told you I cannot help.'

'You did, but I have come to request a favour. I am in Hong Kong for two weeks and wish to see Fong while I am here. I have much to explain to her, and need her address to make her a beneficiary of my Will. Would you be kind enough to see she gets these flowers; the attached card explains and has details of where I am staying and my phone number should she wish to speak to me.'

'She will not see you. You hurt her in the past and she will not risk being hurt again.'

'Please Mr Zhou, make sure she gets the flowers to give her the option of contacting me. If you could stand them in water, they will keep better.'

'Okay,' he said, with a shrug.

'Thank you Mr Zhou, Fong will not have cause for regret.'

He opened a door at the back of the shop revealing a toilet. He lifted the seat and dropped in the bouquet. I wasn't sure if this was a gesture of disrespect or the only source of water. The shop was small enough to give him the benefit of the doubt. Fortunately the transmitter was waterproof. Out of site of the shop, I checked my mobile. The tracker pulsed like a tiny heart, but not as excitedly as mine.

I decided to take a look at Fong's home town, assuming Tai Po to be the eventual destination of the flowers. I headed down Nathan Road towards Victoria Harbour and Tsim Sha East station to board the KCR (Kowloon Canton Railway) train. The journey took thirty minutes, the views mainly the backs of buildings and security fencing before bursting into the hilly, lush greenery of the New Territories.

Tai Po station was 1970s style white painted concrete minimalism. A convoy of green and white taxis congested the street and the first driver attempted to solicit my custom. I shook my head and raised my hand palm outwards before walking away to consult my map. Most of the street directions were dual signed in Cantonese and English. As I reached the old town centre a few familiar western names – McDonald's, Price Rite, 7-Eleven, Starbucks – intruded like infidels upon the sanctum of a mosque.

According to my guide book Tai Po was one of the so-called "new towns" developed in the late 1970s and 80s with a mix of public and private housing and industrial estates. Formerly a forested area – now a forest of high-rise blocks of flats – this once small market town of twenty-five-thousand inhabitants had rapidly morphed into a thriving city of three-hundred-thousand.

I strolled around the town taking in the more attractive side streets and observed the locals going about their daily chores. I paid attention to the women; some young faces were beautiful but most treated less kindly by their plain parental genes. Older faces had deeply etched lines like the hilly contours of an ordinance survey map; in vain I navigated their features in search of Fong.

The town was split wide by the Tai Po River; huge industrial estates tucked away on the far side, home to familiar names including Motorola, manufacturer of my mobile. On my side a waterfront park with cascading waterfalls, shading trees and enough exotic plants to impersonate a botanical garden. Like a soulless graveyard of giant tombstones, the residential estates stretched into the distance towards the backdrop of bluish mountains penetrating the lingering haze.

I wandered into Heung Sze Wui Street to see the enormous Tai Po Hui Market. In this modern, cavernous hall you could buy almost anything, from meat to greengrocery, fish to eggs (and fish eggs), confectionery to bread and hardware to haberdashery. The hall echoed with the thrum of chatter and trade from the horde of mainly women shoppers. I wandered the aisles impressed by the shear vibrancy of the place and variety of produce, all the time looking for a familiar face.

A bewildering array of colourful fruits and vegetables decorated a legion of central stalls. Dozens of eggs – chicken, duck, goose, pigeon, quail, and plover – were precariously piled in pyramids.

Whole fish lay cold and staring on wet slabs or desperately squirmed and slithered and flapped and gasped in shallow water tanks. Children huddled around the sweet displays tugging at parental clothes and resolve. Hung raw meat carcasses buzzed with cavorting flies and pig's heads dripped blood onto the floor. Chickens in bamboo coops clucked anxiously awaiting the stall holder's cleaver.

Around the edge of the market, tea houses clattered with shuffling mah-jong tablets; old men smoked, drank tea, argued and passed the time of day. There were street markets in Tai Po but nothing on this scale, a definite possibility that Fong would shop there.

Parched and hungry for lunch I was keen to relive an experience in London's China Town decades ago after seeing a café with a bank of glistening reddish-brown crispy baked ducks hung from skewers in the window, fat dripping into trays. I perched on a barstool and ordered half a duck and rice and a pot of green tea. The chef took down a duck and wielding his razor sharp cleaver chopped the carcass into bite-sized pieces on a wooden block, scraped the bits onto a plate and added a large dollop of steamed rice from a cauldron. It was lip licking delicious and ridiculously cheap at the equivalent of a couple-of-quid.

Late afternoon the market quietened and the stalls closed, so I walked back to the older town centre. Hungry again, I stopped at the Lin Yuen Tea House, sat at a communal table and chose from the English translated menu displayed on an illuminated panel above the serving staff.

When called, I collected a bamboo steamer of shrimp filled rice rolls and quail egg dumplings and a plate of fluffy bao buns filled with aromatic pork and diced vegetables with a soy based sauce for dipping, each bite an ambrosial union of delicacy and savour. I replenished the Jasmine tea from a self-serve samovar. I checked my mobile; the electronic heart remained pulsating in the Kowloon loo.

Late afternoon from a café in a nearby square, I supped tea and prudently observed the locals wondering what they thought of me, if at all. Fong lived somewhere in this city, but doubt about meeting her seeped into my thoughts. Perhaps she was definite in her refusal to see me. Perhaps there was some perverse feminine form of jealousy in having chosen my children over her. Perhaps she intended to exact revenge, though this would be out of character. Perhaps life had changed her character. Perhaps she didn't want to expose her faded beauty. Perhaps ... oh, who invented this bleeding word *perhaps*?

I boarded the KCR to return to my hotel and again checked the electronic heart. The flowers were on the move! They were coming towards me! They must be on a train towards Tai Po. At Fo Tan station the two trains drew side by side with the platform between. It was rush hour and people thronged the carriages and platform. The electronic heart pulsed into overdrive, and there, as the other train departed, propped up against a window was the bouquet. I could not see who held it. At the next station, Sha Tin, I changed trains and caught the next back to Tai Po.

It was dusk, but the streets well lit. The flowers had stopped moving on the Tai Yuen Estate, walkable from the town centre. The electronic pulses emanated from a late 1970s style greyish block of twenty or so floors, dwarfed by the thirty or more floors of the white high risers of later years. The external air conditioning units were painted in pigeon pooh in the drip-and-splash style of Jackson Pollock. No wonder smoked pigeon was a local delicacy. I called the lift; nothing arrived so I took to the stairs.

Chapter 29

The pulses indicated the third floor, flat 319. I raised my hand to knock on the door I had always wished to open since the hotel door in Watford closed. Doubt intruded my thoughts as my hand suspended above the knocker. Would I still love her as much as I did thirty-seven years ago? Would I love her less and destroy the precious memories I had harboured since Grimsby? If she proved unworthy of my enduring love I would be devastated. Was it better not to know, to keep my precious memories? They could be sullied like those of Mr H.

I had come too far to turn back now. I took a deep breath, knocked and waited. Her deep brown eyes were questioning, tinged with anxiety and resignation but not surprise. Her face showed the wear and tear of motherhood and a life of working fatigue, crow's feet to the eyes and corners of her mouth, etched furrows to her brow, hair lacking the raven's wing sheen of my remembrance. She remained attractive, her figure fuller than before but shapely.

'I knew you would come,' she said in a tone of acquiescence. 'Mr Zhou told me of your visit. How did you know my address?'

'I followed the flowers. Saw you with them on the train.'

'Ah ... a resourceful ploy,' she commended with a wry smile.

'It's good to see you again.'

'You too Chris. Come in.'

The front door led straight into the lounge-dining-kitchen area and I cast my estate agents eye about. Two doors ajar off to the left revealed a shower room and toilet, the other a bedroom. There was no sign of joint occupancy although the bed was a double. The kitchenette was basic with white Formica units, gas hob and microwave, but no oven. The apartment was, in estate agency jargon, "compact and would benefit from modernization." The view from the rear balcony glimpsed the sea of To Lo Harbour between the surrounding blocks. She busied herself making tea.

'I'm here to see Fong. Where does she live?'

'I promised not to tell you; she is my elder, I cannot break my word.'

'I have to explain why I was unable to answer her letters ... I have never stopped loving her. Please Mai, I must see her.'

'She has decided against seeing you. She has her reasons.'

'I will find her Mai; I know she is here in Tai Po. It's only a matter of time.'

'Yes, but how much time do you have in Hong Kong?'

'Two weeks.'

'Not much time to find her if she doesn't want to be found.'

'I will come again if necessary. I have so much to explain, so much to tell her. I have to find her.'

'We knew you were looking a few months ago,' she said with a sigh.

From a drawer she withdrew a newspaper cutting, the advert I had placed.

'Why didn't you reply? At least we could have corresponded.'

'It was Fong's decision; I'm not saying I agreed with her.'

'Will you see Fong gets the flowers?'

'I think the flowers better stay here,' she said shrewdly.

'Come on Mai, don't you owe me a favour?'

'I cannot tell you Fong's address, but ...'

'Yes?' I said, expectantly.

'Do you know the Hui market in Tai Po?'

'Yes, I was there this afternoon looking for Fong. She once said to me, as we walked the market in Louth, she shopped everyday for fresh food.'

'Well ... people tend to food shop in the mornings,' she hinted. 'She is likely to be there with friends, if so you should not approach; it would be extremely embarrassing for her.' I moved to give her a cuddle of thanks; she did not resist. She excused herself to use the bathroom and I took the opportunity to recover the tracking transmitter. 'Now drink your tea and tell me why you stopped writing. Fong was deeply hurt, not knowing your reason.'

I related the whole sorry story and a brief résumé of my life and how I had desperately tried to find Fong years ago, but without her date of birth it had proved impossible.

'When is her birthday?'

'Twenty-second of January, 1952.'

'Fong sent photos of her wedding; the marriage certificate would have given me the all important date of birth, but the registrar was unable to find her marriage.'

'She married in Guangzhou on the mainland so relatives of her husband not allowed into Hong Kong could attend.'

I plucked Fong's photo from my wallet.

'Look. We were so happy; we knew we loved each other.' I turned it over to show her the address. 'I can't imagine why I didn't think of trying the address earlier. It was the last resort. Tell me about her life; is she still married, does she have children, does she work?'

'Her husband died many years ago. Fong no longer works at Motorola.'

'Motorola. The last I knew she worked in a clothing factory.'

'She changed jobs when Motorola opened their new factory

offering better conditions, pay and pension.'

'I'm relieved to hear she wasn't a slave in a garment sweat shop. What about children? I remember her husband was a single parent with a daughter.'

'Yes, she's called Chi Mai. Will you stay for dinner? A quick chicken and vegetable stir-fry.'

'Yes, thank you. Any other children?'

'I must start preparing the meal.'

She looked nervous and busied herself chopping vegetables. I asked again.

'A daughter,' she admitted reluctantly, 'Chi Wah, three years younger than Chi Mai.'

'Do they live with Fong?'

'No, they live in Kowloon.'

I paused in thought, a little uncertain how to continue. It seemed impolite not to enquire about Mai Ling's voyage through the decades.

'Tell me about your life. Where are Wei Ling and your husband?'

'Husband inherited some money and bought a younger model. Good riddance!' she scowled. 'Wei Ling married a businessman.'

'I remember Wei, the shy little girl in Watford.'

'She has her own shy little girl now,' she smiled, 'but I don't see them often ... they live in Singapore.'

'You never remarried?'

'Never again', she said firmly. 'Wei Ling was the only good to come out of the marriage.'

'My marriage was the same, no real love except for the kids.'

I paused to drink tea and she refilled my cup.

'Do you still work?'

'Yes, on the production line at Motorola; Fong and I worked there until her retirement last year. I retire next year.'

'I saw the factory across the river; my mobile is Motorola.'

She gave me a cloth and cutlery to lay the table and dished up the stir-fry. We chatted generally about aspects of my life, my move to Eastbourne, my former relationship with Janet. We discussed the worsening political situation under Xi Jinping's rule; she and Fong had taken part in the Umbrella Movement with their cousin, Edward, and half-brother Zhi Ming. She made more tea and we sat on the two seat sofa.

'What do you hope to achieve by seeing Fong?'

'Reconciliation. As I said, for her to know I never stopped loving ... peace of mind for both of us ... maybe a life together in some way.'

She nodded thoughtfully and took a deep breath.

'There is something you should know; the reason Fong is reluctant to see you.'

She took my right hand in hers and fixed my gaze with a look of apprehension. 'Chris ... Chi Wah is your daughter.'

'Oh no! No; not my child.' Tears misted my eyes, my face quivered with involuntarily grimaces. 'It can't be true, she would have told me,' I protested.

'It is true Chris.'

'Oh God! I had a premonition ... a recurring dream she was pregnant ... I knew something was wrong ... the tone of her letters, the quick marriage. Why didn't she tell me?'

I bent forward elbows on knees, head in my hands. Mai Ling put an arm across my shoulders to comfort.

'Fong did not want to ruin your life with the children you loved. She saw no hope of family life with you here and thought it best not to burden you by knowing. It was a decision taken out of love for you. In retrospect it may not have been the right decision, but it was a confusing and distressing time for her. As you know, her mother had a similar experience with a British soldier and she advised Fong to take the safe option and marry her priest's brother;

our father insisted.

She paused, as if to allow her explanation time to sink in. 'Would you like more tea?' she said sympathetically.

I thought brandy more appropriate, but accepted the tea.

'After the baby was born, you stopped writing. She didn't know what to think, except you wanted to forget her because of the marriage and were involved with someone new. Unless you had died from an accident or illness, why else would you refuse the pleas in her letters to keep writing? She couldn't believe you would stop writing without explanation.

The watery essence was of no comfort. Perhaps it has to be black tea with milk, accompanied by the ritual decorum only the British can occasion. I needed to acclimatize to this revelation, my mind a confusion of bewildered reasoning and conflicting emotions.

Amazingly, the graphologist's surmise all those years ago had been proven. At least it explained the wedding, the older man she married and the resigned expression. Casting my mind back to the wedding photos, I thought she had put on weight, but dismissed it to the Chinese diet. Her hands had been clasped in front of her holding a spray of flowers covering her belly. Like pieces of a jigsaw the picture was emerging.

A love child may well have influenced my decision regarding my children with Mary. The allusion was I would have joined Fong in Hong Kong, the reality less certain, a quandary I'm glad not to have faced. Nevertheless I should have had the opportunity to be involved in her upbringing, to have known her through childhood and adolescence, for my daughter to have known me. On the other hand, If Fong had told me by letter without her address, the cruelty would have been unbearable.

'I want to meet Chi Wah. 'She has to know I'm her father.'

'Yes you should; I'm sure she will want to get to know you.

She will be your go-between with Fong.' She paused. 'I trust you understand Fong is frightened as to how you would react to knowing you are Chi Wah's father; her motives were love for you and a family life for your daughter. Being a single mother is a stigma in Chinese society.'

'I do understand; a decision out of love and pragmatism. Can you not prevail upon Fong to meet me?'

'I have already tried. I cannot do more now she knows you are in Hong Kong. Find her in the market tomorrow and follow her home. Tell her you know about Chi Wah and as her father you insist on meeting her. I'm sure the bond of family will triumph; Chi Wah would not forgive Fong if she missed the chance to meet her father. All will be well Chris, believe me.'

'I'm beginning to believe you. Erm ... do you have a photo of Chi Wah?'

'Wait until you see her, your meeting will be all the more rewarding.'

'Do you have a recent photo of Fong? It might help to pick her out in the crowded market.'

'I'm sure her features are indelibly imprinted on your mind. Trust your heart, it will skip a beat and you will know.'

We hugged and cheek kissed as I expressed my thanks. We parted with some reluctance; she looked into my eyes and said, 'I have never forgotten the night we spent together.'

Her tone implied the regret of only one night. Over her shoulder I could see her inviting double bed. Was she testing my resolve, my loyalty to Fong? I took my leave. I had a restless night, thirty-seven years of frustration and yearning about to be liberated.

Chapter 30

The market teemed with women shoppers, so busy I had doubts I would find her. Like a private eye from an old movie I picked up a free newspaper to hide my face if necessary. For an hour I trolled the aisles scrutinising every face. I stopped for tea in one of the cafés on the edge of the market, apprehension building she had not come, or had been and gone before my arrival. I wandered around peering into the other cafés and mah-jong parlours.

Back amongst the stalls, wandering the aisles and yes, my heart did seem to skip a beat; there she was, with two friends acting like chaperones. My eyes were moist with joy, I wanted to holler her name, rush up and hug her and shower her with kisses but remembered Mai Ling's caution.

I kept my distance, following from stall to stall. They stopped to buy vegetables, Fong dropping her purchases into a red canvas shopping bag. She laughed and playfully elbow nudged a friend in response to something funny or saucy. As I observed, a young lad ran into me, scurrying away from a chasing friend.

'Sorry mister.'

'Hey, I called, you speak English. You want to earn twenty dollars?'

'For what,' he replied warily.

I turned him around and pointed.

'You see the lady in the blue jacket. I want you to drop this button into her red shopping bag without her knowing.'

'Hmm, okay but forty dollars,' he said cheekily. Twenty for my friend to distract her.'

'Okay, agreed.'

I gave them twenty each and the transmitter and watched them complete their task as deftly as a couple of Fagin's pickpockets. They looked back and I gave them the thumbs up. I fumbled with my phone to turn on the App. I was so nervous I dropped the phone, but broke its fall with my foot.

I followed Fong at a discrete distance, shielded by the throng of shoppers and my newspaper. Her last stop was to buy a chicken. She pointed to a cage; the stall holder grabbed the bird by its neck. The frantic flutter of wings and flying feathers – the last desperate struggle for life – ended with a quick chop of a cleaver. With mechanical efficiency the carcass was soon as bald as a patient from chemo.

The three of them inched through the crowd to a mah-jong parlour and, tea served, sat to shuffle the tablets. So as not to be noticed I went for lunch – another portion of crispy duck and rice. I had difficulty containing my excitement, ate too fast and felt the indigestion.

At around one-o'clock the bag was on the move, it's pace indicating a taxi or bus. I walked following the signal, trying to calm my elation. The electronic heart was stationary, the same estate as Mai Ling, the same block as Mai Ling, the same floor as Mai Ling. Perhaps she was visiting her sister, but no, the pulse came from further along the passage. With all the trepidation of a teenager on a first date I took a deep breath and knocked on the door.

Those few seconds before the click of the lock were an eternity; the door opened ajar, she peered out.

'Hello Fong.'

'Chris,' she gasped.

She tried to close the door but my salesman's foot prevented. The pressure relaxed and the door slowly swung open. She had retreated to the lounge, silhouetted against the bright light of the window, arms folded defiantly.

'Why have you come, after all these years,' her voice raised, the tone aggrieved. 'Too late; I have nothing to say to you.'

'I've plenty to say to you. I never stopped loving you.'

'No love here anymore,' she said, patting her chest, 'only hurt.'

'If you allow me a little time I can explain and take the hurt away. You owe it to me for not telling me about our daughter.'

'You know,' she said surprised. 'I can explain ...'

'Mai Ling told me.' I interrupted. 'I understand your reasons why you thought it best I not know. That's in the past; I'm here to create a future for us.'

'Did Mai Ling tell you my address?'

'No, she refused ... sister loyalty.'

'Then how did you find me?'

'A ruse I had seen in some film or other. I left a bouquet of flowers for you with Mr Zhou. Inside the bunch I placed a tracking device. Mai Ling collected the flowers which led me to her flat.'

'It doesn't explain how you knew my address?'

'A bit of subterfuge; in the market this morning I saw you shopping and bribed a young lad to plant the tracking transmitter in your shopping bag. If you look it's still there.'

She recovered the small button. I held out my hand. She closed her hand around it.

'Souvenir,' she insisted. 'How did you know I would be at the market?'

'When we visited Louth market, you told me you bought fresh food daily. So yesterday and today I looked for you at the market. By the way, isn't it customary to make tea when you have a visitor?'

'Only if visitor welcome.'

'Am I not welcome as Chi Wah's father?'

She frowned and didn't answer but moved to the kitchen to fill the kettle. Away from the window I could better see her face with the delicate crazing of an antique piece of porcelain, hair tarnished and greying cut shorter than I remembered, figure more rounded at the waist, breasts of motherly fullness.

Her hostility waned into questioning: 'Why ... What ... When ... How?'

I poured out the answers over several cups of tea. 'I know how hurt you must feel about my not replying to your letters in 1977, but during a house move my wife found and burnt them, incinerating your address. I could not remember your Tai Po address so I was unable to reply. If only you had written your address on them I would still be writing. I was heartbroken like you; I have your last three unanswered letters.

The day my wife burnt your letters was the day I left her and I divorced in 1981.' I paused and frowned in dismay. 'When you sent me photographs of your marriage I was devastated, but I noticed you were wearing my ring and I knew you still loved me and it was an arranged marriage. I never remarried; no one could ever replace you in my heart. I have always worn your ring.'

I held up my left hand. 'In fact I can't get it off, swollen finger joints. Do you still have your ring?'

'Somewhere,' she said dismissively.

'You wear the watch I gave you.'

'I need to know the time,' she said, as if stating the obvious, before defiantly unstrapping and placing on the table.

'True love never dies, never grows old, it's never too late. The ring I gave you was for eternity; I meant it then, I mean it now. You rightly doubted my feelings when I stopped writing, but needing to explain my silence was the reason I tried repeatedly to find you.

A day has not passed I haven't thought of you; every night you were the last of my thoughts before sleeping and the subject of my dreams.

I have lived to regret choosing love and responsibility for my children over our love and happiness. It seemed the decision I had to take at the time; with hindsight it proved to be wrong and I have suffered a life sentence of torment and remorse. I am so sorry.'

I paused as the emotion threatened to overwhelm me. A tear escaped my eye. I had been crying inside and it was about to spill out. My moist gaze pleaded with her for understanding and forgiveness. I was coming to terms with the grief I had lived the wrong life and compelled her to do the same.

'Sorry is never enough,' she said, 'so let there be no *sorry*. There is only what happened; it can never be undone.'

I sniffed and dabbed my eyes with a handkerchief.

'The destruction of your letters changed everything in my life; I not only lost you but it led to the death of my children.'

'No parent should outlive their children,' she said sagely. 'What happened?'

'A road accident, thirty years ago. Son killed; daughter paralysed from the waist down. She died last year.'

'Was the accident your fault?'

'Indirectly yes. I wasn't driving, but if I hadn't left them and divorced it would not have happened. My parents are dead, I have no one.'

'You have Chi Wah.'

'Yes ... child of our love. When can I meet her?'

'I will tell her you are here and see what she says.'

Mai Ling was right; Chi Wah was the olive branch towards rekindling some form of relationship again with Fong. I had to give Fong time, for her to accept my feelings are unchanged, our unfortunate interlude not entirely of my making and therefore a case for forgiveness.

'I always carried your photograph with me, concealed in the lining of my wallet, the reason it survived my wife's bonfire. Look, I have it here. I was never happier than the first night we made love.'

'Me too,' she said quietly. 'The future promised so much, but we lived the wrong lives.'

'We could start to live the right life now,' I said optimistically.

'I think not; too many years, too much heartache.'

'I have explained!'

'Yes you have; but it doesn't change what happened.'

'I can try and make amends if you will let me.'

We sat in silence, gazing at each other. I broke the uneasy pause.

'Our situation has uncanny parallels with actors Vanessa Redgrave and Franco Nero. They fell in love in 1967 – she thirty, he twenty-six – but didn't get together for another thirty-seven years, even though she bore him a son. In 2010, in a case of art imitating life, they starred in *Letters to Juliet,* a beautifully filmed romance set in Italy. Have you seen it?'

She shook her head.

'A retired woman, Redgrave, seeks out a lost love, Nero, regretting she lacked the courage to commit in her youth. She eventually finds him and their feelings are unchanged. Upon meeting she apologises for being late; he responds: "No, when you are speaking about love, it is never too late." They marry and live happily ever after.'

For the first time Fong's eyes betrayed the glimmer of a smile, her mood softening.

'I want us to live happily ever after,' I said, my voice quivering, 'to salvage what we can in the years we have left. If Chi Wah is willing we would be a family.'

We were interrupted by a knock at the door. Fong moved to

answer it. Amidst a torrent of Cantonese and flaying arms from Fong, Mai Ling entered.

'Perhaps I had better leave,' I said, foiled when I thought I was making progress. 'Think on what I have said. Here's my card with my mobile number. Let me know when I can meet Chi Wah.'

As I moved past Mai Ling we politely embraced. Fong kept her distance. I held out my arms to her. She folded her arms and didn't move. I had not the excuse of an ice skating rink to put my arms about her as I longed to do even more so than on our first date. As I walked away towards the stairs Mai Ling called after me and approached.

'Give her time Chris, it's been a big shock; she's emotionally confused. I will talk to Chi Wah and phone you tomorrow.'

'I'm grateful for your help.'

'I owe you.'

Chapter 31

The meeting with Fong was not as envisaged, with a *Letters to Juliet* style joyous reunion. She was to open the door and, overwhelmed with emotion, fall into my arms; we would cry, we would laugh, we would make love. Everything would be happy-ever-after. Perhaps it only happens in films.

In an emotional turmoil unsure what to do, I spent the next day sightseeing although distracted by yesterday's encounter and concerned as to how my meeting with Chi Wah would play out.

The funicular tram took eight minutes in its near vertical climb to Victoria Peak, but well over an hour of queuing to board, packed as tightly as cigarettes in a pack. The two carriages had the external look of the Victorian versions but blandly modern interiors. I spilled out with the crowd into the ill-conceived mall teeming with shops, restaurants and chattering visitors. In the 1950s film *Love Is a Many-Splendored Thing,* the Peak was serene, grassed and undeveloped.

To get away from the hordes I strolled along Lugard Road for a quieter appreciation of one of the world's great city views. The hundreds of skyscrapers resembled an overcrowded graveyard mirroring the demise of my 1960s cinema nostalgia. Toy sized boats and ferries littered the harbour leaving white wakes like aeroplane contrails.

The winding roads, steep pathways and steps led down past old colonial mansions, elite executive houses and exclusive apartment blocks clinging to the sides of the mountain like ivy to an oak.

In the afternoon I boarded the MTR (Mass transit Railway) to Tung Chung Station on Lantau Island, and took a bus to the west coast to experience the time capsule attractive fishing port of Tai O. The village offered a glimpse of pre-colonial life. Families lived in abject poverty on moored houseboats or in tiny rickety houses precariously built on stilts in the shallow inshore.

On the quayside women sorted the meagre catch, descaled fish with wire brushes and hung the fillets on wooden racks to dry in the sun. Others sat repairing nets and bamboo lobster cages for the night's voyage by their men. It played to my nostalgia generated by old movies, but this traditional way of life was fast disappearing in a village under siege from tourism and encroaching high-rise apartment blocks.

Lantau Island retained much of its rural and wooded character, with Buddhist monasteries perched on hill tops, despite the airport's transport links and tourist venues. I had intended to visit the famous Po Lin (Precious Lotus) Monastery but there was no time to see its famous Big Buddha, I needed to return to the hotel, shower and change to meet my new daughter. Mai Ling had phoned with directions to meet Chi Wah at her flat for dinner. I hoped Fong would be present.

Around half-past-seven I took a taxi from the hotel to her apartment block, a 1990s development near the water front extending to twenty or more floors. A security guard directed me to the tenth floor, fortunately the lift worked. I was greeted by Chi Mai, Fong's step daughter. We shook hands with polite formality and she explained Chi Wah had been delayed at work and would join us later.

Her smile was all engaging and yet she was an amalgam

of attractiveness tempered by plainness. She wore make-up, skin foundation and eye liner. Her lips were bright red and her complexion pale, redolent of a Japanese geisha. Her raven black hair was immaculately sculptured into a fashionable helmet style. She was slim, not quite tall, clothed in a dark blue dress with an apron over. She poured tea and we made polite conversation.

'What line of work are you in?'

'I'm a translator at Kai Electronics. They make white goods, sold all over the world. And you?'

'Retired from estate agency.'

'Zhi Ming works for an estate agent; he helped get this flat.'

'I believe your father was the elder brother of Fong's priest.'

'Yes. How did you know?'

'One day in England Fong and I discussed relationships and she mentioned your father as a single parent. Later, she sent me photos of the wedding. Your father died I believe.'

'Yes, an accident driving his taxi one night during a typhoon storm.'

'I'm sorry,' I said softly, lowering my eyes in respect.

'It's okay now,' she replied chirpily, 'many years ago.'

She asked how long I was staying in Hong Kong and about my impressions so far but kept off the subject of my relationship with Fong. She excused herself.

'I must cook or we will not eat.'

I wasn't hungry, my stomach filled with apprehension, the nervousness of a first date. I looked around the pint-sized apartment. The lounge – open plan to the kitchen area – housed a dining table with four folding chairs in one half and a two-seat sofa and wall mounted TV in the other. The bedroom had built-in wardrobes and drawer units, the double bed taking up the remaining space. A door accessed an en suite shower room and toilet. The emulsioned walls were a delicate shade of pink, the floor grey ceramic tiles, the windows screened with matching Venetian blinds; all coolly feminine. A framed cinema poster of *Casablanca* adorned the wall opposite the kitchen area.

'My favourite film,' I said indicating.

'A present from Fong.'

I wandered out onto the balcony, wide enough for a small circular table and two chairs, a restricted view of the harbour visible through the gap between two apartment blocks. Dusk had descended, the sky a deep slate blue; the only stars visible through the smog and light-haze the illuminated green and white ferries chugging back and forth between Kowloon and Central. A wall mounted air conditioning unit toiled, whirring and wheezing incessantly and I failed to hear the front door close. I turned to go back into the lounge. She must have been watching, wary of approaching.

'Hello, pleased to meet you,' she said bowing. 'Do I call you father or Chris?'

I opened my mouth to speak but my voice didn't respond; emotion welled up in my chest, my legs rooted like tree stumps. Sensing the struggle being lost, she moved to me with a broad smile, her eyes brimming with sympathy; she took my hands, as if to start a country dance. Her arms moved about my waist and hugged, her head on my chest. My arms carefully wrapped around her shoulders as if handling a fragile sculpture.

'Call me Chris,' I mumbled tearfully.

Her tears mirrored mine. Chi Mai joins to embrace us. Tears are replaced by relief, smiles and laughter at our reactions; a lost father and a found daughter rejoicing.

'Let me look at you.' I held her hands, arms outstretched.

She was a little taller than her half-sister and more generously built and curved in the Fong mould. She had the engaging beauty and skin tone often witnessed in persons of mixed race. There were resemblances to Fong – her broad, naturally engaging smile and seductively dark eyes – without the wholly Chinese facial look. Like Chi Mai she wore make-up and eye liner although she didn't need to.

She worked as a currency trader at HSBC, monitoring the movements of foreign currency rates and trading to make a profit on the Bank's holdings. Based in the Norman Foster designed iconic office block facing the harbour, she offered to show me her office and the renowned atrium.

She knew little about me, except how Fong and I met and I had been married with children. After the meal we sipped green tea and I related parts of my life history. Chi Wah wanted to know why I had broken up with her mother, how I lost contact, why I had not come to Hong Kong to find her sooner. At times it was an uncomfortable inquisition although nothing accusative, purely the desire to know.

It was an emotional couple of hours, especially when they opened the family photo album, a chronicle of Fong's life: from toothy grinning kid, to adolescent student, to full womanhood, family gatherings, friends, parties, summers on the beach. Images of her time in England, scenes in Watford with her sister, of the Lotus House restaurant, and two of me, one I had given her and one at the celebration meal at the Lotus House with all the staff. How boyish I looked.

Hong Kong again, with Mai Ling and colleagues at Motorola. I recognised two marriage photos. Chi Wah, a few hours old, held in her mother's arms at the hospital maternity unit, with little Chi Mai and her sullen father looking on. I no longer had any animosity towards the man who made an honest woman of her. Her parents declined steadily, the children grew-up through school and college life and into careers. As I turned the pages Fong matured gracefully, retaining the joyful radiance and kiss me smile which had first captured me body and soul.

The time was approaching eleven and I suggested they call a taxi to return me to the hotel. 'Can I give you a lift Chi Mai?'

'A lift,' she said, somewhat puzzled, 'You want me to come to your hotel?'

'No no, a lift to your place.'

'I live here.'

'Ah ... I did wonder.'

'I hope you not embarrassed,' said Chi Wah.

'No,' I replied, shaking my head.

'Chi Mai was always an older sister to me, looked after me at school. In those days people of mixed race were not looked upon kindly by Chinese; I was made to feel I did not belong. We grew close to combat the discrimination and stayed together. We're happy; we love each other.'

'I'm happy for you.' I had no qualms about their relationship; the simple sensuous companionship bonding them since childhood. 'Won't you want children?'

'Maybe in the future we adopt or try IVF treatment. We could always borrow a man to father,' suggested Chi Wah with a chuckle. 'Chris, you could donate your sperm. I'll get a bottle.' She grinned ruefully.

I flushed with embarrassment even as I realized the joke.

'Oh Chris, you should see your face.' They laughed.

Chi Wah had inherited Fong's mischievous sense of humour.

'Do you have any plans for this weekend?'

'Sightseeing of some of the older districts and hopefully to spend time with you and Fong.'

'I will speak to my mother, see what can be arranged. Meanwhile I will be your guide for the weekend.'

Chapter 32

Hong Kong proved an amazing destination: everything from the shops of Bond Street and skyline of New York, to the hedonism of Las Vegas and strip joints of Soho, to world class museums and art galleries, to majestic Buddhist temples, to white sandy beaches rivalling the Caribbean. British colonial influences remained in architecture, place and street names and dual language signage.

Unfortunately, the overall experience tainted my nostalgia for the orient of the Suzie Wong era. Hong Kong was now a conglomeration of nine thousand monoliths flooded by a tsunami of fluorescent neon and advertising hoardings, alien to the romance of the bygone colonial era I had gleaned from films of the fifties and sixties. Much of the mystery and exoticness of the orient had been lost to the imperative drive of westernization and property development.

Chi Wah understood my nostalgia and took me to a few pockets of streets on Kowloon side affording a flavour of the past: the congested grid of narrow lanes, night markets and seedy brothels of Mong Kok and the working class area and squalid accommodation blocks of Yau Ma Tei. Outdoor markets and traditional retailers of time honoured Chinese trades were in evidence, including fortune tellers, ivory and jade stalls, mah-jong parlours, paper votive shops, herbalists and opium dens. Cafés, bars and restaurants around every corner tempted the palate, catering to locals instead of tourists.

With their sense of timeless romance, the one constant from the days of Suzie Wong were the Star Ferries, their green and white livery churning and rumbling back and forth every few minutes across the harbour defying progress and the rivalry of alternative transports.

Chi Wah took me inside the emblematic HSBC building, the famous soaring atrium a cathedral to capitalism. Two lion statues guarded the entrance which we stroked for luck, a local tradition. Her corner office had her name on the door and boasted views over the harbour across to Kowloon.

Close by she pointed out Jardine House – built for Jardine Matheson, one of the colony's oldest trading companies with a dubious history of trafficking opium in exchange for tea, cotton and silk shipped to Britain. Punctured by porthole windows, the building resembled a huge block of Swiss cheese. Chi Wah said the locals nicknamed it "The House of a Thousand Arseholes." She apologised for the vernacular adding it was apparently as much a reference to the occupants as to the facade. The building's exterior stood in for the headquarters of trading company Struan – based on Jardine Matheson – in the 1988 filmed series of James Clavell's *Noble House.*

The myth of Suzie Wong was also linked with Wan Chai, but Suzie's "Nam Kok Hotel" had been demolished in 1988 and replaced by a gleaming glass-and-steel tower block. A neighbouring warren of cramped streets survived, valleys dwarfed by ageing blocks of flats on which air conditioning units clung like barnacles to an old ship's hull. Street level retail units harboured workshops and traditional sundry trades. A wet market of stalls spilled into several back streets providing fresh food; fresh because much of it was still alive, clucking nervously in bamboo cages or floundering in shallow water tanks. Cheap cafés whetted the appetite with enticing aromas and the locals drank "milk tea" – an adulterated speciality of filtering boiling hot black tea through muslin and whitening with condensed milk – a smooth concoction, but not my cup of tea.

Chi Wah, like her mother, had evolved a keen interest in the cinema and whilst in Wanchai we visited the Hong Kong Film Archive, a shrine to local films and related paraphernalia. In the 1980s Hong Kong was known as the "Hollywood of the East", churning out hundreds of films annually, eclipsed only by Hollywood and Mumbai. The industry was initially fuelled by the emergence of the Kung Fu genre with the combative exploits of Bruce Lee and comedic parodies from Jackie Chan. The 1990s saw a new wave of blood-and-bullets crime stories, comedies and romances attracting critical acclaim from worldwide audiences.

Several Hong Kong stars made it across the Pacific pond to the real Hollywood: Anna May Wong (*The Lady from Chunking*); Fong's namesake Tony Leung (*In the Mood for Love*); Jackie Chan (*Shanghai Noon*); Chow Yun Fat (*Anna and the King*); Jet Li (*Romeo Must Die*) and Nancy Kwan, aka Suzie Wong.

The archive listed nearly one-hundred foreign made films shot with Hong Kong locations, many preserving familiar scenes of the past: narrow streets overhung with a jungle of colourful bilingual sign boards; street markets and open fronted shops selling everything and anything; rickshaws and pedicabs negotiating streets teeming with locals; coolies shouldering heavy basket loads on bamboo yokes; the harbour alive with bobbing sampans, junks, Star Ferries and fishing boats under sail.

On Monday, following Chi Wah's suggestion, I took a bus trip through the mountains to the rocky southern shores of Hong Kong Island, to the harbour town of Aberdeen, where remnants of "boat people" and traditional trades remained in evidence, another nostalgic glimpse into the past. The tranquil peace of

Stanley Beach and laid-back fishing villages were a remarkable contrast to the heavily urbanised northern shoreline.

Chi Wah was a clone of Fong in character if not wholly in looks; we bonded easily and I fell in love with her as if we had always been together. I knew over the weekend she and Mai Ling had spoken to Fong in support of my case for reconciliation but Fong was playing hard ball, hopefully part of the age-old posturing in the game of love.

On Tuesday, I decided to take the initiative; I was running out of time. I took the KCR to Tai Po and sat drinking tea in the café where Fong played mah-jong. She came in with her two friends and stopped when she saw me. I smiled. She covertly swished her hand ushering me out of the café. I shook my head and continued drinking. I watched them play. Fong deliberately sat with her back to me but regularly stole glances across the café to check my presence. The first game finished, signalled by the clatter of reshuffled tiles, and I approached the table.

'Hello ladies, do any of you speak English?'

Fong pursed her lips as if stop herself exploding from indignation.

'A little,' said one of her friends, 'Fong, you do.'

'What do you want?' Fong snapped.

'I learned to play mah-jong from a friend in England,' I said, looking at Fong. 'I wondered if I might join your game, four players are better than three.'

'Please, sit,' gestured her friend. 'What is your name?'

'Chris. And yours?'

'Suzie,' she indicated to herself, 'Fong,' she gestured left, 'and Ling.'

I shook hands, leaving Fong until last. I held her hand until she pulled away. I didn't win a round but acquitted myself well enough. Fong and I exchanged conspiratorial looks and she grudgingly returned my smile. The ice was thawing.

'You work in Tai Po?' enquired Suzie.

'No, visiting Hong Kong to see my daughter. She works for HSBC in Central.'

Fong's brow furrowed with concern and she gave me a pleading look with a slow shake of her head, her lips miming 'no.'

'What a coincidence; Fong's daughter works for HSBC,' said Suzie.

'It's a huge employer, many thousands work there,' I said dismissively.

I could see a suspicious look of intrigue in Suzie's glance. Suzie would know Chi Wah to be of mixed parentage; hopefully Suzie's scepticism would induce Fong to reveal our relationship.

I looked at my watch. 'I must be going, things to do.' I locked eyes with Fong. 'Not much time left here in Hong Kong,' I emphasised. 'Thank you for the games ladies.' I bowed and nodded to them and took my leave. As I walked away there was a burst of chatter between Suzie and Fong.

I crossed over to the other side of the market hall for another satisfying lunch of crispy duck and rice. After lunch I headed off to the station and caught the 64K bus to the nearby village of Lam Tsuen and the famous Banyan wishing tree, renowned for granting wishes and good fortune according to my guidebook.

The original banyan tree was subject to conservation from overuse; in its place a realistic plastic replica with gnarled trunk and evergreen foliage – Banyan trees drop their leaves in autumn. In the past joss paper wrapped about a mandarin (fruit variety) was tossed into the tree until it attached to a branch. I purchased a plastic mandarin and wishing tag, upon which I wrote my desire for reconciliation with Fong.

Not having much faith in the plastic replica I looked about in search of the original tree. Away from the throng of tourists a short alley between two non-descript single storey buildings opened on to a space with the tree cordoned off by ropes. Signs in several languages prohibited its use. With no one on guard I bent under the rope to get closer and after four attempts my "mandarin" was withheld by the tree, the string tangled in its bare branches.

An irate elderly woman in a blue uniform strode up waving her arms amid a torrent of Cantonese scolding me for trespassing. I produced a HK$50 bill and put a finger to my lips to indicate shush. She held out her hand and continued to bawl. I produced another HK$50. The notes disappeared down her cleavage like a prostitute's fee. Before being ushered away, I photographed my lone "mandarin" forlornly dangling like the last fruit to be picked.

I sat and took tea and a bowl of dim sum from one of the on-site eateries as I waited for the return bus. Fong phoned. Had the banyan tree worked its spell?

'Are you still in Tai Po?'

'Yes.'

'Why do you not come to see me this afternoon?'

'Would I be welcome?'

'You can come,' she said in an off-hand tone.

I arrived an hour later and Fong made tea, an encouraging start.

'Did Suzie say anything about me after I left; was she suspicious?'

'Yes, I had to reveal you were Chi Wah's father. She knows her too well. It was a clever ploy.'

'Not so much clever as desperate. I've told you of my feelings; I never stopped loving you. If you don't feel the same about me or can't put aside what happened I will at least have a clear conscience when I return to England, I found you and tried to atone.'

I was now playing hard ball. We sat and gazed at each other for the eternity of a few seconds before she diverted her eyes and dipped her head.

'I've been to Lam Tsuen this afternoon to make a wish,' I said, interrupting the silence.

'The tree is impotent, a plastic replica, no power,' she scoffed.

'Yes, so I discovered, but I hung my wish on the original old tree.' I took out my mobile. 'I'll show you the photograph.'

She looked to check out my claim. 'What did you wish?'

'You would again wear my ring.'

She nodded thoughtfully, maintaining eye contact, before getting up and going to the bedroom, returning with a wooden casket. She rummaged inside, took out the ring and placed it on the table between us.

'You can see if it still fits,' she said, her voice quavering, eyes liquid with tears.

I held out my hand, she placed her left hand on mine. I eased on the ring. Tears trickled down her cheeks. I moved around the table and took her in my arms, calling her name. We hugged and kissed; she cried, of course she did. I cried, of course I did. We made love, of course we did.

Whilst cuddled in Fong's arms I noticed a bare picture hook on the wall at the end of the bed.

'A print of the Chagall painting we saw at the hotel when we first made love was hung there. It meant so much to me.'

'I remember it well. What happened to it?'

'When you stopped writing I threw it away ... the memory too hurtful.'

I decided to replace the painting. Next morning, the hotel receptionist directed me to a print shop off Nathan Road. An obliging young technician downloaded a copy off the internet, printed it, cut a mount, and framed it whilst I drank a coffee in a café opposite. With Mai Ling's connivance, the picture was hung whilst Fong and I were out food shopping.

When we returned, Fong went to the bedroom to change and I made tea, trying to keep a straight face. She came to the door in a dressing gown, and with a coy smile suggested my presence was required in the bedroom.

Chapter 33

I returned to Eastbourne in a state of elation: reconciled with Fong, her love revived. We had both drained our reservoirs of disappointments, frustrations and regrets and felt a great weight removed from our consciences. My last few days in Hong Kong were a glorious celebration of found love and bonding with our daughter.

My final evening saw a gathering of kith and kin at a restaurant in Wanchai cementing my position within the family. A dozen of us sat around a circular table and a veritable feast appeared, the dishes continually replenished. Zhi Ming was present, a business like personality with no obvious warmth accompanied by an equally cool girlfriend. I thought of revealing his father but decided against, instead having an interesting discussion concerning the Hong Kong and UK property markets. He boasted he had secured the purchase of Chi Wah's flat at an advantageous price, without it being offered on the open market.

"Old trees have deep roots" the Chinese say and Fong and I decided her living in England or my moving to Tai Po were both impractical and not what either of us wanted. Instead, in the spring of 2015, I sold the flat in Coventry to fund extended regular stays in Hong Kong and holidays for Fong and Chi Wah in England. Meanwhile social media and Skype video phone calls kept us in daily contact while I made arrangements to return for an extended stay in the autumn – the temperate season in Hong Kong.

Lodging with Fong or overnight stays was not a regular option, a matter of propriety. When accompanying Fong out and about in Tai Po we observed a social formality devoid of obvious familiarity; an eligible widow to be seen out with a non Chinese man would be frowned upon. Outside of Tai Po, where she was not known, we acted the courting couple in effect we were, getting to know each other again. We had both changed on the outside as the years had taken their toll, but not changed on the inside in how we felt about each other.

I stayed in what the Italians would call a pensione, frequented by backpackers hiking the New Territories. The single storey building was in much need of repair, but the basic accommodation clean. Each morning I reluctantly ploughed through a bowl of sticky congee and cruller sticks and pickled vegetables. I longed for a bacon-and-eggs fry-up, but Fong's friends, whose family owned the place, were keen on integrating me into Chinese life. Afterwards I would catch the 64K bus into Tai Po and meet up with Fong to shop or sightsee, play mah-jong with friends or dine with Mai Ling and Chi Wah.

Under Fong's guidance I experienced the sights and sounds, tastes and aromas particular to the various districts and ancient walled villages of the New Territories, the verdant scenery and country walks a total contrast to the bustling concrete city. I adopted the mantle of an experienced ex-pat colonial as I gradually assimilated into provincial life and Fong's circle of friends. I learned a few greetings and useful phrases in Cantonese, although with no hope of fluency even at conversational level.

We were happy together, making up for the lost decades as best we could, making love when the sap rose, although I had to admit to a frustrating libido, the mind willing the body less so.

'My first orgasms in thirty-seven years,' she sighed as we lay together.

'I cannot claim the same record but in thirty-seven years I've never been happier.' Never happier because I had once more recognised the look of unconditional love.

The extended holiday arrangement obliged us to make each precious day count, as it had in our halcyon days in Grimsby. It was not the romantic Utopia I had dreamed, unlike the ending of *Letters to Juliet,* but a welcome compromised reality. Vanessa Redgrave and Franco Nero's film painted a happily-ever-after picture, but their reality was also compromised, beset by tragedy. Within a few months Vanessa's sister, Lynn, and brother, Colin, died unexpectedly and Vanessa suffered a debilitating heart attack.

The misfortunes of their story and ours had disturbing parallels: a brief affair, unable to commit, siring a child, reconciling after thirty-seven years, and loss of a daughter. It was as if seeing the film had brought our lives together by ominous coincidences or by a menacing paranormal phenomenon. I had no brother or sister but I had lost a daughter and son. Fong and I watched a DVD of *Letters to Juliet* and afterwards I casually enquired the reason for Fong's mother's death.

'Heart attack,' she said soulfully.

'Does your family have a history of heart conditions?'

'Not to my knowledge.'

'What about your father?'

'He died in car crash.'

'Yes I know, but could a heart attack have been the cause?'

'There was no autopsy ... the crash blamed on the typhoon weather. Why do you ask?'

'I think you and Mai Ling should have a medical check up.'

I told her my reasons, the film and Vanessa Redgrave's heart attack and the ominous life coincidences. Fong remained sceptical but with a superstitious nature and to placate my concerns agreed to be checked out. To my relief a couple of weeks later, she reported an electrocardiogram (ECG) revealed no heart abnormalities.

I never envisaged marrying again but wanting more of our precious time together on my visits, to live as a couple, was only possible if we married to maintain Fong's reputation. So it came to pass I was led to the registrar's altar in Tai Po, clad in a dark suit tailored locally – none of my casual clothes appropriate.

The ceremony was a brief, no frills, formal affair attended by a handful of relatives and friends. At the end of the service a red silk band was wrapped about us symbolically binding us together as established by Yue Lao, the God of love and marriage.

After the ceremony we hailed a taxi to the Laochouxing Temple in Kowloon to pray for a long life (Laoshouxing the God of Longevity). We had been given a veritable collection of Laochouxing effigies and icons as wedding presents.

The cab dropped us at the head of a narrow side street congested with vehicles and locals. We trudged up the hill and after fifty metres or so entered the temple entrance via a wide alley sided by ramshackle buildings with every balcony strewn with washing. Here we ran the gauntlet of stalls selling statuettes and pictures of Laoshouxing and Buddha idols, but our proverbial mantelpiece was full. Two beggars, a scrawny, wizened old woman and a ragged amputee with one leg, tugged at my conscience and emptied my pockets of loose change.

The ornately painted and sculpted entrance arch opened on to a courtyard set behind high white stone walls. A bell and drum tower lay silent to one side.

In front of us steps led to the outer hall of the temple. A life size ceramic effigy of Laoshouxing confronted us: an elderly bald gent with wispy beard cloaked in a colourful gown laden with symbolic images. To the side, a row of larger than life golden Buddha stared critically, with one exception: a monastically clad, pot-bellied, laughing portrayal. I paused, engaged by the smile and remembered Fong mentioning the resemblance to her priest. Fong explained this Buddha was laughing at the unimportance of human adversity.

We climbed a short run of steps to the dimly lit inner temple and removed our shoes. The air was heavy with the aroma of tallow from huge candles. Fragrant incense wafted from bulbous bronze censers. Hallowed shuffling of feet and dutiful murmuring of prayers whispered from the gloom. Three giant gilded Buddha representing the three ages – past, present and future – dominated the rear wall.

The altar took centre stage, replete with a myriad of pots and vases, miniature figures, sprigs of lotus blossom and offerings of fruit. Elderly women, clad in black like Italian widows, pottered replacing withered fruit and wilted blooms. Beside a stone cauldron, a solemn young woman tossed in offerings of votive money, burned for a departed relative.

Fong knelt and quietly murmured her prayer requesting Laochouxing to grant us a long marriage. I stood and watched, sceptical of her belief in one of hundreds of Gods worshipped by the Chinese. We collected our shoes and made our way to the garden of meditation and remembrance. As we entered the garden Fong paused and gazed up into the canopy of branches and leaves.

'Trees house spirits,' she remarked, 'this is a feng shui grove, a place for good spirits to live. The trees were planted by relatives in honour of dear departed, some hundreds of years ago. I wish for my ashes to be buried here.'

I looked around. An elaborately carved and painted wooden bridge arched over an ornamental pool overhung by a weeping willow. The bridge led to a miniature replica of the ancient pagoda which once towered over the area, destroyed by fire during the Japanese occupation in 1937. Tree stumps and smooth rocks afforded rustic seating. A wafting breeze cooled the air and the towering trees shaded the midday sun. The high surrounding walls muffled the cacophony from the neighbourhood streets and an essence of tranquillity prevailed: birds tweeted, butterflies fluttered, leaves rustled, water trickled.

'I visit here regularly to contemplate life and memories,' she said quietly.

'I remember you mentioning it at the café in Lincoln; the *Willow Pattern* crockery reminded you of this garden. I can see why.'

We sat in contemplation for a few minutes before returning to Tai Po whereupon I dutifully carried Fong over the threshold and consummated the marriage. Later, we took a taxi with Mai Ling to a local restaurant, where we were joined by the wedding guests for a sumptuous feast.

Chapter 34

For the next three years I became a "frequent flyer" travelling back and forth to Hong Kong, staying up to three months in the better seasons of the years. The gaps back in England made us hungry for each other's company and allowed space to live out the lives and friendships accustomed to prior to our reunion.

Hong Kong was not a happy place; the populace rising up against Beijing's stifling of free speech and in support of the semblance of democracy bequeathed by the British which Beijing was determined to erode. It had all started back in 2014. I remember it well because it rained.

Friday 14 November 2014, I pandered to the folderol of another birthday, my sixty-sixth, with a meal at a Cantonese restaurant accompanied by a handful of friends. It rained and we needed umbrellas. In Hong Kong, the Sun shone, the temperature thirty degrees, but tens-of-thousands needed umbrellas to deflect the rain of pepper spray and tear gas fired by Hong Kong's police.

Thus the "Umbrella Movement" formed, in protest at the Government's changes to Hong Kong's electoral system denying universal suffrage, ensuring only pro-Beijing candidates could contest the office of Chief Executive. Edward Leung, Fong's cousin – espousing pro-independence and democracy – was denied candidacy and Beijing's puppet, Carrie Lam (Cheng Yuet-ngor), elected in 2017.

The Government made no concessions and the "Umbrella Movement" petered out after seventy nine days of relatively peaceful protest. Fong, Chi Wah, Chi Mai and Mai Ling had involved themselves in the protests in support of their cousin, Edward.

Fast forward to 2019 and Chi Wah wrote she had again raised her umbrella in concert with hundreds-of-thousands of others. The pro-democracy demonstrations were triggered by the Government's introduction of "The Fugitive Offenders Amendment Bill" allowing the transfer of Hong Kong miscreants and political activists to mainland China to face trial and incarceration. The Bill undermined the region's autonomy and its people's civil liberties. The Hong Kong judiciary was accepted as largely independent, the mainland judiciary corrupt at the behest of the regime.

People remembered peaceful protest did not achieve concessions in 2014 and the 2019 activists resorted to violence to further their aims and in retaliation to disproportionate police force. In October, the government withdrew the Extradition Bill, but the demonstrations morphed into a movement for democracy and a halt to the steady erosion of civil rights enshrined in the 1997 Sino-British treaty.

Sustained disruption and violence had produced results but violence also brought tragedies: two young student protester fatalities, Chan Yim-lam and Alex Chow Tsz-lok. Many thousands were arrested and hundreds injured requiring hospital treatment. A girl student lost an eye from a bean-bag round fired by police, creating the #Eye4HK martyr campaign on social media. Many protesters took to wearing symbolic red eye patches.

As the new decade commenced the protests continued in pursuit of other key demands: an inquiry into police conduct, the release of jailed protesters and the resignation of Carrie Lam. Chi Wah advised I postpone my intended visit because the protests were causing disruption at the airport and she was involved in a support capacity, supplying food, water, medical aid, and filming police counteroffensives.

I sympathised with the democratic aims of the movement and applauded the heroism of its supporters but, with fatherly concern, pleaded with her to limit her involvement. The news media reported an escalation of police brutality and increasing use of munitions: rubber bullets, sponge grenades, bean bag rounds, pepper spray, dyed water cannons and tear gas. There were allegations of torture and gang-rape of women. The Chinese government pressurised employers to sack employees involved in the protests. Chi Wah promised to be careful; she and Fong would come to England in the summer of 2020.

They never arrived.

Chi Wah became the third protester fatality and symbol of the #Life4FreeHK martyr campaign on social media. She was filming a demonstration from a bridge – for propaganda – when a policeman, cornered by protesters, drew his pistol and fired a warning shot into the air. The bullet ricocheted off a lamp post and hit Chi Wah in the chest, causing her to topple from the bridge to her death.

Fong and I were engulfed by despair, broken-hearted, our love child gone, and by such a freak accident. Apart from tearful commiserating phone conversations, we were unable to comfort each other in our grief, separated by the travel restrictions imposed because of the Covid-19 virus pandemic. Perversely, Covid-19 did, for a few months, what the Chinese authorities failed to do in stopping the protest marches.

'It was written by the Gods,' Fong cried.

It was certainly following the Redgrave script, whose daughter

Lynn had also died in an unforeseen bizarre accident.

I sought solace in the nostalgic comfort blanket of *Casablanca*, first watched in awe aged seven. The film had always acted as a comfort line on which to hang the memories of my washed out and, for the most part, washed-up amorphous life. It was the movie I returned to in periods of depression and need, from the death of my father, to the death of Simon, to the demise of Samantha, to the passing of Janet. It helped to assuage the dark periods after the loss of Fong's address; the melancholy of Sam's singing brought on tears for all the miles and years of separation Fong and I suffered and the missed childhood years of Chi Wah.

For the next few days I binged on a dozen or so of my favourite films and a diet of alcohol and snacks. My appetite dissolved in the alcohol – poor me, pour another syndrome – and I had no inclination to cook. The films and alcohol engendered a ritualistic calm, an emotional consoling distraction away from the hurt and vacuum of her loss.

Hong Kong is renowned for the world's highest property prices and with the loss of Chi Wah's income, Chi Mai was unable to finance the mortgage. I offered to help and from the proceeds of sale of the Coventry flat transferred $HK 1,000,000 (approx £110,000) to reduce her mortgage liability in exchange for a twenty-five per cent share.

Chi Mai tested positive for Covid-19 but with the benefit of youth her symptoms were relatively mild. Fong and Mai Ling thankfully remained unaffected. In the spring of 2020, despite the risks of Covid-19 contagion, there were fresh protests against the proposed National Security Law, imposed on 30 June. The provisions were so draconian – criminalising almost all opposition and dissent – meaningful protest was stifled. A police hotline allowed the anonymous reportage of fellow citizens for breaches of the legislation.

'Every citizen now lives in fear of his neighbour,' Fong commented, 'a throwback to the division and mistrust of the Cultural Revolution. State interference is more oppressive than the humidity of the typhoon season.'

The protest motivators were rounded up and the independent members of the legislature resigned en-bloc in protest at the arrest of their leader and the barring of pro-democracy legislators from standing in future elections.

All this was deeply concerning and Fong kept me informed with digital copies of *Apple Daily*, the pro-democracy tabloid newspaper. However, there was no reason to further delay my visit and I eagerly pined for Fong's company and to share her bed again. I had not seen her for eighteen months, although we had kept in almost daily contact by video link over Skype.

The Covid-19 restrictions were largely lifted during the autumn 2020 and with the new Covid testing facility at Heathrow I would not need to quarantine upon arrival in Hong Kong. I booked my flight for a three month stay to celebrate Christmas and Chinese New Year the following February.

In November, as I sat sipping coffee and reading *The Times* in a café in Eastbourne, the uncanny premonition of a heart attack materialised. The Redgrave curse completed. I had a phone call from Mai Ling. She was sobbing uncontrollably, hardly able to speak, but eventually blurted out her message.

'Fong was dead ... a heart condition.'

She died on my birthday and my will to live died with her. The devastation felt reached the core of my being, seeped into the marrow of my bones, coursed with the blood to my heart. I experienced an unpleasant shivering sensation and for a few seconds suspected a heart attack. Tears blurred my vision and I gritted my teeth with the physical effort of desperately trying not to fall apart. Staff and other patrons realising my distress offered help and called a taxi.

At the bungalow I fell upon the bed curling into the foetus position and surrendered to a heaving outpouring of ineffable sorrow. Tears flowed like a severed artery, pouring through fingers veiling my face until the ducts ran dry. I sat upon the edge of the bed gently rocking back and forth, reduced to a shivering numbness as I drowned in overpowering grief and remorse.

After a while, unsure how many hours had passed, I lay on the bed staring at the ceiling, gazing into a distant void stretching back through the decades of my life; a life full of regret for the woman I had loved and hurt and lost, the happiness regained for a few years now cruelly denied its rightful place in our disparate lives. So much for Fong's belief in God Laochouxing; I had been right to be sceptical, as I was of any God. Still wearing day clothes, I eventually succumbed to the exhaustion of sleep.

Next morning, I peered at the bathroom mirror. A crumpled, ghostly clone stared back, with puffed-up eyelids, blotchy cheeks and matted hair. I rubbed my hands roughly across my face as if expecting to erase the stain of grief. The pale reflection in the unsparing halogen lights stared back questioning what to do next.

Chinese mythology asserts life on Earth is insignificant, ancient scripts, poems and paintings depicting another world of pleasure and contentment where couples love and co-exist unto eternity. I may not believe in God but I had to believe in an afterlife; there I would make amends by loving and looking after Fong.

Charles Boyer was a great screen lover spanning forty years and had held in his arms all the great and beautiful actresses of the day. But he fell in love at first sight with my namesake, actress Elizabeth (Pat) Patterson. Pat died of a brain tumour and two days later Charles committed suicide. Pat was half of everything in Charles's life; consumed with grief he rejoined with her in the afterlife. Fong was my Pat. Like Charles, fate had dealt me the cruellest of cards and I saw only the ace of spades in my hand.

Chapter 35

I told Mai Ling of my intention to join Fong in the afterlife, but in a heartfelt plead she persuaded me to use my booked flight to attend the burial ceremony of Fong's ashes in the Laoshouxing Temple's garden of remembrance.

The first evening of my arrival, Mai Ling invited me to dinner at her flat. We hugged and sobbed the moment she opened the door. Dinner was postponed and we ended up in bed. Neither of us knew why, we had no intention of pursuing a relationship; the intimacy of nakedness seemed consoling, a measure of love in our time of need. Later, when our emotions could bear the sorrow I asked what happened to Fong.

'How ... why did she die?'

'She collapsed at home while preparing lunch ... I found her after work. The pathologist found no heart abnormalities and the verdict was death from cardiac arrest due to Sudden Arrhythmic Death Syndrome.'

'I've never heard of that.'

'Apparently it's quite common, many people die from it in Hong Kong each year. Our doctor said she had no chance to call for help; she would have been dead before she hit the floor. It's probably a genetic condition. I am to attend the hospital for screening to see if I'm also at risk.'

'I did suggest a couple of years ago you and Fong have a heart check-up because your mother succumbed to a heart attack.'

'Yes, and Fong did have a check up but it revealed nothing untoward.'

'Cruelly ironic to be the cause of her demise; a good heart her defining attribute.'

'Perhaps she gave too much of her heart away to others,' she mused.

The next day we arranged to meet at the Laoshouxing Temple for a meeting with Fong's priest, primarily to request permission for the interring of Fong's ashes, a mere formality according to Mai Ling. I wanted to meet him since he was instrumental in Fong coming to England. When I arrived Mai Ling was sat on a wooden bench in the courtyard with Chi Mai.

'Before our meeting, we will pay our respects to Chi Wah's grave,' said Mai Ling. We entered the garden of meditation and remembrance. 'Chi Wah's ashes are buried over there near the stream,' she said, pointing.

A plum tree sapling with small plaque beneath marked the spot.

"Chi Wah
(1977 – 2019)
#Life4FreeHK"

'A whole life expressed between two brackets and a forlorn hope attached to a hash.' I sighed.

'The hash will give her life immortality,' said Chi Mai.

We stood, eyes closed, in contemplation of her abbreviated life. Chi Mai watered the sapling from the stream. Mai Ling glanced at her watch and indicated it was time for our audience. Through a side gate we crossed a courtyard and entered the monks' refectory, an austere bare brick hall with vaulted ceiling rafters, housing plain wooden tables and benches as hard as Lincoln's oak pews.

Mai Ling introduced herself to an orange robed young acolyte who reverentially bowed and scurried off. He soon returned and ushered us into a smaller adjoining room. A half opened window captured shafts of sunlight which cut through the mist of incense and tallow.

The priest shuffled in, his timeworn face and stooped gait placed his birth into the last imperial dynasty. A long, silken, silvery beard hung from his shaven head. As Fong once remarked he had the rotund shape and fatherly countenance of the smiling Buddha, a resemblance no doubt influential with the local congregation. He acknowledged us with a bow and grimaced with pain as he sat cross-legged, but there was no denying the sparkle of joviality in his moist eyes. He gestured we join him and sit on the mats provided. I also grimaced with discomfort as I mirrored his pose.

He spoke to Mai Ling and Chi Mai in Cantonese. From a heavy cast iron kettle the young assistant poured green tea into small porcelain cups before retiring to sit cross-legged on the floor, apparently adopting a meditative trance. My apprehension evaporated with the priest's kindly smile and perfect English.

'You are most welcome Chris.'

'I'm relieved you speak English. I'm told you were educated in Britain.'

'Yes, I took a degree in English at Cambridge and studied theology in London.'

'Thank you for encouraging Fong to come to England.'

'I wanted to broaden her life experience before her father obliged she marry. I understand the two of you formed a deep attachment, but misfortune separated you. I was pleased to hear of your subsequent marriage and few years of happiness. Her passing is a tragic loss.' He paused to sip tea.

'I knew Fong well as my brother's wife and enjoyed her company and hospitality. She was kind and considerate, sensitive and generous. Her life had not been easy, working long hours, catering to the demands of a family and coping with my brother's premature demise. She regularly worshipped at this temple and sought enlightenment through meditation in our garden.'

'Enlightenment?'

'Peace within herself Chris, through emotional and moral self transformation. After meeting you and experiencing the allure of love and the prospect of a more liberated life in England, she suffered the heartbreak of your separation and pending birth of your child. She reluctantly had to accept an arranged marriage and life of traditional Chinese values. It was a traumatic time for her and she came to me for guidance.'

He paused with a despairing sigh and drank tea. 'You see Chris, much of what life throws at us is not under our control, but Fong came to realise what Buddha understood, we can control the way our minds react to those things, leading to spiritual harmony and a contentment with life despite its many disappointments. This was Fong's way of surviving in the absence of a great love to support and nourish her in an otherwise bland cuisine of life.'

He sipped more tea and offered refills to our cups; Mai Ling obliged.

'Fong was what we Chinese call *ru*, meaning someone of genuine gentle nature. She was compassionate but not submissive; she had the strength of mind to forebear a life she did not desire and devote herself to her family. Attaining enlightenment – nirvana – was her means of reducing the pain and torment of memories, but they would not leave her however much she tried to erase them.'

'I suffered the torment of memories of her,' I said quietly, 'but I never wanted to erase them; they're the most treasured memories of my life. It's why I desperately sought to find her, to make sure she knew how much I loved her, to make amends for us living the wrong lives.'

We sat motionless as if absorbing the sorrow.

'Chris, Mai Ling has confided her concern you feel you have no reason to live now Fong has been taken from you. No matter how special Fong was to you, she is but one person. You cannot be serious in thinking now she has departed the whole world is empty of persons who matter to you. Your love for her cannot conquer death, so it must take its place in life. Love does not mean belonging for all time; death is a separation.'

'She should have been my life,' I protested. 'I have to believe in the afterlife and join her to give her the love denied for most of this life. Does not Chinese culture assert love will endure after death, life is transient and we pass from this life to another?'

'Ah yes, we all have to believe in the afterlife, although a potential reunion with a loved one on the other side may not be so for you. God may not look kindly upon your extramarital affair with Fong, breaking the vows you made in His house on your wedding day. I am sorry to play the role of ... ahem ... devil's advocate, but your dubious rationale for joining Fong may not be substantiated in the eyes of God.'

'I thought God's profession was forgiveness and compassion,' I responded, 'after all we did eventually marry. However it matters not; I can believe in an afterlife, but not in a God capable of inflicting the torment of our separated lives and ending our reconciliation so soon. I can't believe in a God who allowed the senseless death of Chi Wah by a freak event.'

'I think you need to reappraise your idea of the concept of God as a being with human emotions and attributes; God is a higher being who does not meddle in the everyday lives of us humans. We are left to decide our own destiny.'

He paused in thought and offered more tea before continuing.

'It is an established romantic notion to take one's life during a period of despair when love has been denied. But you have a duty to life. Life is sacrosanct, a gift no one except God has the right to take away,' he said, raising an admonishing finger.

'Some Christians seek death in imitation of Jesus who died voluntarily on the cross,' I responded. 'They believe if life has become unbearable you are justified in ending it.'

'Your life is by no measure too hard to bear Chris; it's only *almost* unbearable. When one love is thwarted another blossoms in its wake; you have two people here who care for you,' he gestured with an open hand towards Mai Ling and Chi Mai. 'I'm sure their need for your life is greater than your need for death.'

I looked across to Mai Ling and Chi Mai who both smiled and nodded agreement. I returned their smiles. I had to admit life was bearable but I no longer wished to bear it, preferring to believe that I would live with Fong and Chi Wah in another life, in a better world. My mind made up, I would join them upon my return to England.

'Regarding the burial of Fong's ashes,' he continued, 'I agree she should be interred here. You have my permission and blessing. Now if you will excuse me, I need to rest before my other duties.'

He stood with arthritic discomfort and placed his hands palm to palm in front of his chest, bowing slightly to us as he did so.

We stood and I thanked him for enlightening me on Fong's life and for his life affirming counsel. I proffered a hand which he took in both his.

'Do think on what I have said. I can tell you are loved by Chi Mai and Mai Ling,' he said seriously. He turned and shuffled out followed by his young assistant.

We took a taxi to Chi Mai's flat in Kowloon. After brewing tea we visited a local street market for provisions and the women cooked dinner while I again enjoyed the photo album. After dinner they made a proposal.

'We wish to commemorate Fong's death with a living life form as we have done for Chi Wah. When a loved one dies an ancient Chinese custom is to plant a sapling in the soil above their grave. Their bodies morph into a living organism of leaves, blossom and fruit. In some parts of China there are sacred woodlands of such trees where people's spirits live on in this world. Do you know the mythical tale of lovers Philemon and Baucis?'

'I'm afraid not,' I replied, shaking my head.

'God granted their wish to die and be reunited for eternity, turning them into trees – Philemon to an oak and Baucis to a linden – planted side by side for their roots and branches to intertwine. If we plant trees for you and Fong they will intertwine as your limbs did when you loved Fong and conceived Chi Wah.'

'What a lovely notion and befitting Fong's interest in Greek mythology. In Vienna lived an artist, Friedenreich Hundertwasser, who was a passionate green ecology activist. Hundertwasser advocated the planting of a tree over a person's grave; not only would this help in the fight against global warming, but relatives could imagine the person's spirit living on in an alternative life form. Hundertwasser envisioned vast consecrated forests of people's spirits. It will be comforting to think Fong and I will be remembered in a rejuvenated life form, a symbol of resurrection.'

'We Chinese have a strong belief in the afterlife. We make offerings to our dearly departed to continue our respect. Her spiritual plum tree will be our shrine; we will burn incense in constant remembrance. When it blossoms we will know she is happy, it will bear fruit so she can eat, we will water it so she can drink.'

'Why a plum blossom tree?'

'Plum blossom is beloved flower in Chinese culture and represents the transitory nature of this life and fruition towards the next life.'

'Will my ashes be accepted for burial? I'm neither Chinese nor a

Buddhist believer.'

'Father Cheung Mah will not be with us much longer,' replied Mai Ling. 'Your ashes will be presented to his replacement for interment and blessing as Fong's husband and Chi Wah's father. All will be okay.' They nodded assuredly.

'Where are Fong's ashes now?'

'They are here. Would you like to see them?'

'I would love to hold them.'

She handed the small ceramic urn with conical lid, decorated with a blue-and-white pattern of intertwined blossom. I hugged it to my heart. I felt my eyes fill and tears escaped down my cheek; my body heaved, overwhelmed with sadness.

Mai Ling embraced me.

'It's good to let all the emotion out,' she said sympathetically.

I kissed the urn, handed it back to Chi Mai and dried my eyes.

'Why doesn't Chris accompany you to hospital tomorrow,' said Chi Mai. Give you more time together and he will meet Andy Yeo.'

'Who is Andy Yeo?'

'Andy is Consultant Cardiologist at Nathan Park Hospital, a family friend. He can explain Fong's death.'

'I would like to meet him.'

We bid Chi Mai goodnight and I walked Mai Ling to the KCR station.

'Where shall we meet tomorrow?'

'My appointment is ten o'clock. You could stay at my flat and we could go together.'

'You only have one bed.'

'Yes ... one bed.' She nodded, smiling shyly.

Chapter 36

The clinically white edifice of Nathan Park Hospital soared to thirty floors, the reception area as large and busy as a main railway station concourse. A sea of sober Chinese impatiently waited like passengers from a cancelled train. A white coated Asian doctor headed a procession of students, hurrying through like a train not stopping at this station.

A lift whooshes us up eight floors to Cardiology where assuring smiles from nurses prevailed upon patients to reciprocate with nervous simpers of hope. We registered and waited to be called by the dual language digital display.

Andy Yeo, aged about forty, grey suit, glasses, short black hair, listened intently between smiles and nods as Mai Ling rattled away in Cantonese explaining my presence.

He turned to me. 'Let me explain Chris. Yuk Fong died of cardiac arrest. She had no previous symptoms and the pathologist found no physical heart abnormality. In such cases we attribute death to Sudden Arrhythmia Death Syndrome, SADS for short, a catch all term for conditions of irregular heart rhythm leading to ventricular failure.

It's a genetic defect and can be hereditary which is why Mai Ling is here to be screened. The procedure takes but a few minutes and is non invasive. An electrocardiogram (ECG) tests for the heart's electrical activity to detect abnormal heart rhythms affecting the blood supply to the ventricles, the two main cavities of the heart. This condition, known as ventricle fibrillation, leads to cardiac arrest or brain damage. A sonic scan using an echocardiograph will allows us to look at the condition of Mai's heart and how well it's performing.'

'Fong had an ECG a few years ago and it showed no abnormality,' I said accusingly.

'Unfortunately an ECG only shows the rhythm of the heart at the time performed. In Fong's case there were no symptoms to indicate the necessity for further evaluation. The condition has a high degree of unpredictability; in Hong Kong over two-hundred persons die each year from unexplained cardiac arrest.'

'Thank you for the explanation, but I can't help thinking more tests should have been completed, knowing her mother also died of cardiac arrest.'

'In retrospect maybe; but probably Fong did not have a detectable defect at the time, three or more years ago. Gene defects technology and data incidence within a family line has advanced in recent years.'

There was a resigned pause and I could sense he was not amenable to further discuss Fong's case and we left his office to get Mai Ling tested.

An hour later Andy Yeo looked at Mai's test results. 'We know you have the same defective gene as Fong and the computer has measured a small electrical disturbance, fibrillation, in your heart but nothing serious. There are a variety of medicines available to restore normal heart rhythm.

The condition can also be caused by an overactive thyroid gland.' He scribbled notes on a form and handed it to Mai Ling. 'Take this form down to haematology for a blood test. If your thyroid is okay I would prescribe a beta blocker to stabilise your heart beat, and low dose Aspirin to reduce the chance of blood clots.'

After giving her ampoule of blood we were glad to exit into glorious sunshine.

'We will eat now,' she said, 'I know a good restaurant in the next parade.'

After lunch we spent the rest of the day sightseeing. She took a message from Chi Mai on her mobile; priest Cheung Mah had agreed to conduct Fong's ashes ceremony in two days time. The girls had probably made a donation to the temple for the privilege, but would not hear of my contributing.

Witnessed by Mai Ling, Chi Mai, Zhi Ming, Edward Leung and me, Fong's ashes were reverently poured into the shallow earth work around the roots of a cherry sapling. The ashes were covered with soil and Father Cheung Mah blessed the ground and recited a prayer commemorating Fong's life and the goodness of her soul. I kissed a leaf and watered the tree. At its base, a simple ceramic plaque:

"Leung Yuk Fong
Beloved
1952 – 2021"

Despite Father Chung Mah's impassioned plea regarding the sacrosanctity of life, my life, I confided in Mai Ling that I would not return to Hong Kong to witness Fong's tree bear fruit. As a believer in the next life, she understood. I would make arrangements for my ashes to be sent to her for interment alongside Fong. My Will would make her the main beneficiary of my estate. The night before I left I again shared her bed. I wasn't sure why, but the intimacy seemed right for us in the knowledge we would not see each other again. It was a tearful farewell at Chek Lap Kok airport.

Chapter 37

After Fong's demise I began to write a memoir, a saga of my life told from the day I met her. It proved cathartic, emotionally heart-rending at times but overall heart-warming – recalling events, expressing feelings, musing on remembrances, feeding my nostalgia – as if writing letters to her. I hoped it would be read after my death.

The day after I returned from Hong Kong I awoke with a feeling of pervasive reluctance towards the future in this life. Calling upon the Grim Reaper to wield his scythe with the belief of being reunited with Fong and Chi Wah in the next life was, in the best literary romantic tradition, proof of my undying love. Melodramatic to be sure, but the essence of a great love is inevitably overemotional and often tragic.

From the days of my mother's milk, food and drink had nurtured every significant occasion in my life and I wasn't about to depart this world without a last meal, breakfast. I wondered what other people chose for their final repast. Surfing the internet for inspiration produced a list of last suppers requested by condemned prisoners, a customary right preceding execution. There was nothing of gastronomic inspiration nurtured by fine hospitality, merely a philistine litany of fast food loaded with carbohydrates.

A healthy diet is hardly priority for a last supper, even if you believed in an afterlife. *The* Last Supper, unleavened bread and red wine, whilst appropriate for a devout Christian, was unpalatably chaste for a carnivorous atheist and unbefitting for a hearty breakfast.

Were there any movie last breakfast scenarios? I recalled one, a tour de force by actor Dennis Price in *Kind Hearts and Coronets*. The film opens with Louis D'Ascoyne imbibing claret and writing his memoires in a prison cell. To avenge his mother's rejection by her titled relatives for marrying a commoner, Louis has scythed his way through the male line of the aristocratic D'Ascoyne family to inherit the mantle of 10th Duke of Chalfont. His grace is due to be hung at 8 am. The prison warden enquires of his wishes for what would be his last breakfast. "Just coffee and a slice of toast thank you. Oh and perhaps a few grapes."

Louis considers it indecently early for a conventional breakfast. I had no such qualms at 8 am and I'm almost ashamed to admit to my favourite meal, a traditional breakfast redolent of a greasy spoon café: a fry-up of bacon and eggs and tomatoes and mushrooms and fried bread. An hour later I was scraping the plate of this scrumptious fare which I hoped would be on the menu in the afterlife café at the end of the galaxy, or wherever.

I wondered if Auguste Pahud breakfasted before his hanging suicide. My loss of Fong was as deeply unbearable as his beloved Annie. I had considered joining Auguste by his method, but didn't fancy the slow suffocation depicted in films when the noose failed to break the spinal cord.

Opening my veins in a soothing warm bath and drifting slowly away as the water coloured red, would have been an option except the bungalow had only a shower cubicle.

Shovelling tablets down my throat was not particularly appetising and there was the danger of survival with brain or other organ damage.

In deciding upon an acceptable modus operandi the sagacity of an elderly acquaintance came to mind. The tempo of Eastbourne had agreed with my intended andante lifestyle of retirement, but I was persuaded to work part time for an independent estate agency after socialising with the owner.

Following a valuation I befriended the elderly lady who was considering selling her flat and moving to a residential care home. She was still active, although had recently given up driving, both on the roads and on the golf course. She was compos mentis – reading *The Times* every day – managed her finances, shopped for and cooked her own meals. I liked her and encouraged her not to sell and to retain her independence for as long as possible.

The sale of her flat would provide about five years in a care home, at ninety, long enough you may think, except her family tree propagated branches of exceptional longevity.

'What will you do when the money runs out?'

'Jump into a taxi to Beachy Head,' she replied. 'You wouldn't even have to pay the driver, ask him to wait.'

I telephoned for a taxi to catch the noon low tide.

While I waited I made a final entry into my memoir. I decided I would pay the taxi fare not wanting to leave this world indebted or to occasion anyone's ill will towards my memory. I will have to look cheerful; it's known taxi drivers are on the lookout for singles with ulterior motives destined for Beachy Head. If asked, I would use the excuse of a walk and lunch at the pub as I've done a few times in the past.

Like a fixated lemming I will head determinedly up the familiar grassy slope, bending into the inevitable stiff breeze, past one of the cowered sparsely leafed trees leaning in the opposite direction. At the cliff edge I will check for the highest point with the eponymous red and white striped lighthouse below.

When younger I had no fear of heights, but in recent years

vertigo had been an unwelcome companion, but I don't think my annoying antagonist will care to accompany today, fear renounced along with the desire for life. Five-hundred-and-thirty-feet below, the rocky tombstones of the legion before will beckon.

I don't fear death and I'm convinced I will have the courage to dive into space and complete the short journey – about five seconds – to another life.

There is a tradition of bereaved friends or relatives planting a wooden cross in the clifftop grass in remembrance. There should be a whole cemetery of crosses but someone must be charged with removing them. There will be no one to plant a cross for me.

As I approach the cliff edge I think the situation will seem somewhat surreal as if acting out a scene in a movie; I nostalgically muse about the many films to have used these infamous cliffs.

In the opening sequence to James Bond's *The Living Daylights*, the cliffs deputized for Gibraltar. *Chitty Chitty Bang Bang,* also written by Bond creator Ian Fleming, witnessed the car driving off the cliff top only to take flight like a 'Q' invention.

Thinking of 'Q' reminds me of *Quadrophenia*, in which a disillusioned mod drives his nemesis' motor scooter over the edge. The British 'B' movie *Smokescreen* opens with a blazing car hurtling over the edge in a tale of insurance fraud and murder.

The 2010 remake of Graham Greene's novel *Brighton Rock* and Enid Bagnold's *The Chalk Garden* used Beachy Head backdrops as did the tragic romance *Now is Good*, from a Jenny Downham novel.

One of my favourite comedy thrillers, *Hopscotch* – with the wonderful duo of Walter Matthau and Glenda Jackson – featured a staged mid-air explosion over the cliffs showering the sea around the lighthouse with aircraft debris.

I also recalled a disturbing documentary, *Beachy Head* (2002), featuring Bill Hull, the only person to have survived the big jump. One out of thousands; the odds are stacked as high as the cliffs in favour of my denouement.

I suppose there must be other films, unseen or forgotten. In all these films the cliffs and lighthouse produced a dramatic back drop but there were no deaths to live up to its reputation. In *The Living Daylights, Hopscotch* and *Smokescreen,* the deaths were faked.

Trolling through my film memories brought to mind one of cinema's most iconic deaths in Monty Python's *The Meaning of Life.* A man, Arthur Jarrett, is sentenced to death by a manner of his own choosing. He is chased by twelve topless, busty young women to a clifftop (at Dover) where he dives straight into his waiting grave – and funeral service – on the beach far below. Unfortunately there are no naked ladies to chase me. I will miss such wonderful interludes of silver screen escapism. Hopefully a cinema will be attached to the restaurant at the end of the galaxy or wherever the afterlife resides.

I have left my affairs in good order: my Will prominently displayed on my desk along with instructions for my cremation, the ashes to be sent to Mai Ling in Hong Kong.

Two letters await collection in the local postbox: a heartfelt goodbye to Mai Ling and Chi Mai with a copy of my will listing them as beneficiaries, and a few personal details for my obituary addressed to the *Eastbourne Standard.* My death will not attract a national headline, nor warrant an obituary entry in *The Times,* but the local rag? Maybe.

Yesterday I posted a package – a tobacco tin with the ashes of long ago letters and photographs – with an explanation addressed to the Museum of Broken Relationships, 6751 Hollywood Boulevard, Los Angeles, California. Similar museums exist elsewhere but none more appropriately located than Hollywood, where dreams are supposed to come true but more often don't.

The coroner's inquest will no doubt record my cause of death with the platitude: "He took his life whilst the balance of his mind was disturbed," the annoying label applied to anyone who deliberately tops himself. It is variously held by law, society and religion no sane man would take his own life. I must by inference be mad. I am mad, but in the sense of anger and exasperation at a life misspent: of underachievement, of woeful decisions, of wilful regret, of ruining another's life, the love of my life. I lived a life without the courage to seize the day, "carpe diem", as Robin Williams instilled into his students in *The Dead Poets' Society*.

I will look about for a last survey of the familiar vista. Craggy cliffs and rolling downs of the Seven Sisters sweep westward. The cliffs have been in need of a clean or coat of whitewash for years. A distant wind farm out to sea and the defunct clifftop Belle Tout lighthouse are the only interventions upon the natural beauty of this celebrated coastline. Further round the rolling downland fields will be speckled with grazing sheep, their shepherd's farm buildings nestling in a combe.

It's an inclement day and I expect the sea to look cold and grey unless the Sun breaks through the clouds creating bright spangles over towards Seaford. I don't expect ramblers or tourists to pay attention to my intention, but I have to avoid the chaplaincy volunteers.

Despondent souls from all over the country travel to Beachy Head, for it has acquired a perverse cachet of romance as a portal to the next life. Their numbers recently prompted a chaplaincy of volunteer Christians to patrol the cliffs, their duty to intercept and talk-out the dispirited leapers. I'm in no mood to be engaged by their persuasive patter: the grief counselling, the belief and saviour of religion.

I hope they will not feel too upset failing in their voluntary soul saving mission. I'm glad they will report my demise to the coast guard. Seagulls usually circle in front of the cliffs like expectant vultures for carrion and I take comfort in knowing my body will be recovered before satisfying their carnivorous appetites or being washed out to sea. My ashes have a journey to make.

The door bell chimes, the taxi awaits. From my desk I withdraw the faded dog-eared photo of Fong's smiling face. The photo, from the morning after the first night at the Laceby Hotel, was confirmation of the happiest hours of our lives. I kiss her lips and paste it onto the last page of my memoir.

Chapter 38

'You okay sir? Look as if you're going to a funeral,' I said with a chuckle.

'Yes, fine thank you,' he assured, 'often come up here for the view, a walk and pub lunch.'

'We have to be on the lookout for singles with ulterior motives up here,' I continued. 'Last month I brought a guy up here who never returned, if you get my drift.'

'I know what you mean mate,' he said, nodding with a thoughtful frown.

'My name is Eddie, ask for me when you want to come back, I'll give you a discount.'

He paid the £8 on the meter, gave me a tenner and refused the change. I thanked him and watched as he steadily climbed the slope towards the cliff edge. I parked the cab in the pub car park and radioed to tell the office I was off-air for lunch before following him at a discrete distance. I knew he wasn't coming back, despite the denial; he had the look of someone attending a funeral of a dear departed. Last month I'd done another solo trip to Beachy Head, the guy much younger but with the same resigned expression, the twenty-ninth to jump this year.

I looked on expectantly, waiting as he stood on the edge. Was he having second thoughts? A chaplain volunteer had noticed him, his agitated yellow jacket and swinging binoculars indicating the urgency of his stride as he hurried forward calling and waving.

'Go on you old fool. Get on with it. Don't want the bleeding chaplain talking you out of it,' I muttered to myself, pushing forward with my hands as if moving the air to topple him. Perhaps he felt the push of air, plunging as majestically as a diver into the town's swimming pool. I watched him extend his arms to form a cross with his body. Probably a religious nut or maybe a convert on the way down hedging his bets for the afterlife. Pascal's probability wager they call it: "You have more to gain by believing in God than not believing."

I saw the stain of blood and turned away with a faint pang of guilt. He was nothing to me but he had been honourable and paid the fare, I'd known others who didn't.

The chaplain raised both arms in outrage, frustration and disappointment; he also made the sign of the cross before taking out his mobile. I strode back to the cab and drove to the customer's address. If a partner was in I would be the bearer of the sad news. If not, suicides hardly ever lock up when they leave, easier for friends, neighbours and police to gain entry. Easy pickings, no one suspects a taxi parked in the street, the driver carrying a suitcase.

Have to be quick, small high value items, antiques, jewellery, watches and cash. No credit cards or phones, nothing with a traceable history. No televisions or hi-fi; things have to be left undisturbed, none of the usual signs of burglary; the reason I've never been caught, this guy my sixth victim in the past two years.

His bungalow was perfect: affluent area, quiet tree lined street, front door nicely shielded behind evergreen hedging. I rang the bell. No reply. I donned a pair of Marigold latex gloves and after a quick look around turned the door handle and pushed. The door opened.

'What did I tell you?' I muttered.

The wardrobes and bedroom drawers indicated a single male. A music lover, read novels and biographies. Unusual, a whole bookshelf on things Chinese: history, cook books, horoscopes and customs, the Cultural Revolution, Hong Kong travelogues and a copy of *The World of Suzie Wong*. A framed photograph showed him with his arm around a young Anglo-Chinese woman.

'Dirty old sod,' I whispered, 'old enough to be her father.'

On the dining room table a chess board laid with pieces ready to commence a game; a shelf lined with books on opening theory and famous games. A Georgian mantel clock ticked on a mahogany sideboard. It chimed the hour making me jump, for a split second I thought it was the door bell. I opened the rear panel door; good quality fusee movement. I detached the pendulum, wrapped the clock in a towel and carefully packed it into the case along with some silver pieces from the sideboard, a laptop computer and a couple of watches. From a desk drawer I removed £50 cash from a wallet.

An A4 leather bound folder sat on the desk. It appeared to be a hand written autobiography. What desperation had induced this guy to end it all? I always made a point of scouring the newspapers for information on previous victims so I added the folder to the suitcase.

Time to go. I zipped up the case and after closing the front door peeled off my yellow gloves. With the suitcase in the boot, I detoured home to hide the booty and clocked back on with the office. Later, I wiped clean the laptop's hard drive and telephoned my fence.

After dinner, I relaxed with a celebratory beer and started to read the memoir.

No one goes to Grimsby unless they have to, the name is so appropriate to the grim unromantic nowheresville on Britain's east coast ...

26 November 2021

EASTBOURNE STANDARD

ANOTHER VICTIM CLAIMED BY BEACHY HEAD

The Eastbourne lifeboat was summoned by the Beachy Head Chaplaincy to recover the body of a man later identified as 75 year old Christopher Patterson from the Upperton area of Eastbourne. He lived alone and had been suffering from depression since the death of his daughter in 2020 and second wife (of Chinese descent) in 2021. Mr Patterson's first wife, whom he divorced in 1981, and two children from that marriage also predeceased him.

Mr Patterson left a letter of explanation for his decision to take his own life with a request that he be cremated and his ashes sent to Hong Kong for burial.

Mr Patterson is the thirtieth victim this year prompting further calls for the South Downs National Park Authority to install preventative measures.

Chapter 39

Two years later, in a corner of the meditation garden of the Laoshouxing Temple, Hong Kong, three plum tree saplings burst into pink blossom. Two Chinese women reverently kneel before them in homage; tears of sadness and joy trickle down their cheeks.

Acknowledgements

I am grateful to the following without whom this book would not have been completed and published.

Julian Bailey, artist, for kind permission to use his artwork for the cover illustration.
Julian Sutherland-Beatson, artist and graphic designer, for advice and assistance with cover design and typography, and suggestions after reading of the script.
Jacq Malloy, creative writing tutor, for her tuition in the art of writing fiction, her encouragement, advice and editing of the narrative.
Janet McCallum, graphic designer for the layout of the text and advice.
Mike Tann, Ian Stopher and Peggy Westwood for reading the script and suggestions from a readers' perspective.
Viv Cecil, artist and website designer, for kindly designing and updating my two websites.

And

Ewa O'Donoghue, my long suffering partner, best friend and supporter for forty years.

Julian Bailey

The cover image, 'A Girl Looking Away', a drypoint etching and gouache artwork by Julian Bailey. Julian's recent works have focussed on the contemporary figure with an economy and freedom of line.

Julian has exhibited throughout the West Country and with many prestigious London galleries including the Royal Academy, Mall Galleries and Bankside gallery. In 1986 he won the Gold Medal prize for the Royal Academy Schools and in 2011 was elected member of the New English Art Club and awarded the David Messum prize.

www.julianbailey.co.uk

Future works to be published
by John Silverton

A Murder of Crows

A police procedural crime thriller. The hunt for a serial, ritualistic killer compromises the integrity of Detective Inspector Boyd when the next victim is his girlfriend.

Chapter 1

She was naked. She was blonde. She was dead.

The pictures from the drone showed a once a beautiful woman, blonde yes, but not all over. She was tied to a cartwheel and the crows had pecked out her eyes and scavenged her fractured, flagellated body. The crows looked down upon the disturbed scene like agents of death, mocking with their "caw" calls, angrily denied further pickings. They seem bemused by the commotion and flashing lights, observing every detail of the police operation.

They had seen the murderer . . .

Every Painting Tells a Story

A collection of flash fiction (Maximum 250 words) stories inspired by works of art. Six examples are displayed on www.johnsilvertonwrite.co.uk together with background details of the artwork and artist.

Printed in Great Britain
by Amazon